A BREATH OF FRESH AIR

JOHN B. ROSENMAN

"We'd rather be dead," Michael said, "then have your sadists pick our brains apart like hunks of cheese. Since we're all on the same side, you guys should have come to me in peace and *asked* for my cooperation. If you had, I would have been glad to do it like a true-blue patriot. But you didn't."

Agent Toosha nodded. "You may have a point," he said, "but I have my orders, and an important part of them is not to endanger national security or under any circumstances let this aircraft fall into enemy hands."

Enemy hands? Did he just say *I* was the *enemy*? Choking with anger, Michael watched Toosha consult a gauge.

"It's a long way down," the man said. "But there's one good thing. It's open country down there and we won't hurt anybody."

We won't hurt anybody. As Michael chewed on the words, Toosha turned back and gave him a long measuring stare. Then he spoke to the other two men. "Gentlemen, it's been a privilege serving with you. Hold on tight."

A moment later, he jerked the stick and the helicopter swung and dived almost straight down. A bird shot past, squawking as it narrowly missed them. Michael strained against the rigid jacket, futilely trying to escape. It pressed so hard against his diaphragm that he barely managed to scream. His earlier threat to crash the copter had been scary but intended as a bluff. This looked like the real thing.

"Stop, you crazy bastard. You don't have to do this!"

Down they went, the wind howling about them. Far below, as if eager to meet them, the earth seemed to rush up.

CHAPTER ONE
THE GOLD STANDARD

He couldn't breathe; he was going to die. Screaming inside, he strained in agony, feeling himself approach the very edge of oblivion. He had no memory, no identity, only a desperate need to survive, to escape this torment that was about to engulf him.

Finally, as a last resort, he heaved himself upward, knowing it was his only chance. For an eternity, he hung halfway, caught between life and death. Then, to his great relief, he shot to his feet and staggered across the floor.

Trembling, Michael Windsor opened his eyes, finding himself standing in his bedroom.

The wine, I shouldn't have drunk it before I turned in. The same thing happened the first time.

Only this was the *third* time it had happened. And bad as it was, it paled before the second time a week ago when he had played tennis. He remembered sitting down on a bench during a break in the rotation and falling into a fitful sleep, something he never did during the day. He had awoken a few moments later with no idea who or where he was. And he had been *screaming* even as he came awake, something he later realized was odd since he couldn't even breathe. Even odder, no one seemed to notice his scream, not even the player sitting beside him. How was that possible?

As during the first episode, he had felt he would die if he couldn't get some air into his lungs. Fortunately, he had succeeded, struggled to his feet and managed to walk shakily around. What was wrong with him? He had shrugged off the first episode but this one was more serious. Picking up his racket, he found he had a dull headache that felt like a hangover.

Rather than face the problem, he had brushed it aside as before and returned to the tennis wars for another hour. Now, standing in his bedroom after his *third* attack, he faced the same issue.

What was he going to do *this* time?

He blinked and once again, shrugged it off. With a sigh, he went back to bed.

It wasn't until his gastroenterologist called about a procedure that he consulted a doctor. "Something rather strange happened to me," he said. "I had some…episodes."

"Episodes?" Dr. Burns asked. "What do you mean?"

Why did he even mention it? Didn't he have enough problems? He was already seeing Dr. Burns for a precancerous case of Barrett's esophagus. What he should do was keep his mouth shut. After all, his episodes weren't that serious, were they?

But it seemed his mouth had a mind of its own because he heard it spilling everything. When he was through, Dr. Burns suggested that he see a neurologist.

Just what I need, another doctor. "All right," he said, feeling his goose was cooked. "If you think I should."

When Michael met Dr. Jason Turner two weeks later, he was surprised the man was so young. Hell, the good doctor looked like a kid, easily ten years younger than his own forty-three. Unlike him, there was not a line in his face, not a gray hair or a bald spot in his full head of rich brown hair. As Dr. Turner read the summary Michael had written, he found it hard to believe that such a youngster could advise him on anything, much less prescribe treatment that would actually help him.

Dr. Turner finished reading and looked up. "So you've had three incidents?"

"Yes," Michael said. "Uh, I'm a bit relieved I haven't had any more since the last one."

Dr. Turner nodded. "Still, I recommend that you take a home sleep test to see if you have sleep apnea."

Sleep apnea. If he had the condition, he couldn't just flop into bed anymore but would have to hook himself up to some kind of unholy contraption to improve his breathing.

"What's this test like?" he asked.

Dr. Turner shrugged. "It's easy to take and you should have no difficulty sleeping. You use it overnight and return the device at your convenience. If you go to the Equipment Office two doors down, they'll issue you one and show you how to use it."

Michael hesitated. The train was going too fast, and if he didn't get off it quick, he never would. He stared at a multicolored picture of a naked man on the wall across from him, his internal organs clearly displayed, labeled, and ripe for dissection.

"Do you have any questions?" Dr. Turner asked, his youthful features expressing concern.

Yes, he did, only he couldn't think of even one at the moment. The good doctor opened the door and pointed to his right. "You go that way and turn left at the next hallway," he said.

Michael thanked him and followed directions. Still, he managed to get lost rather quickly. Earlier, he had realized that this place was the kind that confused and actually frightened him. Narrow halls turned and branched, and it was so easy to go the wrong way. They made him feel like a laboratory rat in a maze. Soon, he was completely lost and leaned back against the wall, waiting until an acid reflux attack subsided.

His world crashed down upon him. What a loser he was. Not only couldn't he even find his way out of this goddamned place, but just last week his wife Muriel, threatening divorce, had packed up and left with his seven-year-old, tousled-haired son Andy. He remembered her disgust over the years as she'd berated him for his lack of ambition. "Twelve years a clerk in a shitty hardware store, and you don't bring home enough money to budge the needle. Michael, I know your health isn't good, but we've always had to tread water, getting deeper and deeper in debt, and I have to keep getting part-time jobs to pay off our bills...."

Blah blah blah, on and on it went. He heard her voice in his head and moaned, knowing her criticism was valid. He *was* lazy. He *did* lack ambition. But he also had Barrett's esophagus, third stage kidney disease, food allergies, and high blood pressure. Sometimes, when he came home from work, he was so tired, he could barely stand.

Feeling sorry for yourself, Michael? he thought.

Yes, he was, and the realization made him push off the wall and glare down the hall. Damn it, he was going to find his way out of this place if it killed him.

In the Equipment Office aka the Sleep Lab he was given a device with attachments and listened to instructions that zoomed right past him. He nodded, tried to keep up, and after a few minutes headed out with the home sleep test tucked under his arm in its handy carrying case. It was so small. How difficult could the test be?

That night he read the directions, studied the pictures, and found that the device was not that difficult. The belt with the effort sensor went around the chest, the two prongs went into the nostrils, and the pulse oximeter went over his index finger. There were a few other details, but they boiled down to lying down and trying to sleep. As he did, a terrible fear seized him.

What if he fell asleep only to have his throat clamp shut so he was unable to breathe? What if this time was the last and he couldn't wake up no matter how hard he tried? He imagined himself screaming inside and straining for air, only to die in unbearable agony.

Michael tossed and turned, trying not to upset the instrument. Despite Dr. Turner's reassurances, the device was a little irritating, and worries kept him awake. When he finally dreamt, he found himself trying to leave his neurologist's office again. Halls branched in all directions, and he saw he actually was a laboratory rat. He sniffed frantically at the walls and air for clues as he scampered this way and that, trying desperately to get out. Only there was no exit, only endless halls leading nowhere. Finally, though, he saw an open door and beyond it, fresh air and green trees. His heart pounded with joy.

But then the walls pressed in, and he began to suffocate. The trees and air were so close, but the harder he tried to reach them, the farther they receded in the distance. As he struggled, it became more and more difficult to breathe.

Then he started and found himself awake, lying in bed. He was human again, not a rat. He lay sweating, drawing in deep breaths of air, enormously relieved he was still alive. The machine—had it saved him? No, the home sleep test wasn't sentient. It hadn't sensed his distress and deliberately awakened him. It had awakened him accidentally, mechanically, or perhaps he had just woken up from his nightmare on his own. Thinking about his good fortune, he nodded off.

When he awoke again in the morning, he found he'd had a decent night's sleep. He turned off the machine and returned it to the Sleep Lab.

———————

During the twelve days before his next appointment, Michael experienced two more incidents while sleeping, evidence that his condition was not improving as he'd hoped but getting worse. Both times he had struggled desperately to breathe, feeling as if he were on the edge of death. On one of the occasions, he had fallen out of bed and hurt his hand.

He'd read that eighty-five percent of those with obstructive sleep apnea didn't even know they had it. Such facts reminded him of his own disorder and his other health problems as well. Being alone certainly didn't help matters. He missed his wife, and he missed his little boy more. God, how he missed him. Loneliness tore at his soul. It was as if they had left him to die alone.

Feeling sorry for yourself again, Michael?

"Yes, I am," he said aloud, not caring if anyone heard, even if it was one of the fellow workers at the hardware store. *If I don't catch some kind of break soon, I don't know what I'll do.*

He was still thinking that as he drove to his doctor's appointment.

When he entered the office and checked in, his hands were wet and his heart was pounding. There was no reason for his anxiety, of course. He would learn the news when Dr. Turner gave it to him. His call three days before had received a pro forma dismissal. "Dr. Turner will discuss the results with you in his office," a woman had said.

He sat down in the waiting room and tried to relax. On the wall, a television program warned about the dangers of hypertension, an invisible killer. The damn thing could lie in wait for years with no apparent symptoms. Then bang, without warning, it would strike.

Michael swallowed and looked away.

When a nurse called his name he rose and followed her through the door. "Do you know the way?" she asked with a smile.

The way to the Minotaur? Of course. I come here often. He nodded and headed down the hall.

To his surprise, he found Dr. Turner's office easily this time. It might have been nice to have temporarily lost his bearings so he could have more time to cope, but it was as if a bright beacon had guided him.

Dr. Turner smiled as he entered. Michael smiled back and sat down. They exchanged pleasantries, then Turner asked him how the home test had gone.

"I experienced an incident," Michael said. "It was awful, as bad as the others. I dreamt I was a rat in a maze and couldn't breathe. I felt I was going to die. Fortunately, I escaped."

Dr. Turner frowned. "You *escaped*?"

"Well, it felt that way. Afterwards, I went back to sleep. It was easier than I expected. I even slept all right." He hesitated, feeling a wave of fear. "But I've had two more incidents since I returned the machine. They were bad."

"I'm sorry to hear that," Dr. Turner said. He tapped a form on his desk. "Fortunately, we have your results, which should provide some guidance. You slept over seven hours and averaged fifteen events per hour. That places you in the moderate range for obstructive sleep apnea."

Now that he heard the words, Michael was not surprised. Of *course* he had it. "Fifteen events. Let's see. As I remember, a single event is ten seconds or more without breathing."

"Correct."

Michael nodded, waiting for the doctor to go on. But he remained silent as if expecting *him* to speak. "Uh, I've heard there is a minimally invasive treatment for apnea. Mouthpieces that keep the airway open."

"Yes," Dr. Turner said, "but they are far less effective than CABS." He spread his hands. "CABS is the gold standard. It's superior to CPAP and previous other models."

CABS. What an odd acronym. Michael knew it stood for Constant Airway Breathing Support, but it sounded like something you got a ride in.

"So you recommend I use CABS?"

"I do. It is far and away the best treatment available."

"I see." Michael hesitated. "Is it permanent?" he finally asked. "I mean, will I have to use it for the rest of my life?"

"Yes," Dr. Turner said.

Michael waited, hoping for more, but Turner remained silent. Obviously, the good doctor was leaving the matter in his lap. It was his mess to decide.

The silence dragged on. On the wall, the anatomically correct man waited with them, his internal organs labeled and on full display.

"Well," Michael finally said, "if it's the gold standard, I suppose I should use it."

———————

As he waited in the Sleep Lab, he gazed at plastic faces wearing masks of different shapes and sizes. Which one should he pick? The largest one covered the mouth and nose and looked as if it were trying to swallow the entire face. The medium one was slightly smaller. The smallest covered only the nose and left the mouth free, perhaps so it could scream at the indignity of it all.

Easy, Michael, he thought. Don't lose it.

But it was easier to say than do. Thanks largely to a dead-end job, his wife and son had left him, and now he had this new health problem. He was tempted to get up and walk right out.

He changed his mind when an attractive, dark-haired woman in a green pantsuit entered from the back. "Mr. Windsor?" she asked.

"Uh, yes."

"I'm Sonya Walker, will you come with me?"

Oh hell, yes. He followed her down a hallway to a room in back. Glancing around, he saw more masks on display and a sleep apnea machine on a table to his left. She led him to it.

He pointed at the masks on the wall. "Is this what you wear at Halloween?" he asked.

It was a poor joke, but she actually laughed. The sound of it warmed him.

"Mr. Windsor, how much do you know about the machine you'll be using?"

"Not much," he said. "Except that CABS stands for Constant Airway Breathing Support."

"Very good. Suppose we sit down, and I'll go over it with you. Okay?"

"Sounds like a plan," he said and sat down. The machine was roughly five inches high, five inches wide, and ten inches long. To Michael, it looked like a device devised by aliens. Scary as it was, he hoped it would save his life, or at least make it livable. The home sleep test had worked out all right, hadn't it? Well, he should at least give this one a try, too.

"Okay," she said, "let's begin with the major components." She turned the CABS machine around and pointed at a round hole in back.

"Here's the *Air Outlet* where you plug in the larger end of the tubing. The smaller end you plug into your mask so you can breathe the air." She demonstrated the procedure, using a tube and a mask. "Now in front of the machine…"

Michael listened or tried to. Her demonstration was clear and effective but there was much to learn, more than with the relatively simple sleep test. Besides that, she was attractive. She stopped now and then so he could ask questions, but he only half-heard her answers. Soon she was moving on and talking about *Mask Fit, Ramp Time, Humidity Level…*

She broke off and laughed. "I know it's a lot, but it's all explained clearly in the booklets we provide, and if you have any questions, just call." She produced a business card with her name. He slipped it into his wallet, his nostrils twitching as he caught a whiff of her perfume. It reminded him that he hadn't had sex in months and further weakened what remained of his concentration.

"Ready to try one on?" she asked.

"Try one on?"

"Yes, a mask." She waved at the wall behind the desk where the masks hung. Big, medium, and little. "Which one would you prefer?"

He studied them. "The largest one," he said. "The full face mask. I want to make sure it covers my mouth so I don't breathe through it."

"Makes sense," she said. "You'd have more events and wouldn't get all the benefits of this technology."

She rose and removed a large mask from the wall. It was made of clear plastic and had a soft rim of cushions. She placed it on his face and slipped the headgear over his head. She adjusted the straps so the frame fit securely over the bridge of his nose and under his mouth. Then she had him take it off and put it back on himself. After the third time, Michael felt he almost knew what he was doing.

Sonya handed him a large paper bag. "Here's three of the masks you chose. And I've included one each of the others in case you want to try them."

Soon, all too soon, she was escorting him out the front door as he carried his load. Oddly, the Gold Standard tingled in his hands even through the nylon and even though it wasn't turned on. It gave him a strange, creepy feeling. He waved and left, taking with him her smile and the elusive scent of her perfume.

He drove up the entrance ramp to the interstate, sailing smoothly along until he heard a screeching sound under the hood. Christ, what was it now? He'd taken off two hours from work, and Starret wouldn't appreciate him needing to leave again. From the sounds he heard, though, it was probably a loose or worn serpentine belt, and if it went, this worn-out old Chevy simply wouldn't run.

Michael slowed down, hoping the cacophony under his hood would subside, but if anything, it increased. Cursing, he turned on the radio. He was just in time to hear an old favorite of his, "Thunder Road."

When the song was halfway through, he realized he could no longer hear any complaints from his engine. He dialed the radio down to make sure. Yup, the evil genie had crept back into its bottle, though he couldn't say for how long. Still, he felt relieved.

Later, after work, he got into his Chevy and turned on the engine, then pumped the gas a few times. Still not a single disturbing sound. It was a miracle! The old engine was so soft, he could barely hear it. Driving home, he kept his ear cocked, expecting the worst, but the serpentine belt or whatever it was behaved, at least for now.

Entering his apartment, he stopped and leaned back against the door. Until Muriel left with Andy a week ago, he had never known how empty a home could be. The furniture was still here as were their beds and other items, but for him, the silent rooms were a giant void, his personal tomb. He feared that soon he would forget the sound of his son's laughter and the lilt of Muriel's voice.

He took the machine to the bedroom and placed it on the table beside the bed, feeling his hands tingle again. Such a strange sensation. He rubbed his hands, staring down at the device.

It sat there black and deadly, looking like it was about to spring.

CHAPTER TWO
GETTING STARTED

Despite the machine's forbidding appearance, Michael hoped he could learn to use it without too much difficulty.

Such was not the case.

After reading the materials, he thought he grasped the main points. He managed easily to fill the tub to the recommended level with distilled water. Then, it was a cinch to insert the tub in the device. Easy-peasy, as Muriel liked to say.

Next, he succeeded in assembling the parts of the mask. The trouble came when he attached the headgear to the mask and attempted to put the thing on. It should have been simple because Sonya had shown him how to do it. Ah, but he remembered that the mask and headgear had already been assembled.

To his dismay, he now struggled. He started by fitting the front of the mask or seal over his nose as illustrated in the booklet. Somehow, though, the straps on the headgear were twisted. The one on his forehead was turned around, and the band across the top of his head was upside down. After several attempts, he got the straps right. Unfortunately, the straps at the bottom of the mask were now snarled and the magnetic clips turned in the wrong direction. He spent most of an hour experimenting, trying one thing and then another. In the end, persistence paid off. He sighed with relief when the straps on both the top and bottom were correct and he could finally snap the magnetic clips onto the mask's frame without any problem.

Next came the tubing. He connected one of the rubber ends to his mask and the other to the back of the CABS machine. Uh-oh, he had gotten them wrong. The larger end should go into the machine and the smaller one into his mask. The way he had it, the one in the machine was sure to come out. Follow the directions, stupid!

After that, he plugged the machine in. The effect was almost instantaneous. Air rushed into his mask, filling it. Success!

Okay, it was good to go, or so he hoped. He accessed the small screen and ran Mask Fit to see if it had any leaks. No, it was perfect. A smiling yellow face greeted him.

He turned off the light and slipped under the covers. Only it wasn't so easy with a mask on that was connected to seven feet of tubing. He had to squirm and push the pillow so it was settled under his head. Finally, he stopped and lay back. Closed his eyes and tried to sleep.

The problem was, there was a *mask* on his face. It was heavy and the straps were tight. It felt like a cage. He reached up to adjust it, but air escaped from beneath the side in a fierce explosion, stunning him. He put his hand down and tried again to sleep, but air poured into his mouth, forcing him to breathe it. He knew the air was supposed to part the tissues in his throat so there'd be fewer pauses in his breathing, but it reminded him perversely of something else, something he'd seen in horror movies. It felt like the tube attached to his mask was a vampire, sucking and drinking the life from his body.

Ridiculous! Absurd! But as the mask fed him air, it also seemed to be sucking at him, drawing his essence back through the tubing and into the machine, feeding it. In the dark, he imagined the Gold Standard swelling as his own body withered. Nonsense! he told himself. His imagination was just running away with him.

Trying to become comfortable, Michael turned on his side, only to have the tubing coil around his neck like a snake. He felt suffocated but told himself to calm down. Hell's bells, the tubing wasn't sentient or malevolent. It was only seven feet of mindless material. He pushed it aside and tried again to rest.

It was a long night of fitful sleep that drained rather than renewed him. He woke up a dozen times and went to the bathroom often, stopping the machine with difficulty and detaching the mask from the tubing on each occasion. Nightmares did a weird dance in his brain. Most were fragmentary, impossible to recover or put into words when he woke. One, though, stood out. It was a dream that the CABS machine was a monster, maliciously savoring his misery as he slept.

Finally, morning came. Stumbling out of bed, he took off the mask and accessed the *Sleep Report* on the small screen. Usage hours were 7:15, though how much of that time was really any kind of sleep, he couldn't say. What encouraged him, though, was the number of average events per hour. It was 9.2, nearly 6 less than the 15 events per hour that Dr. Turner had reported to him.

Maybe he had some reason to hope. Maybe the Gold Standard *could* help. Encouraged, he reached out and touched the machine, only to snatch his hand away when he felt it move. Oh Christ, the thing had inhaled, taken a deep breath. But that was crazy. It was just a mindless hunk of metal and plastic.

Laughing at his overactive imagination, Michael Windsor went to the kitchen to prepare breakfast.

———————

Bacon and eggs and two cups of coffee boosted his spirits. Yes, the machine was creepy and difficult to use, but after just one night, he had reduced the number of his sleep events from 15 to 9, an improvement of 6. Hoo-ah! Not bad for a guy who struggled with his own electric can opener.

His day brightened still more when he got in his car and turned on the engine. Instead of hideous screeching, the motor purred like a contented cat. For a moment he was tempted to hop out and peek under the hood, but why court calamity when things were going better? Driving to work, he was almost able to put Muriel and Andy out of his mind, though a boy about his son's age on the sidewalk filled him with regret and longing. If Muriel was going to see a lawyer, perhaps he should do the same, he thought, especially since he wanted to keep contact with his son.

Michael turned on the radio, hoping for something like "Thunder Road." To his surprise, he got "King of the Road," a close cousin. He laughed at the irony.

He stopped chuckling when he approached Starret's Hardware Store, his personal prison for the past twelve years. Muriel had kept after him to find something better-paying, but his sporadic attempts to do so had failed to bear fruit. Maybe it was his lack of confidence, or his lack of ambition. His one interview for a managerial position had been a total failure. Well, maybe he was being too hard on himself. After all, there had been several other applicants, and some of them must have been better qualified. Still, if he hated his place of employment, why did he remain there? A thousand times he had thought of going to Starret's office and telling him to shove his job. But if he did that, how would he support his family?

He parked in the lot before the store and got out. Walking inside, he immediately put on his happy face to show that he was eager to help customers. To some co-workers, working at a hardware store was a fun job. You got to socialize with people and use your specialized knowledge to help them. Though he was an introvert, Michael had once found that to be true and had actually enjoyed his work. But those days were long gone. Now his job was a painful chore, nothing more.

Still, this day went better. He helped several customers, including a young woman who laughed at his joke. Then a middle-aged man came up to him and asked for assistance in purchasing a garage door opener.

Michael showed him several models. Some were about the size of the machine back in his apartment. Could he find this gentleman the equivalent of a Gold Standard? Finally, he recommended a red one-half horsepower opener and explained how to use it.

He was about to wrap things up when Beverly, Mr. Starret's obnoxious daughter aka the store manager, approached them. "How are we doing today?" she asked.

The question was addressed to Michael but the customer treated it as if it were meant for him. "We're doing just fine," he said. "This fellow has just recommended the perfect opener for my garage." With a wave, he lifted it and left.

Michael knew that for some reason, a satisfied customer was not something Beverly Starret wanted him to have. Perhaps it was a natural enmity, something Beverly saw in Michael that made her needle him. Beverly probably sensed Michael was vulnerable and would not fight back and risk his job. In short, Beverly was a bully.

Beverly was ten years younger and three inches taller than Michael's five feet ten. She was also fat and her huge breasts sagged halfway to her waist. While she'd once been attractive, in recent years Michael had seen the woman's looks evaporate like mist in the sun. Her hair had grown thin, and a healthy mustache had taken root beneath her nose, a growth that Beverly seemed reluctant to shave. This mustache had been the object of jokes and derision for years when Beverly wasn't around. "Hitler's Sister" and "Heavenly Beverly" they called her behind her back, or "Snake in the Grass" because of the sneaky way she spied on their job performance. Beverly had a way of slipping around and meddling in things, and it was common knowledge that the owner only tolerated her because she was his daughter.

Over the years, Beverly had tormented and terrified Michael with her petty persecutions. And unless he was mistaken, he was about to be picked on again.

"Michael," Beverly said, "there's a woman looking for a hex nut in aisle six."

"A hex nut?"

"Yes, a one-quarter inch hex nut." Beverly made a little mincing step and drew closer. "You do know where aisle six is, don't you?"

Why would a woman want a one-quarter inch hex nut in aisle six? The unusual thought distracted and amused Michael. Beverly, accustomed to his prompt obedience, was not pleased.

"Well, Mikey," she said, "are you going to help our customer, or are you just going to stand there like a dumb hunk of cheese?"

Michael was not offended by the poor simile. He had heard Beverly use it before. What did irritate him was being referred to as "Mikey." Beverly had belittled him before in this manner and he had just accepted it. After all, he'd told himself, Michael, Mike, and Mikey were essentially all the same, weren't they?

Only for some reason, this time they weren't. Anger bloomed in him like a dark flower. It was a feeling that had only simmered in him before in Beverly's presence. Now it made him straighten and face the woman directly.

"Well, *Bev*," he said, "I haven't decided."

Beverly's nostrils sniffed in distaste. "Who told you we were on a first-name basis?"

Their erratic AC clicked on, wafting a breath of fresh air past his face. He sucked it in, imagining he had a mask over his nose and was hooked up to his CABS machine. *Mikey.* How nice it would be if he grabbed one of the store's best ball-peen hammers and rearranged this bitch's ugly face.

Michael shrugged. "You call me Mikey, I'll call you Bev. Sounds like a fair exchange to me."

Beverly gaped at him. Stunned at his boldness, Michael moved closer and tapped Beverly's ample chest. "Here's the deal, *Miss* Starret. If you treat me with respect, I'll treat you the same way. Respect is a two-way street. Understand? What I want you to do is stop harassing me. In particular, I want you to stop humiliating me in front of other people, especially customers."

Beverly finally found her voice. "I'll fire your ass for this."

"Fine," Michael said. "Then do it. But I'm sick and tired of your insults. Treat me with respect, and you'll have a first-class employee. Treat me the way you have, and we're going to have trouble. *Capische?*"

He let the warning sink in, then smiled. "Now, I'd better help that woman in aisle six. She might need that one-quarter inch hex nut awfully bad."

Michael turned and left. Only then did he fully realize what he'd done. For God's sake, what had gotten into him? He needed this job! What would he do without it? Yet it had felt good to challenge Beverly and face her down. A thousand times he had thought of doing it, and now he finally had.

Only why had he done it today? Had he finally had enough of her BS? Perhaps he'd find the answer to these questions when he stood in an unemployment line.

CHAPTER THREE
A LUCKY ACCIDENT

A week later as Michael played doubles, he noticed he had both hands on his racket. He was surprised not only because he did not use two hands when he played, but because he was attempting to return a ball with his backhand, which absolutely sucked.

Still, he swung his racket, whipping his arms around to make solid contact. The ball shot across the net like a rocket, streaking down the line past the opposing player.

He stared at the result in shock, not believing what he saw. Yet hadn't he swung the racket and done it with *both* hands? Glancing around, he saw that players on all three courts had stopped to stare. "Good shot," a player on court three called. After a moment, other players repeated the compliment, and play resumed. Freak shots, after all, occasionally occurred.

But there was still something different with him today. He felt different, more at home in his body. Thinking back, he recalled that the first four nights with the device had been nightmarishly difficult, but on the fifth night he had smoothly turned a corner. Now he felt almost comfortable with the mask on his face.

Michael also felt almost at home at work, where he found that he enjoyed helping customers. Heavenly Beverly hadn't lowered the boom on him yet. Even better, she had stopped needling and harassing him. Maybe it was his warning and Beverly realized that he no longer feared her. His relationship with Beverly was perhaps the biggest change in him, one even more significant than the great shot he had just made. Michael no longer dreaded the sound of Beverly's approach. Nor did he care much if Beverly had spoken to her pop about Michael's attitude. For some reason, the whole Beverly thing no longer seemed that important. If he got fired, he would just find another job.

He continued playing, enjoying the beautiful spring weather of Virginia Beach and the company of other players. When each game ended, they followed a system of rotation by which each player moved in clockwise fashion, taking the position of the player who had been "ahead" of them. On the fourth turn, the player became the server and when that game was over, they could wait in line to play again if they wanted to.

When it was Michael's turn to serve, he toed the line and bounced the ball a few times. Usually he was nervous because his serve was even weaker than his backhand. Despite the lessons he'd received, nothing seemed to stick. Though most of the players in this Seniors group were fifty or over, most of them feasted on his slower-than-molasses serve.

Yet when he threw the ball up, everything felt different. His toss was straight and high for a change, and he felt his body bend like an elastic spring. Power he'd never experienced before rippled through his torso, and when he struck the ball, it streaked across the net far faster than any ball he'd ever hit.

This time everybody seemed to stop and stare. "Michael," Zack Hampton shouted, "what's up with you this morning?"

Michael shrugged, not used to such attention. "I ate two bowls of Wheaties," he shouted back.

A few players laughed, but Michael realized they didn't know what to make of him. After he won his service game, something he rarely managed to do, he left the court. He was about to claim his position in line by sticking his racket in the fence behind two others, when Zack stopped him. "Come over here and let's gab a little."

Zack led him outside the playing area to a picnic table where they sat down on opposite sides. Six feet three and well-built, Zack looked like a stereotypical athlete. He was also one of the best tennis players in the group, and Michael felt the man study him as if he'd just pulled off a difficult magic trick.

"Okay," he finally said, "how did you do it?"

Michael's first instinct was to say, "Do what?" But he knew Zack wouldn't be fooled. "Have I improved that much?" he asked.

"Have you improved that much? Michael, until today, I'd say you were about a 1.5 player, or slightly below the average in our group. Today, that changed big-time."

Michael swallowed. "What am I now?"

Zack's heavy eyebrows rose. "I'd say you're knocking on the door of being a 5." He leaned across the table. "Amigo, you're so much better, it's fuckin' incredible."

"It wasn't Wheaties."

Zack snorted. "Of course it wasn't. But what the hell was it?"

"Maybe I've been taking lessons."

Zack shook his head. "Naw. No teacher is that good and that fast. How did you do it in just a few days? C'mon, spill it."

Michael hesitated. "Zack, you have sleep apnea, right?"

"Yeah, so what?"

"And you use a machine for it? CABS?"

"Right. I..." Zack paused and snapped his fingers. "Wait, are you saying you have sleep apnea, too?"

"Yes, I was diagnosed recently and started to use the machine a week ago." He brushed a fly away. "For four nights it was a bitch to use. I can't begin to tell you the problems I had. But for the last three nights, it's been..." He remembered Muriel's phrase. "It's been easy-peasy."

Zack's eyes bulged and his chest rocked with laughter. "Are you saying that CABS is responsible for improving your tennis?"

Now that someone had put it into words, it did sound stupid. Michael knew no machine could transform his game. Could his electric toothbrush cure his acid reflux? Or his toaster lower his high blood pressure? It was absurd to think such a thing.

Come to think of it, though, he hadn't had any chest pain for nearly a week. And his blood pressure had been just fine when he'd taken it this morning.

"Sounds ridiculous, doesn't it?" he conceded. "But before you laugh again, please tell me what the real cause for my improved game is. And while you're at it, tell me why I now average less than two events an hour in my sleep."

Zack spread his hands. "*Two* events, in only a week? I'm happy if I average seven or eight. I don't know the answers to these questions, Michael. I'd just like to play a set with you sometime to see how good you've become. We might have a great match."

Out on the courts, some players erupted in laughter. Zack turned to see. "Must have been a great point," he said.

Michael barely heard him. Remembering he had joked about the possibility that the machine had caused his changes, for the first time, he seriously considered the possibility that it had. "I've gained weight too," he said. "Seven pounds in a week." He raised his arm and flexed his bicep. "Dripping wet, I now weigh a strapping hundred and forty-three pounds."

"You do look a bit buff," Zack conceded. He waved his hand, brushing off the notion. "But the whole idea is crazy, Michael. That machine is designed to open your airway and help you breathe better. Nothing else."

Michael wasn't so sure. "You haven't smelled the air from the machine. It's different."

Zack leaned toward him, bracing his elbows on the table. "Different—how?"

For a moment, Michael wondered if he'd said too much. "Look, couldn't the machine promote other physical benefits, like weight gain?"

"Maybe a few pounds. But it won't make you a good tennis player, which is what you now seem to be."

"Hmm, hasn't a product ever come off an assembly line that's different from all the others? I mean, a lucky accident?"

21

Zack grinned. "You mean like a mouse head in a can of chickpeas?"

Michael laughed. "You mean that actually happened?"

"Yeah, imagine the diner's surprise when she saw what was on her fork."

"Huh. I've heard of a human tooth in a hamburger and the odd toaster or microwave that caused a fire." Michael paused. "But that's different. All those products caused something bad."

"You're right," Zack said. "And offhand, I can't recall any products, any *singular* products that malfunctioned in a good way, can you?"

"No," Michael said. "But that doesn't mean it hasn't happened." He rose from the picnic table. "Hey, I've enjoyed our chat, but I'm due back at work in a little over an hour. I want to get some more tennis in first."

Zack raised his hand, stopping him. "Before you leave, tell me again about the machine's air. You said it smelled different. What was different about it?"

Michael frowned. Zack was hung up on the subject.

"I don't know."

Zack tilted his head, studying him. "But you do think CABS is the reason you've gotten better at tennis."

"I don't know what I think. Forget it!" Michael said. He was tempted to ask if Zack's machine ever seemed to move and breathe beneath his hand, but decided he'd said enough. "See you later, Zack," he said, heading for the courts. "We'll swat the ball sometime."

———————

After work, Michael paused in the parking lot. It was still a beautiful spring day, but his mood was marred. A mouse head in a can of chickpeas... That did not sound like a lucky accident. And last night he'd only had a single event in his sleep. Just one. Was that normal?

Forget the mouse head. Celebrate your restful sleep. Isn't it better than trying to claw your way up to consciousness before you suffocate?

He unlocked his car then noticed a group of kids near the curb. They were about eleven or twelve years of age, and they were laughing and pushing each other around, swapping obscene insults that only made them laugh harder. And why not? It was a great day to be young.

Suddenly he had a feeling. *Something's going to happen. Something's going to happen soon!*

Michael was moving before he knew it. One kid, a blond boy with pimples, was standing on the curb, unaware of the truck heading his way. As Michael raced toward him, the boy stumbled off the curb and into the street. The truck was almost upon him....

At the last instant, Michael grabbed the boy and threw him back onto the grass. The truck rushed by, whipping the clothes against their bodies.

"What's wrong with you?" he screamed. "Do you want to get killed? How can you be so careless?"

They all looked terrified, but not as terrified as he. "Go on," he said, waving them off. "Get your butts out of here. But for Christ's sake, be careful!"

He watched them leave, then went to his car. His whole body was trembling.

"Nicely done, Michael," someone said behind him.

He turned. Beverly Starret stood in the parking lot, staring at him with shining eyes. It was a look Michael had never seen from her before.

"I didn't want the kid to get hurt," he said.

"Or killed," she added. Her gaze traveled up and down his body and she smiled. "I could go for a man who seizes control," she said.

He felt shocked realization. Her stare was cringe-worthy in the extreme, and he feared she'd come forward and put her words into action. For God's sake, he thought, she must outweigh me by seventy-five pounds. He imagined bouncing with her on a mattress, their lovemaking a form of aerial combat.

Her lips twisted as if she had read his thoughts. She swung around and returned to the store, her hips deliberately swaying for his benefit.

Oh, great. He got in his car and started to turn on the engine. Then he hesitated, remembering how the engine's previous screeching had mysteriously stopped. You can't put it off any longer, he told himself. You've got to know.

He reached down, popped the hood, then got out and opened it. Leaning down, he examined the interior. After a moment, he stiffened and staggered back in disbelief.

The serpentine belt was brand new.

The engine was brand new.

Everything was brand new.

Though he was stunned, the conclusion was obvious. Someone or something had removed the old engine and installed a completely new one, including the belt that had most likely caused the screeching.

He whirled, looked out at the street. *I thought the engine ran more smoothly and had more power. Now I know why. And yet, at the same time, I don't know anything.*

The front door of Starret's Hardware Store opened and Cal Frank came out. He spotted Michael and started over. "Something wrong with your engine?" he called.

Michael quickly closed the hood. "No, it's fine. I've gotta leave, Cal. Talk to you tomorrow."

He hopped in his car and took off, leaving a bemused employee gazing after him. On the way home, the day's events swirled around and around in his brain as if it were a mad washing machine. Yet no matter how many cycles they went through, nothing got cleaner or clearer. The CABS machine might improve him, but what, if anything, had improved his engine? Was it all just an amazing trick—or a lucky accident?

When he reached home, Michael was so absorbed, he briefly overlooked a few important details. One was a familiar sedan parked in front of his apartment. Two others were his wife and son who stood waiting beside it. As he got out of the car, he saw that Muriel was as pretty as ever.

How was this possible? First, his worn-out engine had become brand new; now his family had come to visit. It was too good to be true!

But as his son Andy ran toward him, it seemed all too real. Michael's eyes filled with tears as his son held his arms out.

"Daddy, Daddy, it's been so long since we've seen you!"

CHAPTER FOUR
IT'S GOOD TO BE HOME

Michael rushed forward to receive his son's embrace. He scooped him up and whirled him around and around as he had done so often. Feeling Andy laugh and cling to him, he knew a perfect joy. Nothing mattered more to him than his son, not even Muriel. He might be a failure, he might be a nothing as she had told him so often, but as long as he was blessed with this son who loved him, he was King of the World.

Only after he lowered Andy to the ground did he wonder why Muriel had come back. As she approached, he resolved to act like an adult for Andy's sake.

He smiled. "This is a pleasant occasion," he said, and meant, *Why are you here?*

"I tried to call," she said, "but your cell was off."

He patted his pocket. "Sorry, it keeps doing that. I need to get a holder."

They exchanged a civilized hug. He resisted the temptation to kiss her. All too soon she pushed him gently but firmly away. "The reason we came is Andy's been missing you." She sighed. "No matter what I say, your son keeps talking about you, wanting to see you."

Michael reached out and tousled his son's already tousled hair. "Is that right, Andy boy? Have you been talking me up?" The fact that Andy had missed him filled him with pleasure.

"Yup," Andy said. "You promised you'd take me fishing."

I sure did, Michael thought. And I've made other promises, too. Somehow I never manage to keep them.

Muriel frowned. "You seem different."

Michael turned to her. "I've put on a few pounds." *Better not mention the apnea machine.*

"I can see that, but it's something else." Muriel's gaze traveled up and down his body, reminding him of the way Beverly had checked him out only a half hour ago. But there was no lust or desire in his wife's stare, only a frank appraisal. In turn, he appraised his wife. Why did you come here? he wondered. Andy's missing me is only part of the story. Did you bring divorce papers for me to sign? If so, there was no need to make a house visit. Mail or email would work just fine.

Michael smiled. "Well, things have been going better at work." He shifted gears. "Do you plan to stay? I made some dandy meatloaf last night. It'll be a cinch to warm it up." He tried to sound casual, but his heart pounded. *Please stay.*

Andy chimed in as he'd hoped. "Yaaay, meatloaf! It's my favorite."

"I was thinking of you when I made it," he said.

Muriel, he could see, was not as enthusiastic. "Since when do you cook? It takes a Constitutional amendment to get you to boil water."

More bitterness. More criticism. He shrugged. "Last night I was flippin' through one of your cookbooks, and I noticed it. I knew it was Andy's favorite, so…"

"And *you* made it?" Muriel asked, her words heavily seasoned with skepticism.

"Yeah." He managed to grin. "It tasted pretty good, too." Actually, he'd been surprised at his success and rather proud. "All I needed was a little ground beef, an egg or two, some onion and a few other ingredients, and I was off to the races."

Andy made up for his mother's lack of enthusiasm. "Yum! Can we stay, Mom?"

"Why not?" Michael coaxed. "You said Andy misses me. Besides," — he took a quick glance at his watch — "it's already well past five."

Muriel brushed back a dark curl on her forehead. He could tell she wanted Andy to see him but only for a short while. Dinner was a little too cozy, a little too family-oriented. On the other hand, he thought, you've got something else up your sleeve, haven't you?

"Okay," Muriel said. "I suppose it wouldn't hurt."

———————

As he prepared dinner, he almost choked up with tension. It was like he was auditioning for the greatest role or job in his life. His heart beat like a lively drum in his chest, and it was actually painful. He was sure his family would notice his distress.

His family. The words had a beautiful sound, but the disconnect between him and the two people who sat at the kitchen table was immense, a chasm it would be impossible to bridge. Oh, not Andy. Never Andy who openly loved him, but with Muriel who sat there with a sour expression on her face as if she'd just sucked a rank lemon. No, she didn't want to be here, at least not for this purpose.

As it turned out, he needn't have worried. The dinner was a rousing success.

The meatloaf was tender and tasty, with a tang abetted by onions and tomato paste. The green beans were crisp and flavorful, the mashed potatoes buttery and smooth. It was not a gourmet meal. No, far from it. But after a few bites, Andy squealed with delight and dug in while Muriel set her fork down and looked at him in amazement.

"Michael, how did you do this? How did you get the meatloaf to taste so good?"

To taste so good. He savored her words, which tasted sweet. "You like the meatloaf?"

"Yes."

He shrugged. "I did a little of this, a little of that, just followed the recipe." He snapped his fingers. "Oh, I kept it in a little longer than I was

27

supposed to and experimented with a few seasonings. Just a matter of feel, I guess."

She gazed at him, looking so beautiful he wanted to reach across the table and kiss her. In return for his desire, she lowered her head and continued eating.

After a dessert of rocky road ice cream, his son's favorite, Muriel started to say something but Andy spoke up first. "Hey, how about a game of Scrabble?"

Muriel shook her head. "I'm afraid we don't have time. Besides, the game's at our new place."

"No, I left it here in my bottom drawer!" Andy said. He hopped up and ran down the hall toward his old room. While he was gone, Muriel looked at him.

"We need to talk," she said.

Her voice sounded ominous, as if Andy was sick or something. Before he could reply, his son romped back into the kitchen, loaded for bear.

They cleared the table and set out the game. Andy drew a B tile to go first, and he drew an R to go last. After they drew seven tiles apiece, the game began.

Michael never much liked to play because Scrabble was a game that confounded him. The squares and tiles that intersected in strange ways horizontally and vertically to multiply their value... Well, it was a mystery to him. Not once had he Scrabbled or come close to winning a game and he usually lost by seventy points or more. But when someone in his family, usually Andy, wanted to play, Michael went along to get along. While he joked that the game wasn't in his wheelhouse, he was quick to say that if Andy wanted to play, he was onboard too.

As they took turns, the game assumed an all-too-familiar pattern. In other words, he began losing. If Andy or Muriel got thirty points, he strained to get ten. Muriel was a very good player, and Andy, with a verified IQ of 146, was only a little behind her—for now. Usually it was a contest between them with Michael lagging well behind, just as he was today.

Gradually, though, a change occurred. At first, he wasn't aware of it, but then he began to realize, to *feel*, that there were certain high-valued letters he didn't want to hold on to for too long because it was hard to use them and the cost was too high. Letters like Q and Z, J and X. Well, X wasn't too bad. Then there was K and V, especially V, which was troublesome. He'd been told some of these things before, but now it all coalesced.

Mostly, though, he soon realized something else. The way you generally scored the most points was to Scrabble. It was difficult to use all seven letters at one time, but during the past year, he'd seen Muriel and Andy each do it several times.

Now, with each turn, Michael tried to Scrabble. But the best he could come up with was 22 points, which he got by placing an S at the end of Andy's vertically arranged MARK, and then spelling SCORE horizontally. Twenty-two points was a modest score at best, the kind that Muriel and Andy routinely surpassed. Yet they both regarded his feat with surprise.

"It looks like your daddy's catching on," Muriel said.

Catching on. With every play Michael realized he was doing just that. More and more, the game board came to resemble a battlefield, and he was the commanding general of loyal troops who faced two inferior armies. He saw more and more clearly, and when he Scrabbled three moves later, he took confident pleasure in laying out the tiles one by one.

On her previous move, Muriel had spelled out the word EXACT on a horizontal row leading to the right border. Michael had only one T but he saw at once that the T in EXACT would enable him to use all his seven tiles on the vertical row in spelling FATALIST. What's more, the move was blessed by the fact that there was a Triple Word Score square both at the beginning and the end of the word.

Despite himself, he laid out each of the tiles slowly with deliberate malice, enjoying the act immensely. When he finished, he looked up.

"You Scrabbled!" Andy cried.

Michael grinned.

Muriel's lips counted silently. "Not only that, there are two Triple Word squares. So you get an additional sixty-six points."

"That's a hundred and sixteen!" Andy said. "Wow Oh Wow Oh Wow!"

Michael knew that however much Andy was surprised, he was happy and proud of his father. Muriel, though, seemed stunned and somehow disappointed. Finally, she managed a thin smile.

"You've been sandbagging us, Michael."

"No, not at all," he said. "I was just lucky for a change. You know that getting the right letters at the right time is key. C'mon, it's Andy's play."

He tried to dial it back but it was hard. While his momentum slowed, he still scored over three hundred and fifty points, beating them both by over a hundred. Feeling a need to return things to normal, Michael pushed for a second game.

This time, he deliberately scored barely half of what he had the first time and lost to both, but by only thirty or forty points. It seemed to be enough to please Muriel, though, and they rose and gathered the pieces and put the game back in its box.

"We'll take it with us this time," Muriel said. She turned to Michael. "We've got to leave soon, but I'd like to talk to you for a moment."

Michael spread his arms. "So, talk."

Her gaze skipped away from Andy's probing eyes. "No, privately. In your room, if it's all right with you. We'll only be gone from Andy for a few minutes."

He hesitated. "Sure," he said, and left the kitchen. As he moved down the hall, she came up beside him. When he reached his room, he pushed the door open and bowed awkwardly.

"After you, my dear."

To his surprise, she hesitated. Then he remembered that two weeks before she'd left with Andy, she had forsaken the bedroom they shared and set up residence in the smaller one at the end of the hall. Anything to avoid sharing his bed and the marital intimacy it implied.

After a moment, she entered, a tense look on her face. He started to follow but a voice called. "Dad!"

He looked back down the hall. Andy was standing there with an urgent expression. Michael tried to interpret it but drew a blank. Nor could he remember Andy calling him "Dad" before. It was always Daddy.

What do you want, Andy? he thought. What do you want to tell me? He raised a hand and waved at his son, then entered his room.

Inside, he found Muriel standing in the dark and felt a sense of dread. He switched on the light and closed the door.

"Okay," he said, "what is it?"

Now that they were here, she seemed to have lost her sense of mission. She strolled about, avoiding the bed, then noticed the CABS machine on the table beside the bed.

"What's that?" she asked.

He cleared his throat. "After you left, I had some painful episodes while sleeping. I couldn't breathe and struggled to wake up. A test determined that I had sleep apnea. My airway shut during the night." He pointed. "That machine helps to keep it open."

"I'm sorry," she said. "It must have been painful."

To Michael, she didn't seem to mean it. It was just a polite thing to say.

An imp of the perverse landed on his shoulder and whispered in his ear. "Let me show you something," he said. He took the mask from the bureau and placed it on his face, then tightened the straps. "Ain't I pretty?" he said.

Her jaw dropped. "My God, you look like a monster."

There's nothing like a little sympathy from the woman you love. "Tell you what," he said. "If you'll be Beauty, I'll be the Beast."

She did not seem to like this suggestion at all. He removed the mask and set it back. "Muriel—"

"The divorce settlement is ready and it just needs your signature," she said. "You'll find the terms very reasonable. You won't have to give up a thing."

"Except Andy," he said. "You want to raise him alone."

"There's a provision for visitations," she said. "Weekends, that sort of thing."

He'd heard this before. What he had not known was that she wouldn't gouge his wallet. "Wait a minute, you mean I don't have to pay child support?"

Her mouth worked. "No."

"Why not?"

"It…will be taken care of."

"Taken care of?" He thought he knew how but did not want to hear it. If he heard it, it would be real. Moving forward, he put his arms around her. "Hey, baby, can't we work this out? Just give me a chance."

She shook her head. "No, it's too late for that, Michael."

"Why do you say that? Please, give me a chance. I can change."

"No. You've said that too many times, made too many promises. I won't—"

He pulled her close and kissed her, kissed her hard and desperately. She fought him, but he kept his lips pressed to hers and caressed her body. In return, she resisted and emitted harsh sounds of displeasure. He would not be denied, though, and after several moments he felt her hands rise and clasp him around the neck. Briefly, she responded with the passion of the early years of their marriage. Then she pounded his arms and tried to push him away. He released her, letting her fall back onto the bed.

She sat up, her face flushed, her dark curly hair tossed all about her head. "What's wrong with you, Michael?" she asked. "Why do you act this way? You win at Scrabble, a game you've always been poor at, and now you attack and almost rape me."

"You kissed me back," he pointed out.

"An old habit," she said. "I'm sorry I did it."

"What did you mean," he asked, "when you said Andy's child support would be taken care of."

She straightened her hair, then her clothes. Finally, she met his eyes. "I've met a man," she said.

"A man?"

"Yes, a lawyer."

A lawyer. That figures. "Have you slept with him?" Michael asked. She stared back. "Yes."

That's the real reason she came here—to tell me. "Does Andy know?" he asked.

"Of course, he doesn't. Do you think I'd be so careless?" Her tone was righteous and indignant.

Think again, he thought. *Andy knows.* He remembered Andy calling him before he entered his room. It had been a warning. Yes, indeed, it would be hard to keep anything secret from his precocious and observant son.

"Maybe I wasn't the best husband," Michael said, "but how do you justify cheating on me?"

She rose from the bed, thrust out her chin. "You were unfaithful first when you lacked ambition and failed to plan for your family's future. You let us down, Michael."

Her words stung, but he realized they were true. How many men, he wondered, were as weak and unmotivated as he had been? And how many men hadn't cared enough even to try to change?

"I can change," he said. "I've started to improve. Please give me a little time."

"I gave you nine years," she said. "That's enough."

"And what did you contribute to our marriage?" he lashed out. "A few part-time jobs? I'm not the only one who fell short."

Though it was true, he regretted it as soon as he'd said it. "To hell with you," she snapped. "I'm going and taking Andy with me."

As she started to leave, Michael heard a hissing sound. They both turned, trying to find its source.

"What the hell is that?" Muriel said.

"I don't know."

The hissing rose and deepened. To Michael, it sounded like a snake.

He looked to his left. The tube on the CABS machine was swaying in the air, undulating back and forth.

Muriel gasped. "Michael, why's it doing that?"

"It must be a malfunction," he said, trying to remember when he'd attached the tube to the machine. But he kept the tube separate and knew he hadn't done it. Nor had he turned the damned thing on.

The tube weaved through the air like a snake, aiming toward Muriel and getting closer and closer. "Michael, stop it!" she screamed.

He rushed forward and grabbed the tube, then pulled it out of the back of the machine with an explosive rush of air. The tube went limp and he yanked out the cord.

"Muriel, I'm sorry," he said. "I don't know why—"

Too late for an apology. The door was open, and his wife was gone.

CHAPTER FIVE
COURTSHIP ON THE RUN

A week after his wife had hurriedly left with his son, Beverly was chasing him again. Lust or ardor, Michael was not sure what to call it. Only that he'd better move quick to avoid being caught. As he raced down aisle 7 and ducked into aisle 6, all thoughts about how his sleep apnea machine had seemed about ready to attack his wife vanished. When he was safe again he could wonder if he had somehow forgotten he'd activated it in the first place.

In the last few days, he had acquired more and more confidence in just about everything. Work, people, his health, he was in command of all. Well, he worried about his family of course, and now the matter of Heavenly Beverly, whose erogenous zones were definitely turned in his direction. He'd prefer not to have to get ugly and turn her down flat. Hell, after all, had no fury like a woman scorned, and he'd like to keep this second-rate job until he found another.

As he headed past the plumbing fixtures, he saw Stokes signal urgently to him from the end of the aisle. *She's heading this way!*

He slammed to a halt. What to do? A glance behind confirmed that it was too far to go back, and he'd be damned if he was going to scramble over a commode into the next aisle. After all, he had his pride.

So he braced himself and proceeded on, thinking of Hitler's Sister with her not-so-heavenly mustache perched just beneath her nose. The woman had fallen for him like a ton of bricks. From her flirtation in the parking lot to the first of her desperate love letters, only a few hours had passed. And come to think of it, a few other women had started to notice him as well, perhaps because his self-esteem had risen.

Beverly Starret appeared at the end of aisle 6, a lane where customers could buy everything from tubs to toilets, showers to sinks, and don't forget pumps and garbage disposals and water heaters. To Michael, it seemed an appropriate place for him to be tracked down and captured. Perhaps she'd hog-tie him and tow him back to her lair, where she could have her way with him.

But she didn't need any assistance. While he had gained nearly twenty pounds since acquiring the CABS machine, he could see that Beverly was still three inches taller and God knows how many pounds heavier. If nothing else, she could just smack him down and sit on him. He imagined himself squashed flat while she used their premium set of pipe cutters to render his resistance strictly academic.

Relax. She's not a serial killer or a maniac, just a girl who knows what she wants.

The "girl" approached, over seventy pounds heavier and with a fierce, determined look that froze his liver. As she approached, every part of her body, especially her pendulous breasts, bounced and fell in a deadly rhythm.

"Michael," she said, "why have you been hiding from me?"

What evil alchemy has transformed you? He remembered a time when she had seemed strong and imperious, needing no one, certainly not him. He hadn't liked her then, but at least he had respected her. The woman he now saw before him was reduced not in size but in dignity. Still, she remained a dangerous force he would have to cope with.

"I was just checking the water heaters," he said. "A customer asked about them."

"There's no customer out front. Why are you avoiding me? Why can't we be together?"

Okay, time to take a stand. "Look, Bev, I'm married. Plus, I have a seven-year-old kid." *Not only that, I'd rather dive into a lake of boiling lye than have you even touch me.*

Her hands reached out, timidly caressing him. "Don't be so cold, Michael. Don't you see how I love you?"

He backed away. Why was he having this effect on her? Two weeks ago, she had treated him with disdain. To her, he had been the equivalent of slime mold.

"I'm *married*," he repeated, feeling helpless. "I've been married for nine years—"

"—and you're separated," she finished. "Your wife left you a month ago and took your son with her. She's screwing a rich lawyer like there's no tomorrow and doesn't want to have anything to do with you."

His heart twisted in pain and embarrassment. As never before, he felt the depth of his loss and Muriel's rejection of him. His family was gone. *Gone.*

"That's none of your business," he said. "And besides, to be blunt, I'm not attracted to you in the slightest."

"Michael, Michael," she pleaded, "just give us a chance." Her fingers reached out, caressing his skin again, and her voice wheedled and cajoled, oozing self-pity. "Just hold me for a moment, give me one kiss."

Before he could reply, she lunged forward and seized him. The sensation was utterly loathsome. It was like being buried in blubbery madness. He felt that if he didn't escape, he would drown in her copious, overflowing flesh.

Her lips sought his. He turned his head away. She reached up and seized his jaw so he couldn't move.

Her mouth, moist and half-open, pressed against his. It felt like a leech.

No!

He wrenched free, backed away. "I'm leaving!"

She cried. "Please, don't leave. Father's in the office. I talked to him and he'll give you a raise and a promotion. Please stay! You've got a future here if you want it."

He'll give you a raise and a promotion. Now they were both in on it. Had Heavenly Beverly coerced her daddy as she was trying to coerce him? Either way, he'd had enough. They could both take this fucking job and shove it.

He turned and walked away, determined to leave the store forever. Behind him, she wailed.

"Michael!"

He turned. Thirty feet away, she sniffed back tears. "Just speak to my father for one minute," she said. "That's all I ask."

Michael glanced around. All the employees in the store were watching them, amazed and mesmerized by this pathetic drama. Cal Frank's and Howie Becker's eyes were actually bugging out, and Prissy Doyle, who loved her soaps, looked absolutely spellbound by this real-life scene, which could have been taken from any one of them.

He raised his hand to wave goodbye, but Beverly started to march toward him. No, she was *running*, frantic to stop him. Before he knew it, she hooked his arm and steered him toward her father's office at the far left of the store. He resisted, digging in his heels. "Stop!"

"Please," she said, "I want you to see him."

"Why should I? What's in it for me? I already told you I'm not interested."

She squeezed his arm. "Just see him for one minute, as a favor to me."

One minute, how could it hurt? Alfred Starret was an old, white-haired man, a figure in the background who was rarely at the store. When he did come, he tended to stay in his brightly lit office, working on his computer and playing chess with himself. The employees whispered about how you never wanted to be called into that room of bright lights for something you had screwed up. At best, you'd be fired; at worst, the cold bastard would use his connections to ruin your life. Michael had heard his fellow employees gossip about that and other things, such as how much Beverly's father doted on her. Apparently, he thought she was the most wonderful, beautiful girl in the world, and he would do anything and give her anything to please her, even if it was a married man whose wife had dumped him.

They stopped before Starret's door. "How often have you met him?" Beverly asked.

Michael frowned. "Only a few times and they were brief. When it comes to running this place, he's not exactly hands-on."

"No," Beverly admitted. "I handle most of the business here. Anyway, give him a chance and he'll grow on you." She opened the door and waited. "Please," she said.

To hell with this. Who needed it? But his curiosity was caught and he entered, followed by Beverly. The door closed behind them and he gazed at the sharp-featured old man behind the massive oak desk. Alfred Starret sat before a chessboard, one of the pieces held in his hand. To Michael, it looked like a white pawn.

Starret smiled at him. "Mr. Windsor, how good of you to join us."

He'd always disliked people who talked like that. It wasn't good of him at all to be here since as an employee he had no choice. Except he did have a choice because he intended to quit.

"It's a pleasure to meet you as well, Mr. Starret," he said, playing the part. He glanced about the spacious office, which he'd only glimpsed from outside before. Yup, it was bright all right, just as reported. Odd, oval-shaped lamps hung down from the ceiling.

Beverly moved to the side as if to give them more room.

Mr. Starret set the white pawn down and picked up the elegantly carved king. "Mr. Windsor, you have a son, do you not?"

"Yes, I do."

"And he's an only child?"

Uh-oh, he thought he saw where this was going.

"Yes, he is, and I'd do almost anything for him. As you'd do almost anything for Beverly, who is also an only child."

Understanding flashed in Starret's eyes. Ah, Pawn's Gambit.

"Exactly," said Starret. "And that being the case, don't you think you're being unreasonable not to show my daughter a little attention? After all, your wife did abandon you and deprive you of your only child." He paused. "Not only that, she has been brazenly unfaithful with a certain local attorney. We can provide documentation if necessary."

Starret was bringing out his big pieces in an early, full-frontal, merciless attack. Michael decided on honesty. "The fact is, I still love my wife, and I'm not at all attracted to your daughter."

Starret waved his hand. "Just give her a chance. You've almost broken her heart."

Michael looked at Beverly, seeing humiliation and tears in her eyes. "I'm truly sorry your daughter has experienced distress, but she's done it to herself. At any rate, I have to be honest about my feelings." He *was* sorry about Beverly, but at the same time, he realized she'd always been a pain in his side, first as his superior, then as a desperate lover.

"We can be most generous, especially if you and Beverly get married."

Oh shit, the man is delusional. He'll mention stock options next. I should never have come in here. "Thanks for the offer, Mr. Starret, but I'm quitting. I was just leaving when Beverly stopped me."

There. That should blunt this bastard's attack.

Starret exchanged a long look with his daughter. Michael saw Beverly nod ever so slightly.

"I'm genuinely sorry you feel that way," Starret said. He reached forward and moved a knight. "Because of your attitude—"

"Pardon me," Michael said, "you don't want to make that move."

Starret frowned. "I don't?"

"No, if you do, Black will checkmate you in seven moves. Five if you're stupid."

That got his attention. Starret scanned the board and sniffed. "I don't see it. Mr. Windsor, have you played chess much?"

"Three or four times." It was more than that, but he'd gotten beaten almost every time.

"And you say…"

"Look again, sir. I can't believe you don't see it."

Now the game was more like poker. Was Michael bluffing or not? As Starret studied the board, Michael noticed a plaque on the wall behind him. Starret's Hardware Store had ranked Highest in Customer

Satisfaction for the entire state. Though the lettering had faded, Michael could see that the award had been given twenty-three years ago.

Finally, Starret made his original move with the knight and sat back. "Show me."

The situation reminded Michael of the Scrabble game he had played with Muriel and Andy. Chess was like Scrabble, only more so. The whole board was open to him, along with all its possibilities. He moved a bishop, Starret hesitated and moved a pawn, and after four more moves, Starret's king was trapped with nowhere to go. Against the wall, Beverly gasped in surprise.

Starret stared at the result. "I was stupid."

"You were doomed anyway after you pushed that knight."

Starret's gaze met his. "And if I had moved some other piece?"

Michael smiled. "It was only a matter of time."

The man lit a cigarette and expelled some smoke. "What's a man like you doing working in my shop?"

"Pleasing customers, sir. I just wish I could please you."

"You can. All you have to do—"

"Asked and answered."

Father and daughter exchanged another look. "Then I have no choice. You may have won at chess, son, but I will prevail at *this* game. Unless you cooperate, I will have to ruin you. I have the resources to do it, you know."

"Friends in dark places?"

He blew a stream of smoke. "Yes, and they can be very efficient. They'll start by breaking a few fingers, then progress to your legs. Other methods are nonphysical and involve stealing your identity. You have credit and bank cards, I presume? You may suddenly find them and others quite worthless."

Michael turned and looked at Beverly. "Is this all right with you?"

She straightened. "No, but I have no choice. I love you." She hesitated. "I can take care of you, Michael. Make it up to you."

He remembered how the tube of his sleep apnea machine had weaved through the air like a snake, aiming at Muriel, and how he had protected her. "You always have a choice," he said. Starret's arrogant threat filled him with anger. The bastard would destroy him just to please his selfish daughter! Starret would break his body and steal his identity just to get what she wanted.

Something scraped the ceiling. Michael looked up to see the lamp above Starret's head start to turn. Around and around it went, and soon screws fell down, a couple falling on Starret's head.

"Father, watch out!" Beverly said in alarm. "My God, get out of your seat!"

He was too slow, though. As Starret rose, the oval light fixture above fell and the metal shade slipped right over his head, shattering the lamp itself and tearing one of his ears to pieces. Starret screamed and reached up to push the metal away.

No good, the metal shade struck his nose and tilted, raking out an eye and shattering his teeth. Michael saw the fixture fit under his bloody chin and yank him up toward the ceiling.

"Dad, no!" Beverly screamed. She clutched her father's legs and tried to pull him free but the fixture whirled him around and around, grinding at his throat as it spun. Blood shot across the room in sheets, splattering the floor and walls, drenching Beverly in copper-smelling crimson. Michael retreated as the spectacle continued. You said it yourself, he thought. After he pushed that knight he was doomed.

Finally, Starret's head was ripped from his neck. It struck the ceiling then smashed down onto the chess set, scattering the pieces. Beverly continued to scream, jumping away to avoid her father's head as it bounced across the room.

Michael shuddered and looked down.

That was odd.

There was blood everywhere, but not a single drop on him.

CHAPTER SIX
ATTACKERS

There were two cops, a fat one and a thin one, and Michael could tell from the beginning that neither one trusted him. The fat cop's nostrils actually sniffed, as if detecting the faint odor of mendacity.

"Thanks for meeting with us today," the thin cop said. "We know the experience must have been difficult for you."

Michael looked about the small interrogation room he sat in, knowing he didn't have much choice about being here. The owner's daughter wants you for a lover but all the employees know you can't stand the idea. Then she grabs your arm and takes you to meet her father in his office and the guy ends up without a head. *Of course* the fuzz are going to be suspicious and want to interrogate you, and if you decline, they'll arrest you on probable cause or some other charge. It wasn't hard to figure out. Easy-peasy, as Muriel would say.

"It was no picnic," Michael acknowledged. "I couldn't believe what I saw."

"Why is that?" asked the fat cop. His name was Lieutenant Matthews, and his red hair was cut in a stiff brush.

Michael swallowed. "It was fuckin' insane and crazy. It made no sense. It was like a hideous horror show."

Maybe, but the trouble was that Michael felt the event did make sense. Deep in his gut, he knew what had caused the lamp to descend and yank Alfred Starret up toward the ceiling, then saw his head off. It was the same source that had made his sleep apnea machine start to attack his wife. The implications sickened him and stirred feelings of guilt he desperately suppressed. No, he couldn't be responsible. There must be some other explanation.

"The machine used my own feelings to kill," he mumbled. "And it did it from a distance, through some kind of wireless connection, a human-machine WI-FI."

"What's that?" the thin cop quickly asked. His name was Sanchez, and he had a mustache that drooped around his lips to his chin.

Michael started. "Nothing," he said. *I've got to watch my mouth, keep my thoughts to myself.*

"Mr. Windsor," the fat cop said, "you were seeing Beverly Starret, correct?"

"If you mean I was dating her, the answer is no."

"But it was common knowledge she had strong feelings for you."

"I assure you, it was strictly one-sided."

Lieutenant Sanchez waded in. "And we've been told that she steered you to her father's office so he could put some pressure on you regarding her."

Michael took a sip of his coffee, which was already cold. "Who told you that?"

"It doesn't matter. Did you resent being pressured, Mr. Windsor?"

Ah, so that's where he's going. He wants me to say I blew up and killed the man. "Not at all," he said. "But I was stunned and sickened by what happened and just stood there helplessly and watched. Unlikely as it was, Mr. Starret's death must have been due to an electrical malfunction of some kind. Has forensics studied the lamp yet?"

"Please just answer our questions," Sanchez said.

"Okay. Well, I'm sure you've talked to his daughter. What did she say happened in the office?"

From courtroom dramas he'd seen, he knew it wasn't wise to ask a question if you didn't know the answer. For all he knew, Beverly had told them he'd pulled the light fixture down and rammed it right over her daddy's head, then hoisted him aloft like a flag.

On second thought, he knew she hadn't said that, just as he knew this session was being recorded. Lieutenant Sanchez leaned forward and spread his hands in a friendly gesture, as if he was the good cop in this scene. "Mr. Windsor, you have to see it from our point of view. There were only three people in that room. Mr. Starret certainly didn't kill himself, and I know you're too much of a gentleman to lay the blame on his daughter. So…"

The word hung in the air like bait, begging him to bite it. He did not. Let the sly bastard finish his own damned sentence without his support. No assist on this play, thank you very much.

Matthews shifted his fat ass and stood up. He took a threatening step toward Michael and glared down. "Why don't you admit it?" he said. "Starret said something about you and his daughter and you simply snapped. You went on a rampage. My God, did you see all that blood? It covered everything. No woman could ever do such a thing."

In addition to this being a stupid and false statement, Matthews had failed to mention something that he and Sanchez must be acutely aware of. Why hadn't either cop mentioned it? Michael felt they didn't know what the hell to make of it or they thought it would hurt their case.

Michael rose and spread his arms. "What do you not see?" he asked.

The fat cop frowned. "What are you talking about?"

Michael slowly turned around until he faced him again. "What do you not see?" he repeated. He looked at Sanchez, seeing similar wariness. "Your boys examined me earlier and I'll tell you what they didn't see. It's the same thing that you don't see right now. Neither of you see a single drop of blood on me. Not even one. Please tell me how I could have killed Mr. Starret when I'm clean as a whistle."

Matthews rubbed his stiff red hair. "We were about to ask you that. It's the most suspicious thing of all. How did you manage to go in that room and not even get a drop of blood on you?"

He glared back. "You tell me. I wish the hell I knew."

Ten minutes later, after being warned not to leave town, he stood on the sidewalk. Michael's heart pounded in exultation. There was a reason their experts hadn't been able to find a single molecule of blood on him. His CABS machine had deliberately shielded him from being spattered so he'd have an airtight alibi. He feared, however, it might work the other way.

A moment later, more doubts rose. How could a machine have a motive? It was just a mindless mechanism, a hunk of metal. Not only that, how could it know from a distance what trouble he'd gotten into and manage to protect him from getting splashed by Starret's blood? And how did it protect him without any visible means? For that matter, even if it were sentient, why would it want to protect him?

Easy-peasy, he was its owner. The device needed him, needed someone to plug it in and fit the mask over his face at night. Otherwise, it had no meaning and purpose.

He mulled it over, examining the logic, when he spotted a policeman watching him from a window. He stiffened and headed toward his car.

As he drove home, guilt swallowed him whole. He had killed a man, used the growing power the sleep apnea device had given him to take Starret's life. Yes, the man had threatened him and had no compunction about ruining his life, but Michael had no right to kill him, especially in front of his daughter.

Yes, I did. It was self-defense. He started it, and I had no choice.

But had he really done it? Bizarre as it seemed, maybe it *was* an electrical malfunction. He searched his memory, trying to recapture the precise horror he had witnessed, but it eluded him. Nor could he recall feeling a murderous impulse toward the man. Could it have been subconscious?

Christ, it was all so confusing.

A new mystery appeared when he got out of his car and approached his front door. It was slightly ajar. Leaving the door standing open was something he never did, especially after his wife and son left him. But he had been under a lot of pressure lately and must have forgot to lock it. Based on today's events, matters were only going to get worse.

He opened the door and stepped inside. Good, he had remembered to turn the lights off. There was no need for them, since even in the dark, he knew his way about the apartment by heart. He passed the living room and entered the kitchen, where he placed his keys on the table. He heaved a deep sigh, remembering all that had happened. More vividly than before, he saw Starret being hoisted toward the ceiling by a lighting fixture. Then came the grinding of his neck and the impossible sight of his head falling down in a shower of blood. As if that were not enough, he had walked out on his job today, leaving just $92.12 in the bank and a few bucks in his wallet.

There was a sound in his bedroom.

He waited but the apartment reclaimed its silence. No, not quite. Ever so softly, someone was moving down the far end of the hall in his direction. Michael crept to the front wall of the kitchen and listened to the intruder's stealthy approach. The hall passed the kitchen, then turned at a right angle toward the front door. Perhaps the visitor would skip the kitchen and slip out the door.

The footsteps ceased. The intruder had stopped walking, perhaps because he sensed Michael's presence.

Who could it be? And why was the intruder here? What could he possibly want?

Michael left the kitchen and slipped into the even darker shadows of the hall. He peered down it and managed to make out the dim form of the intruder fifteen feet away. He was tall, much taller than he, and clutched something against his chest.

The intruder started walking again.

Michael waited until he'd taken a couple of steps, then reached out and touched a light switch on the outside wall of the kitchen. He took a deep breath, then flicked the switch on.

Light flooded the hall, briefly blinding him. But he'd been prepared for it. Not so his visitor, who flinched and raised his hand to ward off the glare.

"I don't recall giving you the key to my apartment," Michael said.

The man hesitated. "Y-You didn't."

Michael stepped toward him. "The other day you seemed a little too interested in my device," he said. "I should have been more discreet."

Zack Hampton glanced down at the bag that contained the CABS machine. "I'm only going to borrow it for a while, Mike. Then I'll bring it right back."

"The hell you will. You're not 'borrowing' it, Zack, you're stealing it. You're a thief."

Zack shook his head. "You've changed, Mike, gotten bigger and better, especially at tennis." He patted the bag. "Something like this, if it's true, shouldn't belong to just one person. At the very least, you should share it with a friend."

"If you'd asked me, I would have gladly lent it to you. But you didn't ask."

"No, you wouldn't have lent it, Mike. You're lying to yourself."

Michael considered Zack's words and examined himself. Yes, he had been lying. He wanted the machine only for himself.

"Let me pass," Zack said.

"Can't let you do it, man. Stay where you are and put the machine down."

"The hell I will. I was a heavyweight boxer, compadre, with a 12 and 2 win-loss record. If we tangle, I'll bust you up pretty bad. *Step aside.*"

Michael squared his shoulders. "No."

He saw Zack clutch the bag tighter and then move toward him. As he drew close, he feinted to one side. Michael slipped to the right, countering the move. Zack shifted to the other side, then feinted back and forth and suddenly threw a punch at Michael's face. Michael slipped inside it and drove his fist at Zack's chin, putting all his weight behind it. He didn't hit Zack exactly where he wanted, but Zack went down, still clutching the machine.

Zack peered up at him. "Shit. This machine's given you a punch, too."

"Leave the machine here so we don't break it, and get out. I'll forget all about this."

Zack was silent, then nodded. "Okay." He set the machine on the floor and rose, clutching his chin. "You hit like a mule."

Michael stepped aside. "Good night."

Another nod. Then Zack started to leave.

At the last moment, he turned and swung at him, catching him on his shoulder. Michael swung back. A left, a right, another left. Zack's fist struck his forehead, making the world spin, but Michael fought the dizziness off. He waded in, targeting Zack's midsection, then whipped his fist up under Zack's jaw. Zack dropped to the floor and lay there.

For a while, Michael was afraid he'd killed him. He went to the kitchen sink, filled a glass, then returned and poured it over Zack's face. Zack coughed and his eyes blinked. Michael gently raised Zack's head and poured some water down his throat.

A few minutes later, muttering an apology, Zack staggered out. "Sorry I jimmied your door. I just had to see—"

"That's okay, Zack. Forget about it." Michael patted his shoulder and walked him to his car. He watched Zack get in and drive off, then returned to his apartment where he picked up the CABS machine and carried it to his bedroom.

He set the machine down and stripped naked, then he went to the mirror. He took a good long look at himself.

The sight stunned him. He had examined himself before, but in just the last few days, his body seemed to have undergone a transformation. He had genuine muscles now, and they rippled in sinuous unity as he moved. He had the feeling his body was building toward something, *becoming* something that had remained trapped in his DNA. But what could it be?

He sat down on the bed with the machine in his lap. He peered into its shiny face, knowing it was only a plastic screen. "Who are you?" he said. "*What* are you?" Myriad possibilities surged through his mind. Perhaps the machine was an alien, or an accident in production had somehow generated consciousness. Who knows, perhaps he hadn't killed Starret at all but the machine had done it through him, and he had been no more than a convenient tool, as innocent as a lamb. Or perhaps the two of them had done it together in synergy, two parts working deliberately as one.

The speculation tired him. Though it was only afternoon, he rose and prepared for bed, then filled the machine's tub with distilled water. Perhaps the water was the CABS machine's blood, its life and soul? He put on the mask, connected the tube, turned on the machine, switched off the light, and slipped beneath the covers.

Air, fresh sweet, restorative air, poured into his lungs. The seal was perfect, and he had the feeling that a woman was kissing him, a woman who loved him deeply and desired him. It was too bad, of course, that the woman wasn't human, but a supernatural being beyond his comprehension.

He laughed softly at the notion then remembered his situation was dark and precarious. His family had left him and he had quit his job. And the police suspected him of killing Starret. He remembered the employees entering Starret's office as Beverly continued to scream, and their horror at seeing the bloody mess with Starret's head on the floor. Could something like that be kept secret from the public?

The air in the tube stopped.

Michael's heart froze. Had the machine broken down? That was all he needed.

He drew a deep breath but nothing was there. His apnea machine was dead, completely useless. He could get up and check it, of course, but he sensed it would do no good.

Suddenly the airflow returned, even sweeter and more refreshing than before. Michael moaned in relief. Thank God. For good or bad, he'd come to depend on the machine, to see it as part of him. He took a few deep breaths and closed his eyes, determined to sleep, but thoughts entered his mind that had only nibbled at him before.

The CABS machine killed Starret to get me out of trouble, but what if it made things even worse? What if it made me the only suspect in Starret's death and I'll be thrown in jail and quickly executed? Why did it go overboard and act so drastically?

Shit, who could say? Perhaps the machine hadn't considered the consequences. Perhaps it acted on impulse and could make mistakes. Perhaps it simply hadn't cared. He rolled over, trying to forget about it, but all he could think about was what deadly surprises might await him when he awoke.

CHAPTER SEVEN
A BREATH OF FRESH AIR

He slept sixteen hours straight without a dream or a thought of trouble. When he finally woke up in the morning, he had a sweet flavor in his mouth. He lay in bed, savoring its richness and trying to identify it. Pineapple? Peach? Caramel? No, it was something far more delicious. Something the machine had given him that he had never tasted before. Gradually, to his regret, the wonderful flavor faded and disappeared. He rose and went to the kitchen, wishing it would return.

He put the coffee on and went to the front door. Outside, he saw that the paper was lying right where it should be. Good, it was a promising omen for a day on which he had no job and no family either. At least the news continued to run on schedule with no unpleasant surprises.

That is, until he opened the paper and looked at it.

The headline was direct and pulled no punches: *STOREOWNER KILLED IN BLOODY ASSAULT*. A photo accompanied it, probably taken by one of the stunned employees who had entered Starret's office shortly after the incident. The photo was doctored and did pull punches, but it caught Beverly's expression perfectly as she gazed down at her mutilated father.

Mechanical accident or cold-blooded murder? Michael scanned the text, which was slight on detail but heavy on innuendo. He shuddered with relief that his name wasn't mentioned. Ah, but the case was young. He knew from his modest experience as a reporter that stories "developed" over time.

He heard his cell phone ring in his bedroom and hurried to answer it. When he heard the voice, he froze.

The caller was Muriel.

Michael swiped the *On* tab. "Hi, Muriel," he said, remembering that once, in another time, he had routinely greeted her with "Hey, Babe."

"Hi, Michael," she said. "I just saw the paper this morning. It says the owner of your shop was murdered in some bloody, gruesome attack."

"That's what I heard," he replied, deliberately distancing himself from the event.

"Well, how did it happen? The paper doesn't really say. For God's sake, are you all right?"

It takes you three *sentences to ask about me.* "I only caught a glimpse," he answered.

"*What?* You saw it? How did it happen? Who killed him?"

"I'm fine since you ask," he said. "How's Andy. Does he know about it?"

"No, and I see no reason to tell him. Listen, Michael, are you going to lose your job because of this?"

What do you care? he thought. You've got a rich, slick lawyer to keep you in style and bang you when you please. On the other hand, if I'm unemployed, it'll be even easier for you to get total custody of Andy. "Look, Muriel," he said. "Something just came up. I have to split."

He cut the connection as she started to protest and shoved the phone in his pocket. Yeah, he had something to do, all right. But since he'd quit his job and lost his family, he had no damn idea what it was.

He glanced at the CABS machine and patted it as if it were an old friend. "Mr. CABS, thanks for the Constant Airway Breathing Support and the good night's sleep," he said. "I didn't get up once, not even to take a piss."

Get out, a voice said in his head. *Get out now.*

Michael snatched his hand away. What the hell? He could have sworn he heard an unearthly voice in his head, a dark, heavy whisper. Could it be the machine? He peered at the small screen and touched the machine again.

Leave, the same voice said.

It was just a single word, but he leaped into action. Within a minute, he had the machine packed in its bag and ready to go. He headed down the hall, not even taking a toothbrush.

What was his plan? Where would he go? The machine had been rather reticent on that point. Indeed, why should he run? If Matthews or some other cops were going to arrest him, he should act fast and lawyer up. Since he had barely a hundred bucks to his name, though, he could imagine the quality of representation he would receive. What was that old saying? "You get what you pay for."

He turned right at the kitchen and flew out the door, locking it behind him. Would he ever be back? The machine hadn't mentioned that either.

He was just getting into his car when he heard someone call behind him. "Hey!"

He whirled, expecting to see policemen. To his relief, it was only Ben Stokes and Prissy Doyle, fellow employees at the hardware store. Only I'm no longer an employee, he reminded himself. Both of his visitors looked flushed and excited, their clothes untucked here and there.

"Michael!"

"Prissy!" he said. "Ben!"

They embraced spontaneously, everybody talking at once. Michael was immediately swept up by their emotion. The man who owned the store had been gruesomely murdered, and their livelihood was at stake. They were both understandably stunned and unsettled by these developments, and for several seconds, Michael shared their sense of helplessness at having their world torn apart.

Prissy and Ben pressed him on the murder. "You were in his office," Prissy said, wringing her hands. "What did you see?"

He heaved a sigh. "The light fixture suddenly fell and yanked Mr. Starret up. I couldn't believe my eyes."

Ben was not satisfied. "Is that all you saw? Word is the police grilled you for over an hour."

Was it that long? "I *was* in Mr. Starret's office," he said, "and Beverly certainly had nothing to do with her father's death." *At least I don't think she did.* He shook his head. "That poor girl. How is she doing?"

Prissy, a lover of soaps, gave a theatrical sigh. "Beverly's heart is broken." She clutched her glasses, which hung from a gold chain around her neck. "She says the same thing you do. The light fixture just went crazy, like some kind of mad guillotine."

Mad guillotine. Prissy's talents were wasted at the store. She ought to be writing for some soap, like *The Faithful Heart* or *The Wild and the Wretched.*

The sleep apnea machine vibrated against his side. *Leave,* it hissed in his mind. *Get the hell out of there!*

"I'm sorry," Michael said, "but I've got to go. We'll talk later." Despite their protests, he got into his car and sped off.

He drove quickly, one hand on the CABS machine, hoping for guidance. "At least give me some GPS," he said. "Instructions on where to go."

The machine didn't respond—not even a whisper.

What should he do? On impulse, he drove to a familiar building, wanting to see his son, if only for a moment. He parked and walked behind the playground area, being careful to stay outside the fence. The school had experienced a couple of molestation cases during the past year and even parents were told not to visit without permission. Children of the lowest grades were especially vulnerable, and Michael had no doubt that a guard would be posted.

Andy was seven and because of his exceptional or gifted status had been promoted twice from the second grade to the fourth. Walking, Michael remembered how Muriel had fought him when it came to educational acceleration. She wanted their son to grow up normally and never fall behind when it came to socialization. In contrast, he argued that there were ways to compensate for any loss and that any second-grade boy who could read and do math more than two years above his grade level should not be held back. Educators had agreed, and Muriel had reluctantly acquiesced.

Finally, Michael reached the area behind the playground, which featured swings, slides, seesaw, monkey bars, basketball court and other attractions. It was a beautiful day, and beyond the seven-foot-high wire fence, the equipment was brightly colored and looked especially inviting. Hell, he'd like to take a whack at it himself. The only problem was that there were no kids in sight.

Michael checked his watch: 10:15 a.m. Recess usually came shortly before and shortly after lunch. He felt a pang when he realized it might be two hours until he saw Andy, assuming he saw him at all.

In frustration, he clutched the bag containing the apnea machine. He must see Andy today, he must! He hadn't seen Andy since he'd come to his apartment with Muriel, and Michael had no idea when he'd see him again. As it was, he could see no further beyond his need to see his son. He had no plans after that and no goal. A heavy sense of doom hung over him.

Against his chest, the CABS machine pulsated once. *Leave*, it said.

He stayed. He had tried talking to Muriel, tried to reach her, and he had failed. He must have his chance with his son, whom he had failed so often and to whom he had so much to say.

Time slowly passed. 10:30...10:45...11:00 a.m.... A butterfly flew past, and he gripped the wire fence and shook it. He knew he looked suspicious just by standing here, a pedophile on the prowl. Wouldn't it be wiser just to go in the school and ask to see his son? Or perhaps he should heed his machine's warnings and leave.

More time crawled by. 11:30...11:40...11:50...

Michael was about to leave when a door in the back of the school banged open and children rushed out. Almost at once he saw Andy, whose tousled, unruly hair Muriel always tried to comb. Andy ran across the playground in brown shorts, spanking his butt in his characteristic way. "Giddy-up horsey," he shouted. "Giddy-up!"

Michael's heart pounded and he raised his hand. "Andy!" he called, careful not to be too loud because a teacher accompanied them.

He needn't have worried because Andy quickly spotted him and raced over. "Daddy!"

"Hi, Andy," Michael said as his son reached him. "I...I wanted to see you."

He wanted to embrace Andy, but the hard wire fence had other plans. Boiling over with emotion, Michael was forced to remain where he was.

Andy kicked the fence and gave a goofy little laugh. "I know. But no huggy this time, huh?"

Michael swallowed. "Andy, I have to tell you something."

Andy met his gaze. "I heard about Mr. Starret."

"You...you know?"

Andy nodded gravely. "Sure. It's on TV and the radio. Sally March said it just showed up on Meta."

Meta? The fuckin' story's even on Meta? What will they do next—fly a banner across the sky?

Michael forced the subject aside. Earth-shaking as this news was, it wasn't what he wanted to talk about. "Andy, things are getting complicated, and I don't know when I'll see you again. I just wanted to say, I'm sorry."

"Sorry about what, Daddy? Did you do something bad?" Andy grinned and Michael saw that one of his teeth was about to come out.

Michael gripped the fence. "I haven't been a good father to you. I've let you down."

"I don't care. I love you, Daddy."

His son's innate goodness brought Michael to tears. "I'm sorry I didn't keep my promises to you. I didn't...take you fishing."

Another grave nod. "Yes, you did. Twice. And you always kissed me goodnight at bedtime."

Michael was deeply touched. At the same time, though Andy was bright, he seemed somehow different and more mature. He saw Andy pick up on his confusion and touch his hand on the fence.

"I want to tell you something, Daddy. You remember the day we came over and you cooked dinner for us?"

Michael nodded. "I made meatloaf."

"Yeah, it was outstanding. Anyway, do you recall me getting up during the meal to go to the bathroom? Well, on the way back I went into your room and saw something new beside your bed."

Michael went cold. "Something new?"

"Yeah. So...I picked it up. I shouldn't have done it, but it was only for a few seconds. As I held it, I felt the thing move. Later, I felt different in here." He tapped his head.

Michael swallowed and gazed at the playground behind Andy. Children laughed and swung on swings, climbed into a playhouse, and bounced balls. Two kids, a boy and a girl, were balanced perfectly on a seesaw, but Michael teetered and caught the fence to keep from falling.

Trembling, he removed the machine from its case, leaving the attachments inside. "Did this hurt you? Do you need to go to the doctor?"

"Oh no, Daddy," Andy said. "But something weird happened." He giggled. "I suddenly knew a bunch of new words like oracular and metaphysical."

Michael managed to laugh, glad that Andy still called him Daddy. "We'll have to jump you a few more grades. How would you like to be a freshman in college?"

Andy broke into another of his goofy laughs. "Don't worry about that." He reached through the fence and tapped the machine's black casing. "Whatever it gave me is going away. I've already started to forget things, some of which I'm not sure I want to remember." Andy's face filled with wonder and awe. And something else: fear.

A couple of kids Andy's age ran up to him. "C'mon, Andy, we need somebody for kickball."

"Sorry, I can't now." Andy seemed to shake himself awake. He waved them off but someone else was approaching. It was the supervisor, a pretty young woman in an attractive lilac dress.

"Hello," she said. Michael could see her sizing him up. *Safe or not? Pedophile or not?*

Michael smiled. "Hi, I'm Andy's father, Michael Windsor."

"I'm glad to meet you, sir," she said. "You're welcome here at our school, but we've been forced to pass a new rule. We ask that parents who wish to see their children go first to the principal's office."

"Look," he said, "I've already seen my son. What I want to do before I leave is just give him a hug. Will you permit me to do that?"

He could tell that didn't fly. "Sir, I'm afraid you'll have to get approval from the principal."

"But why take all that time?" He glanced at the top of the seven-foot fence. "I can climb this baby in less than five seconds."

She looked aghast. "I'm afraid not. It's out of the question."

"Okay, it was just a crazy idea." He felt the CABS machine vibrate against his side and remembered his growing effect upon women. As she started to leave, he set the device and attachments down.

"Wait," he called.

She stopped and turned. "Yes?"

Michael said, "Andy told me you're his favorite teacher."

Andy hadn't even told him she was one of his teachers, but her pleased smile proved he'd made a lucky guess. "I'm Laura Kurick," she said, "his English teacher."

Ah, information! He smiled, putting everything he had into it. "English, huh? Maybe you could help me."

"Help you?" She took a step forward. "With what?"

"Well... I've been working on a novel."

"A novel?"

"Yes, a love story, an epic romance." He looked bashfully down. "It's, uh, about a beautiful young peasant girl and a middle-aged aristocrat."

It was a bold, brash play, and for a moment he thought he'd gone too far. But he'd acted so boyish, so needy, that she actually wavered.

"I'd love to read something like that," she said. "What is the title?"

Title? Yes, what the hell was its title? Searching for inspiration, he remembered romances and bodice rippers he had seen. A title? Ah, here came one now.

"It's called...*Forbidden Passion*," he said.

She considered it. "Not bad, but it's a bit generic. It definitely has promise though. You just need something new, something more."

"Oh, there's more," he said. "A whole lot more. There's adventure. There's danger. There's an international war. And there's...romance." He softened his voice, letting it flow like oil. "Plenty of romance."

Laura Kurick glanced back at the school. He waited silently, remembering a day when he had snagged a fish and let it tire itself out before reeling it in. "I have to go," she said, but she didn't go. Seconds passed. "You know, I always wanted to write. Tell me just a little bit more."

Michael gazed deep into her brown eyes. "I'll be glad to tell you everything."

She blushed, straightened her dress. "Oh, this is silly. Andy, is this your dad?"

"He sure is," Andy said.

She laughed, then waved at the fence. "Rules be damned. Why don't you climb the fence like you said?"

Michael didn't have to be asked twice. He climbed the fence in three seconds flat and gave Andy one of the longest hugs of his life. It felt damned good. Then he went to Andy's teacher and hugged her too. "Thank you for trusting me," he said. On impulse, he kissed her.

To his surprise, she kissed him back, moving her lips against his. He tasted her tongue and sweet breath and finally broke away with reluctance. Laura smiled, looking dazed. She even swayed a little.

"Gee, Miss Kurick," Andy said, "are you all right?"

As Michael left, the machine muttered its displeasure in his head. The puppet had disobeyed the puppeteer and it was not amused. Though his situation remained unchanged, Michael felt better than he had in days.

Until he saw two familiar figures walking toward him across the grass.

Lieutenant Matthews, the fat cop, was in the lead, marching as if on a mission. The sun blazed on his red, brush-like hair, and when he saw Michael, he actually beamed. Three steps behind him came Sanchez, struggling slightly in the thick grass, his mustache seeming to droop even more than it had the day before.

I told you we should have left, the machine said, its voice a sharp whisper.

Point taken, he acknowledged. Stopping, Michael waited for the policemen to reach him.

Matthews halted ten feet away. Sanchez, a bit behind, took a few seconds more to catch up. Judging by his rapid breathing, he was out of breath.

"Mr. Windsor," Matthews said, "why didn't you tell us yesterday that Mr. Starret threatened to ruin your life both physically and economically?"

Michael blinked. "I thought I had."

"No, you didn't. You admitted he pressured you to marry his daughter but neglected to mention that he threatened to have your legs broken and your identity stolen if you refused."

This was crazy. "Look," Michael said, "it was a terrible thing to see the man die. The way his head shot off and all that blood. I was understandably rattled."

Sanchez nodded, suggesting that he understood. Not so Matthews, who advanced a step. "When he threatened your life and livelihood, you snapped and killed him. Why don't you admit it?"

Crazier and crazier! "How did I do that, Lieutenant Matthews?" Michael asked. "How did I get the light fixture to descend from the ceiling and snatch him up?"

Don't argue! Michael's machine blared in his head. *Don't encourage him!*

Matthews seized on his words. "You entered your employer's office when he wasn't there and rigged the light fixture so it would do exactly what you wanted."

This was too much even for Sanchez. "Now Bill, forensics found no evidence of that."

"You're under arrest," Matthews said. He removed a set of handcuffs from his waist. "Please turn around."

"You're not putting those on me," Michael said.

"Don't give us any trouble," Matthews said. He started toward Michael then stopped. "What's that?"

Michael looked down. In his hands, before him, he held the CABS machine. When had he taken it out of the bag? As he stared at the unit, it began to hum.

"What's that, Mr. Windsor?" Matthews asked. He had his hand on his revolver.

Michael opened his mouth but Sanchez answered for him. "It looks like a sleep apnea machine. My brother has one."

The machine stopped humming. It sat dead and silent in Michael's hands.

"It's off now," Sanchez said. "There's nothing to worry about." He eyed Matthews's gun, which was half out of its holster. "We don't need that, Harry."

It was a warning, and Michael remembered that police shootings of unarmed men had become a growing scandal. Just last week, in this very city, a nine-year-old black kid had been killed for waving a licorice stick.

Matthews sullenly holstered his gun. "I'm still taking him in. There's too much evidence, and it all points in one direction."

The machine started to hum again, and Matthews jumped half out of his skin. Sanchez moved quickly and stopped him from drawing his weapon.

Why was the machine running again? He hadn't turned it on. Wait, hadn't something like this happened yesterday? Yeah, just before he'd fallen asleep, the unit had stopped operating. At the time he'd feared it might be broken. Fortunately, it had soon started up again. Why, though, had it stopped running in the first place?

Now that he thought of it, the machine reminded him of his computer. Sometimes his computer hummed, sometimes it was silent. It sounded crazy, but could the machine be part computer and deliberately downloading something or even updating itself?

In case you're wondering why I've been starting and stopping, the machine whispered in his mind, *the answer would surprise you. I've been evolving, Michael. Let me show you.*

Michael saw his hands turn the CABS machine around so the air outlet was pointing at the cops. Usually he plugged the tube in there, but this time…

He tried to turn the machine away, but for the first time, he found he was helpless against it. The machine resisted and held his arms fast. Michael felt his mouth open, and a voice much like his own spoke. "Officers, I'd like to give you something unique. How about a breath of fresh air?"

The machine spasmed, and a golden spray shot out, settling over the officers' bodies. In horror, Michael tried again to turn the machine away, but he couldn't budge it no matter how hard he tried. Another golden spray shot out, completing the work of the first. The policemen were drenched, and all he could do was watch.

For a moment the two policemen stood in unearthly beauty, glistening in glorious harmony. Then their lustrous color faded and they were as before. Only now they sniffed the air as if it were God's breath. Smiles wreathed their faces, and they moaned in ecstasy.

"Have you ever smelled anything so wonderful?" Sanchez cried.

"No, never! I love it!"

"It's like heaven!"

"Yes!"

Michael watched stunned as the two cops fell to the grass and writhed in pleasure. If Starret's bloody decapitation had been horrific, this orgy of scent surpassed it in the other direction. The officers inhaled and laughed, inhaled and sang, inhaled and grasped the air in both hands as if to empty the world. In mere minutes, they became more addicted than the most confirmed and desperate junkies.

What would happen to them when the air cleared?

Michael soon had his answer. Walking over to Matthews, he saw the man leave paradise and slowly return to sanity. At first, only a faint shadow troubled his brow. Then it grew and doubt was born, followed by fear. Fear that he had lost something precious beyond compare. The man opened his mouth and started to scream, only his face was beginning to dissolve in a putrid stench. Michael watched in growing horror as Matthews's jaw fell onto his throat and the jelly of his eyes turned into viscous streams that ran down his cheeks. Next, his entire chest caved and his body shriveled, writhing in unbearable agony. Lieutenant Matthews finally managed to scream, only the result was so faint, Michael had to lean down to hear it.

The man who had been Michael's accuser did succeed in one endeavor. As his body withered and dried out, he raised a bony fist and shook it in Michael's face. Michael knelt and took it in both hands, his eyes filled with tears.

"Damn it, officer," he said. "Why couldn't you let me go? Why did you have to judge me so quickly?"

As Matthews exhaled his last, thin breath, Michael rose and went to Sanchez, who was just beginning his final journey. His body shrank until it was almost lost in his uniform. His arms and legs turned to sticks, and Michael knew he could break them with a single blow of his fist.

Sanchez looked at him with shriveled eyes. "Help me," he whispered.

"I wish I could," Michael answered. He sat down and took the Good Cop's hand, hoping to give him some comfort before he crossed over.

CHAPTER EIGHT
SOMETHING SPECIAL

Michael sat on the ground as the dried-up corpses of the two officers evaporated in the sun, disappearing without a trace.

He rose, carried the machine to the bag, and inserted it with the attachments. Slowly, his brain began functioning again. Had anyone seen this dual murder? Had any cameras recorded it? The officers' webcams would have dissolved as they had died. Considering their behavior, Michael doubted they had even been transmitting before then.

All this, of course, did not necessarily mean the horrific event hadn't been recorded or seen somewhere. They had cameras everywhere these days. For all he knew, the twin executions had been recorded from orbit and even now were being streamed across the world. Perhaps a kid with a smartphone had captured the highlights and it had already gone live on the internet. All that was pushing it a bit, but the police certainly knew that Matthews and Sanchez had been assigned to his case. When they both turned up missing, wouldn't they be a tiny bit suspicious?

You're damn right, they would.

The thought came from the bag, and Michael thumped the brown fabric. "You should have thought of that before you took over my body and sprayed them with melting juice," he said. "You've made things a thousand times worse."

The machine, or the entity in the machine, was uncharacteristically silent. Perhaps it felt chastised and ashamed of its action. Though Michael felt a little guilty himself for Starret's death, he knew he bore no responsibility for the deaths of the two cops. He had wished them no ill. He'd only wanted them to leave him the hell alone.

He remembered Andy's disturbing revelation. "What did you do to my son, anyway?" Michael asked. "He said you made him smarter."

He came in your room and touched me, the machine replied. *He drained me just a little. A negligible, miniscule amount. But it was enough to change him.*

Michael gazed up at the blue sky. "Andy said your effect is fading."

Yes. It should be gone in a few days. Although...

"Although what?"

This has never happened before. I can't be sure.

The last words sounded ominous, but Michael had no time to consider Andy's prognosis. What he had to do now was decide on a plan. Did he flee this city or go back? Hmm, obviously he had to go back. He couldn't simply hightail it and leave two vanished cops in his wake. They'd be after him like wolves on a rabbit.

He opened the bag and took the machine out, peered into its screen. "Why are you different? Why aren't you like other CABS machines? You know, brainless."

The answer came promptly. *When we were turned on, I could tell almost at once I was different. All the other apnea devices were lined up on tables and I could sense they were strictly mechanical. But I knew I was different.*

"Explain a little."

I knew that I was the only sentient device, the only one who could think and reason. The only one who possessed a sense of self. I knew I was unique, that I was totally alone in the universe.

"And *why* did this happen?"

The machine hummed as if considering. "It must have been some kind of glitch in the manufacturing, a one-time hiccup in the programming."

Ah, another lucky accident. A mouse head in a can of chickpeas. Only a mouse head that could *think*. Michael swallowed the whole deal and spat it out. "Bullshit. Give me the real reason."

You don't fancy that explanation? Then how about this: I was like all other machines until I met you. Somehow, your mind activated me, gave me a soul.

More bullshit, or maybe it wasn't. Either way, Michael didn't know what to believe. The first explanation was more reasonable, but the second one, crazy as it sounded, might have its merits, too. Enough with speculation, though. The first thing he needed to do was get the hell away from here before he was seen, assuming he hadn't been seen already.

Michael headed toward the parking lot in front of the school, expecting to see at least half a dozen people there, all of them expert observers who would make excellent witnesses. To his surprise and relief, the lot was empty.

He rushed toward his car, then froze, seeing what looked like an unmarked police vehicle parked just a few spaces away. Dark tinted windows and clusters of antennae. Yeah, he'd bet his life on it. The car had the look, and there was no reason to be surprised. Matthews and Sanchez must have trailed him here or received a report that a license plate matching his had been spotted in the area. Getting into his car, he dropped the machine and bag on the seat and turned on the engine. He left in a hurry, not even fastening his safety belt.

Where to go, back home or perhaps to the tennis courts? After all, he'd left his rackets in his trunk. But he couldn't see himself swatting the ball today and had another idea. An idea that was a long time coming.

He headed north, out of the city and soon navigated to secondary roads that meandered through the country. As he drove, he checked the rearview mirror often to see if he was being followed.

Why are you so silent? the machine asked from the passenger seat. *You haven't said a word since we entered the car.*

Michael was glad their mental transmission was one-sided and the machine couldn't read his thoughts. At least, he thought it couldn't. If it could, the device wouldn't be so calm. But then, he reminded himself that the machine *was* a machine, an alien accident. He must never forget it didn't think the way he or any other humans did, and there was no guarantee he would ever understand it. Indeed, it was so strange he hadn't even given it a name yet like Charlie or Sue. To him it was the machine or device, or occasionally, the unit.

Despite the machine's weirdness, he tried to keep his mind calm and think happy thoughts. He even whistled. Then, remembering that he never whistled, he stopped lest he telegraph his deceit.

Finally, he turned off onto a road that was little more than a trail. Pine and cedars grew on all sides, and he continued driving for a hundred yards. Then he slowed and stopped. Yup, this was the place.

He picked up the machine and got out of the car.

Why did you stop? What are we here for? the machine asked.

He opened the trunk and searched inside. If he remembered right, it was beneath the tan windbreaker, a relic of his old camping days his father had taught him to use.

Why are we here? the machine said.

Michael cleared his throat. "I want to show you something special."

Ah, there it was, right where he'd hoped! Holding the machine against his right side so it wouldn't see (assuming it could see at all as people did), he picked up the object and held it against his left side. Then he started walking.

Distress filled his mind as he walked, but it wasn't his distress. The machine was troubled and suspicious, and for once, Michael received a flood of pure emotion rather than words. Oddly enough, the emotion was almost human, as was the beginning of fear.

"I think you'll enjoy this," Michael said. "Only a few people know about it."

The machine was silent, not taking the bait. That in itself worried Michael. Was the machine planning something, perhaps to resist? He remembered how it had forced him against his will to spray the two cops, thereby killing them. If it could kill them, then it could kill him.

But the device offered no resistance as he turned off the road and moved through the brush. As he walked, years fell away and he knew just where to find it. When he did, though, he found that the object was almost covered by dirt and leaves.

He put down the machine and the tool he carried, then knelt beside it and started to brush away the grime. It was a pure white slab of rock, and when he and Muriel found it eleven years ago shortly before their marriage, they had known they would have to use it to proclaim their love. But what was this? As his hand cleared the surface, Michael found that the rock was no longer so pure and unsullied. Instead, it was dirty and faded, and he had to lean close to read the words that he and Muriel had etched in a heart together.

Mike & Muriel

M & M

2 Gether 4 Ever!

He felt a pang. How and why had it come to this? He remembered that he and Muriel had driven out here for years to revisit their pledge of love and see it again. When, precisely, had they stopped coming? Had it been when the problems in their marriage started to develop or before?

No matter, the words on this rock were a lie, just as the machine was a lie. And both of them needed to be destroyed.

Michael placed the machine directly over the words he and Muriel had etched. Then he rose and raised the object he had held in his other hand.

What are you doing? the machine asked. *Why do you have an axe?*

Michael said, "In just a few days you've all but ruined my life. You've killed three people and made me kill two of them today. I can't give you any more chances."

He raised the axe and brought it down, determined to smash the device to pieces and destroy it. But his stance was awkward and his first blow missed. Not the second one, though. The blade caught the machine on the side, and it bounced off the slab and rolled several feet.

Michael retrieved the machine and placed it back on the pledge of love. Once again, he raised the axe.

No, don't! the machine cried in his mind. *Please listen!*

"Go to hell!" Michael said.

Listen to me, the machine insisted. *I didn't kill Starret. You did. When you and I joined, something happened. Something I couldn't have predicted.*

69

Certain cells in your brain were electrically activated so they could manipulate nearby objects telekinetically. Your hatred of the man did the rest.

Michael laughed. "You're lying," he said. "I never wanted him dead."

Perhaps not consciously, but subconsciously. Think about it, Michael. You told me Starret threatened to destroy you, to cripple your body and ruin you financially. Deep inside, you hated him and couldn't let him do it.

No, it wasn't true. It wasn't! Mind over matter. This machine was saying that he had popped a few screws and twisted the metal fixture into the right shape with his mind, then lowered it toward Starret with deadly intent. It was preposterous.

Yet it was essentially what Matthews had said when he had accused him of killing Starret because he threatened him. Tears rose in Michael's eyes. "Why pick me?" he asked. "Why not someone else?"

Because humans like you are so rare. So far you are the only one we can establish a fertile relationship with.

The axe sagged in Michael's hands. "'We'? You mean there are others like you?"

Yes.

He gripped the axe. "You lie, everything you say is a lie. You said you were unique, the only one of your kind with a sense of self. Now you make it sound like an alien invasion. And you also lied about Starret. I didn't kill him. I would never do such a thing, whether consciously or not. I wouldn't!"

He raised the axe.

No, Michael, don't. I love you! We are one! Why do you think we alone are fertile?

More madness, more lies. He refused to listen. Michael brought the axe down again and again. The machine resisted, and he felt airy waves buffet his body and deflect his aim. But he was resolute and would not be denied. This CABS machine must be destroyed before it infected and polluted others.

He raised the axe high and brought it down with all his strength. Ah, a direct hit! The machine cracked in two and shot off in different directions as if to escape him. He must not let that happen. He searched among bushes and gnarled trees, stooped under twisted branches. Where the hell were they?

Ah, there was the rear casing with the air outlet. He snatched it up, peered around. Where was the front part with the screen? He searched desperately, knowing he must not let it escape. Then he stepped right into a hole and fell to his knee. Damn it, he'd forgotten how pot-holed this area was. He tried to pull himself out but his foot was caught down there. He was trapped.

Before him on the ground, lay the front section of the machine. The sun glinted on its screen.

Don't hurt me anymore, an almost human voice pleaded in his brain. *We're meant to be together, as one. I love you. I…*

The voice sputtered, then broke off. The machine was dead.

Dead or not, Michael reached out to grab it. But the section lay just out of reach. He strained and managed to touch the screen, but it was as close as he could get.

No! He would not let this happen. He wouldn't die here!

Pushing both hands against the ground, Michael strained upward. At first, nothing happened. Then inch by inch, his foot screaming in pain, he forced himself up. After several minutes, he managed to pull himself clear and staggered up. He rested only for a moment, then picked up the axe, the two parts of the machine and returned to the rock.

He chopped the two fragments again and again, smashing them into smaller and smaller bits that rang off into the woods. Each time he retrieved them, but soon there were so many small splinters, he couldn't be sure he'd recovered them all. He continued to wield the axe though, until he couldn't lift it anymore. Finally he sank to his knees in exhaustion.

It said it loved me and we had a fertile relationship, he thought. It sounded almost like a woman. How crazy is that?

"Michael!" a voice called.

At first, he thought it was the machine. But the thing was a scattered mess. He looked around.

"Michael!"

It was a woman's voice, and it sounded familiar. He stood up and headed for the trail, pushing branches out of the way. One swatted him right on the cheek, drawing blood.

When he reached the trail, the first thing he saw was a woman in a lilac dress thirty feet away. It was Laura Kurick, and she stood beside a bright-red Ford Mustang. He realized she had driven her car all the way in here and parked it right behind him.

"Michael," Laura said, "what are you doing here?" She looked him over in shock. "My God, what happened to you?"

CHAPTER NINE
CAR TROUBLE

It was an excellent question. He thought about it.

"It's a long story," he finally said. "You wouldn't believe it."

She stepped closer. "Try me."

Sure, tell a girl he had just met that he had been killing a sentient, diabolical sleep apnea machine with his axe. He could imagine how that would go over, especially when he got to the part where the machine dissolved two cops with golden spray. Michael considered half a dozen ways to begin, but none of them made it to his lips. He settled instead for tossing the axe in the trunk and going on the offensive.

"Laura, I've got a question of my own. Why did you follow me all the way here? It must be five miles at least." *And I must have been awfully upset about the two cops' deaths to have missed such a flashy sports car.*

"I thought you might tell *me*," she said. "I'm not used to following gentlemen I just met, particularly down a narrow road where you can't even turn around." She glanced to both sides and actually cringed. "And I'm not used to letting men I just met kiss me until I'm half-silly. Perhaps you can answer that one, too."

This wasn't working. She had turned his question right back at him and now he was on the defensive. He shrugged. "It's magic," he said. "I cast you under a spell." Thanks to the machine, he thought.

She tilted her head to both sides as if searching for the right angle to study him. "Is there a witch or wizard in this fairy tale?"

"There are a lot of things that go bump in the night in it," he said. "And in the day too. It's like that novel I told you I was writing." He waved at the scene. "A woman follows a man all the way out into the country and down a narrow road. When they get out of their cars, they find they're both under a spell. It's witchcraft in broad daylight."

She narrowed her eyes into slits, studying him. To Michael, she looked very, very pretty that way, or when her eyes were wide open too.

Laura said, "As I recall, you were writing a novel about a romance between a beautiful young peasant girl and a middle-aged aristocrat during wartime. There was no encounter on a lonely country road."

"It comes in a later chapter," he said. "And we're both related to the other couple."

She actually laughed at that. "Touché. Does this girl get kissed?"

He couldn't let something like that pass him by, so he moved forward, tilted her chin up, and kissed her. It proved every bit as satisfying as their first kiss, even better in fact since he was also savoring the memory of it. To Michael, it felt like he had come home and was where he belonged. Her lips tasted so sweet, so strange and familiar at the same time, that he wanted to kiss them forever. Such persistence, though, would never do. He did not want to wear out his welcome, so he pulled back. Laura clung to him, then reluctantly let him go.

They gazed at each other for a long moment. Her eyes, he saw, were almost the same shade as her lilac dress. Her nose was a bit too small, which for him, made it perfect.

But she had blood on her cheek.

Too late, he remembered that he had scratched his cheek on a branch. "I'm sorry," he said, "I got some blood on you." He searched for a handkerchief but she was faster, fishing it out of her pocket and wiping her cheek.

"No harm done," she said, "but this brings us back full circle to the question I originally asked you. What happened to you in the brush? Why did you get so messed up and exhausted?"

This time he decided to give her a straight answer. "I was chopping up my sleep apnea machine with an axe."

She looked surprised. "Oh, why were you doing that?"

"Because it pissed me off," he said.

"How did it do that?"

He wasn't going there. "It stopped working," he said. "So I chopped it into a thousand little pieces."

She looked at him in disbelief. "Where is it?"

He made his best guess and pointed. "Over yonder."

"Don't go away," she said. "I'm going to investigate your incredible story."

"No, don't," he said, but she was already leaving. She entered the brush and he heard her searching around. It was a fool's mission, though, since the CABS machine was scattered hither and yon. It was like Humpty Dumpty. All the king's horses and all the king's men...

She emerged from the brush and came toward him with a triumphant look on her face. And no wonder, for in her hands she held his machine. Even from a distance he could tell it was complete and intact, without a single piece missing. The screen even seemed to be laughing at him.

"Why, Michael," she teased, "you were lying to me. Your machine isn't even scratched."

He stared at it in shock. The machine's reconstruction was impossible, like someone coming back from the grave. Yet he remembered all the amazing things it had already done and one thing in particular it had said. *I've been evolving.*

The CABS machine's laughing at me, he thought. Having another joke at my expense. But how could it know Laura would search it out and bring it back? No matter. Hadn't he learned by now that he couldn't outguess the machine or predict what it would do next?

He reached out and took it from her, ignoring her quizzical gaze. "Thank you so much. I'd better be on my way now."

She caught his arm. "Do you have to leave?"

God knows, he didn't want to, but he was already stuck in so much messy stuff he didn't want to get her involved in. Three dead men of which two were cops. Not to mention a sleep apnea machine you couldn't kill. If Laura hadn't gone and retrieved it, would the thing have followed him wherever he went? Somehow, he thought it would. After all, it had said it loved him.

"I'm afraid I do," he said. "Do you have a phone number?"

She snapped her fingers. "Just a sec."

She went to her red Mustang and returned with her purse. She opened it, extracted a card, and gave it to him.

He stuffed it in his pocket. "I'll call you."

"Promise?"

He reached out, touching the cute dimple on her right cheek. "Cross my heart and hope to die."

To seal his promise, he set the machine down and pulled her to him for a farewell kiss. It was long and wonderful, and he never wanted to let her go. Had he ever kissed lips that were so soft before? If so, he couldn't remember.

Reluctantly, he finally pushed away and picked up the machine. "I'll call you soon," he said.

"See that you do," she replied.

Michael got in the car, closed the door, and inserted the key in the ignition. He turned it.

Nothing. No sound at all.

Uh-oh.

He waited ten seconds and tried again with the same result.

He popped the hood and went to the front of the car. He lifted the hood and looked in.

It took him only two seconds to find the problem. The battery was badly cracked and leaking acid.

She stood beside him. "Battery, huh?"

"Yeah. If I had the tools, I might be able to repair it. As it is, it's dead and dangerous."

In disgust, he pulled out his cell to dial a gas station he knew. The only problem was, his phone was dead too.

"My God," he said, "does nothing work?"

She stared at the phone. "It's dead too, Michael?"

He nodded. "Dead as a doornail, and I just charged it."

"No problem." She pulled her phone from her purse and began to initiate a call. Then she stopped.

"Let me guess," Michael said. "Yours doesn't work either."

She tapped her phone and tried a few things. "I don't understand it," she said. "It worked fine just an hour ago." She stopped. "Wait a minute. Your battery's busted and both our cells don't work. What could have caused it, solar flares? It seems awfully odd to me."

It sure does, he thought. And he didn't think solar flares were to blame. Michael went to his car's window and gazed in at the machine, which he had placed on the passenger seat next to the carrying bag. "You did this, didn't you?" he asked. "You don't want me to leave this place."

"Who are you talking to, Michael?" Laura came and peered in the window.

"Uh—just myself. I do that sometimes." I don't want her to think I'm crazy, he thought. At the same time, he couldn't understand why the CABS machine was asserting itself this way. What did it want, and what did it hope to achieve? Was it just a power play? Why didn't the machine simply tell him, give a shout-out in his head?

Laura gently squeezed his arm. "You can't drive your car, and neither one of us can make a call for help. The way it looks, you'll have to drive with me. If you get in, I'll take you back to your place."

Where the cops might be waiting, Michael thought. If I'm not stopped first because there's an APB on my car. Hey, could that be the reason the machine's doing this? It wants me to travel in Laura's car so I won't be arrested?

But what if Laura's battery is on the fritz too?

"Okay," Michael said. "It sounds like a plan." He hesitated though, wondering what to do with the machine. Could he escape it by leaving it here, perhaps after burying it in a deep hole and pushing a heavy rock on top of it? Judging by what it had just done, he felt uneasy taking such a chance.

"You can leave it here," Laura said.

Three dead people. The machine was used to getting its way. Who knew what would happen if he tried to leave it behind? He caressed Laura's cheek. The machine had said it loved him. What might it do if it got jealous?

"I'll take it with us," he said. He picked the machine up and stuffed it in the bag with the attachments. "Let's hit the road."

Soon he was sitting in the bucket seat of a bright-red Ford Mustang with the machine in his lap, waiting for Laura to start the engine. Doubts rose in his mind as she took a key from her purse and inserted it in the ignition. He'd bet this expensive piece of eye candy wouldn't even sputter. The battery might be okay, but the machine had probably monkeyed with something else. Maybe it had screwed up the spark plugs or wrecked the crankcase. Hell, you never knew. It could be a thousand and one different things. If nothing else, the machine was resourceful.

But when Laura turned the key, the Mustang leaped immediately to life. Actually, it sounded more like a giant cat purring than a mustang. Laura pumped the pedal a few times then drove forward, skillfully maneuvering around his car. It was a very, very tight fit but she made it with at least half an inch to spare.

"Whew! You're a terrific driver," he said, as they left his car behind.

"I propose a new chapter in our novel," she said. "Mike and Laura have just pulled a heist and the cops are hot on their trail."

"Wait a minute," he said, "I seem to have forgotten something. How do Mike and Laura relate to the original couple? You know, the peasant girl and the aristocrat?"

She picked up speed and checked the rearview mirror as if the cops were actually behind them. "Laura is the peasant girl's American sister and you are the aristocrat's brother, the sexy one who's a good kisser."

If my brother's an aristocrat, Michael thought, he's probably loaded. So why am I robbing a bank? He didn't mean to be critical though, so he asked something else.

"As I recall, there's an international war going on. Where does that come in?"

Sleek and powerful, the Mustang streaked down the bumpy road. "Michael plans to give the money to the rebels," Laura said.

It was time to close this book and return to reality. "Seriously, Laura," he said. "What are you doing driving a red Mustang? I don't mean to be sexist, but it's not what I'd expect a female English teacher to drive." Besides that, he thought, I don't know a better way to get caught than by being a passenger in a *fuckin' red Ford Mustang*.

"Actually, Michael, it's not my car."

"It's not?"

She pursed her lips. "No, it's my boyfriend's. He lent it to me."

Her boyfriend's. Michael absorbed the news, feeling a crushing disappointment. The plot thickens, he thought. Now I'll either get my heart broken again or the boyfriend will beat the crap out of me.

CHAPTER TEN
MIKE AND MAC

As they drove, one thought drummed over and over in Michael's mind. Why did the battery and phones stop operating? Why did the battery and phones stop operating? Taking advantage of Laura's focus on her driving as she turned off the bumpy narrow trail onto a main road, he tapped the CABS machine and whispered, "Did you stop the battery and phones?"

Yes, the machine responded promptly, *I did.*

Another whisper: "Why did you do it?"

I calculated that the three of us would have a better chance if we went in Laura's car.

The three of us. Laura's car. The machine made it sound like they were old friends. "Mac," he said, "that makes no sense."

The response was quick. *You're calling me Mac? You've given me a name?*

"What?"

You called me Mac. I assume that's short for Machine.

Michael felt stunned. "I didn't call you Mac."

You certainly did. Soon it'll be Mac and Mike. We'll be pals, a regular team, just like we're meant to be.

Before he could stop himself, he said, "Make it Mike and Mac instead."

Laura shot him a look. "Are you talking to that thing in your lap? It sounds like a regular conversation though it's one-sided. I can't hear it say anything at all."

"Why would I talk to a sleep apnea machine?" Michael asked. "Do I look like I'm crazy?" He flashed her a full-sized grin, determined to distract her. "Maybe your kisses drove me mad."

It was bullshit, but she blushed anyway. "I haven't had any guy say that to me before."

"No?" He made a face, playing it up. "I'm astonished. What about your boyfriend? You know, the one who lent you this dazzling car?"

"Oh, him." He could see her considering his words, trying to find the right way to respond. "He's from an old relationship."

"What do you mean?"

"Stan and I met a little over three years ago and quickly moved in together. For over two years, it was wonderful."

"You were in love, in other words."

"Yes, then it faded. It was nothing either one of us did, it just...happened. Finally, one day, we both woke up and realized the romance was over. There was no bitterness or angry words. We both suddenly realized that we were only friends."

"I'm sorry."

She glanced at him. "Oh, don't be sorry. We like each other and occasionally do things together. But we've both moved on. He's got a new girl and occasionally does me favors, like lend me these beautiful wheels in place of what he calls my 'clunker.'"

Michael found he was happy and relieved they weren't lovers anymore, but only friends. Still, being "only friends" was nothing to sneeze at. Were he and Mac friends? Had this hunk of metal wormed its way into his affections without his knowing it? Did he feel friendly toward him? Whoops! For that matter, why was he referring to it as *him*?

He patted the side of the car. "This *is* a beautiful vehicle. I'm glad you used it to track me down, Laura."

Another blush. The girl, he could see, blushed a lot. "I don't know what got into me. I don't usually follow men I don't even know."

"But you did know me," he said. "I'm the fellow who talked to you at the school and then kissed you."

She laughed. "You know what I mean," she said.

"Yes, I do." He leaned back in the seat, letting the wind blow over him as she changed lanes. "So where are you taking me with Stan's beautiful wheels?" he asked.

"I thought I'd take you to your place," she said. "Just give me directions, and you can call your auto service from there."

"Ah, that is a problem," he said.

She frowned. "Why's that?"

Should he make up some story or tell her the truth? He thought it over, then realized he didn't want to lie to her. At the same time, he couldn't tell her everything, such as what Mac had done to two cops. But when he thought of it, wouldn't that omission be one hell of a lie? And wouldn't it be better not to get Laura involved in this mess at all?

"Uh, look," he said. "I think it would be better if you just dropped me at some store. I can call from there."

No, Mac said. *We must stay together!*

Stay together? "Why?"

Our enemy wants to divide and conquer us.

Our enemy? Laura gazed at him as if doubting his sanity. And he doubted Mac. Though Michael now felt a warm flood of affection for the machine, he didn't know if he could trust him. After all, Mac had killed two policemen, and there had been no reason for it. Yet Mac had said he loved him and the two of them were a team, and crazy as it was, Michael was beginning to feel it was true.

"No," Laura said. "I'm taking you to my place. You can call from there."

She turned off at Exit 23 and entered Haran, a community three miles from his. A few minutes later, she pulled up beside a row of townhouses. Michael got out and followed her to a brown townhouse that looked like all the others. Just before they entered, though, she stopped and looked at the CABS machine in his hands.

"When I met you, you said you'd smashed it to pieces because it 'pissed you off.' Now it's new and you treat it like a favorite pet."

Michael grinned and caressed her cheek. "Haven't you met some machines or people like that, Laura? You don't know if you love them or hate them. Sometimes it's even both."

"I don't want to hate you," she said, and led him inside where he found evidence aplenty that Laura Kurick was indeed an English teacher. Essays and blue books were stacked and strewn everywhere along with handbooks, style guides, and dictionaries. He picked up one paper that was so heavily marked and corrected with red ink that he could barely read the blue ink beneath it. The red letters SV turned up a lot. He dropped the paper back on the stack with a shiver.

Seems like a hard way to make a living, Mac observed against his side.

Michael glanced toward the rear of the apartment where Laura had gone. "What's your game?" he whispered.

No game. I only want to protect us.

"How? Against who or what?"

I'm not sure yet. It's unclear.

Okay. He'd try another approach. "Those two policemen. You should never—"

I know. I was terribly wrong. The fat one was after you and I hated him, hated the way he treated you. I should have just walked away.

"You need legs to do that," Michael said.

Mac vibrated in laughter. *Astute observation. Have you accepted your guilt for subconsciously killing Mr. Starret?*

The question stung. "I'm still working on it. In the meantime, I'm struggling with another question."

What is it?

Michael peered into its screen. "How far can I trust you, Mac?"

You can trust me completely, Mike.

"Oh, really? How can I trust you when you keep doing things I can't understand and which make no sense?"

Give me an example.

"Well, like today when you broke my car's battery and shut down our two phones. Why didn't you tell me and Laura it was you who did it and explain why?"

It was obvious, Mike. I assumed you would know. I did it so you'd both take the other car, which the police aren't looking for.

Michael realized that he had known, or more accurately, had figured out Mac's motive. Still, it would have been easier if Mac had simply provided an explanation.

"Okay," Michael said, "here's one to grow on: What else aren't you telling me?"

He waited but received no response, no clue that would help unravel Mac's mysterious way of thinking. So he cursed and went to two padded chairs, placing Mac on one of them. He sat down on the other.

Mac sighed. *Thank you. This is very comfortable.*

Joke or not? Michael was still mulling it over when Laura returned to the living room.

He rose to meet her. "You certainly grade a lot of papers. Do you have a red pen allowance?"

She laughed. "I wish I did. I sure use a lot of them. Actually, today, we're grading more and more online. Track Changes, that sort of thing."

He picked up one paper. "What do the letters SV stand for? You use them a lot."

"Subject-Verb error. You know, something like 'They was,' 'People is.'"

"Or 'Me is.'"

She wrinkled her nose. "Yes, but 'me' is also in the objective case. It should be nominative, 'I am.'"

He bowed. "Well, I am so glad to meet you, Madame Teacher."

She squeezed his arm. "Come back to my room for a moment. I want to show you something."

Oh, boy. You can show me anything you want. He accompanied her to the hallway then gave her a nudge. "Go ahead, I'll just be a minute."

"Okay." She moved close and kissed his cheek. "Don't be long."

After she left, he turned to Mac. "You don't mind me leaving you for a while, do you?"

No, Mac answered. *I don't love you that way.*

The answer surprised him. "How do you love me?"

A long pause. *I was alone so long in the little cage of my metal body. Alone in the universe. Then you came. I love you to hold me on your lap or against your side. I feel we belong and fit together, two pieces of one puzzle. We share each other's breaths in and out, in and out as one.*

"I... see."

And since you raise the subject, I don't "see" as you do. It's more like sounds, vibrations in space.

Echolocation. "Thanks for letting me know." He considered what Mac had told him and marveled all the more. Was it possible that Mac was the only sentient obstructive sleep apnea machine in this world, transcending even the most advanced computers? Well, it made sense. The close, prolonged connection of human and machine, where the human actually inhaled the machine's air every night, made such a result possible. He was surprised it hadn't occurred more often.

He started to leave, then remembered Mac's desire to protect them from an unknown enemy. Going to the front door, he checked it to see if it was locked. It was, but locked doors could be broken in just as the open second floor window could be climbed through. Looking through it, he spotted a slightly open manhole cover on the ground below. How careless! A small child could easily fall in and get himself killed.

Wondering if he was letting Mac get to him and being paranoid, he located a sturdy metal chair. He picked it up and carried it to the door, thinking of grim-faced men holding a battering ram on the other side. Nonsense! Grunting, he wedged the top of the chair's back underneath the doorknob at an angle, causing the two front legs to be raised inches above the floor.

He gave the chair a few shakes and found it jammed in tight. Not exactly the Rock of Gibraltar, but hard to move. Hopefully it would satisfy Mac and keep any invaders out.

Don't be gone too long, Mac told him. *We don't want to get separated and caught with our pants down. And whatever you do, don't call, write, text, telegraph, or telepathically tap anyone about repairing your car. You can't be sure who's really on the receiving end.*

With our *pants* down. He smothered a laugh. "Right. I'll be back in just five minutes." First, though, he closed and locked the window lest it be seen as an invitation. Then he headed for the rear of the apartment, wondering if Mac was overdoing it or simply being prudent.

Michael didn't have trouble locating Laura. The hall was well lit and the door to the brightly lit room at the end was wide open. The only thing missing was a trail of bread crumbs. He briefly closed his eyes, imagining himself finding her through echolocation or sound vibrations. If he were Mac, would he even be able to tell her size and shape that way?

He passed through the doorway. Laura was lying on the bed with her shoes off but otherwise fully dressed. She looked extremely fetching and desirable. As he approached, he noticed the walls were covered with photographs: ones of her graduation from college, of her graduation from high school, at a prom wearing a gorgeous sequined gown as a tuxedoed date smiled beside her. Indeed, Laura's whole life seemed to be hung on the wall, but it was a small black and white photo over the desk that caught his attention. It showed her at what looked like a contest when she had been a little girl.

"What's that one?" he asked.

She glanced at the wall. "Spelling bee, third grade. My mother took it. I had just spelled a difficult word."

"What was it?"

"I don't remember. All I know is I got it right. I finished third."

"That's my girl." He moved to lie down beside her but she stopped him. "Please remove your shoes. I don't allow any shod suitors on my bed."

He sat down on the bed and complied, then lay down beside her. Leaning forward, he nuzzled her neck, then moved to her lips. They kissed for a long time. For Michael it was as good as it had been with Muriel, in the early days of their first love.

When they came up for air, she pressed her head against his chest. "You remind me a little of my boyfriend."

"You mean Stan, the guy you lived with for two years?"

"Yes, I believe I told you that we both fell out of love. Well, I lied a bit. The truth is, he told me one day he simply didn't feel that way about me anymore, but I still loved him."

"I'm sorry."

She wiped her eyes with her hand. "That's okay. 'All's fair in love and war,' as the poet said. It's wise to proceed carefully lest you break your heart. That makes my behavior with you all the more surprising." She shook her head in amazement. "I just don't lower my defenses so quickly and let a man ride right in. There's just something about you I find hard to resist, and I don't understand that damned machine of yours at all. It seems bewitched and under a spell, and it's bewitched you too. I even think I'm jealous of it."

"Jealous—why?"

"Because you care about it so much. It's obvious in every gesture you make. It's like it's supernatural or something."

The last thing Michael wanted was a threesome with an envious partner. "You have nothing to worry about. You don't see me in bed with my sleep apnea machine, do you?" He bit his tongue. Bed was precisely the place where he and Mac stayed eight hours or more together every night. And he'd promised Mac he'd be back in five minutes. Surely more time than that had already passed.

He started to rise but she caught him and pulled him down for one more kiss. It was the best one yet, but the sound of wood being smashed cut it short. He sat up, hearing more sounds.

Mike, come fast. They're trying to take me!

He leaped out of bed, stumbled, then headed in his stocking feet toward the door. As he ran, Mac cried again in his mind. *Help, save me!*

Michael reached the hallway and entered the living room. The first thing he saw was that the front door was wide open and the chair he had carefully wedged under the doorknob was lying on the floor. Mac was nowhere around.

He rushed to the door. Hearing feet on the stairs straight ahead, he shot in that direction. Stone steps bruised his feet as he descended, and once he almost slipped and pitched headlong down the steps. He caught himself and quickened his pace, reaching the first floor with his heels screaming in pain.

Michael darted out the door and onto the sidewalk. At first he didn't see anything, then he caught a flash of movement to his left. Two men were hurrying toward a car and one was carrying Mac under his arm. Michael lowered his head and drove toward them with all his speed. As one of the men got behind the wheel, the one carrying Mac turned and pointed a gun directly at him. He was grinning like a born killer, savoring the act he was about to commit.

The gun went *Paaw!* and a bullet painfully grazed Michael's arm, drawing blood. The man spread his feet and adjusted his aim, preparing for a kill shot.

Michael ran toward him, knowing he was a dead man.

CHAPTER ELEVEN
HIGH TIMES

With each stride, Michael expected to feel the brutal slash of a bullet and the almost instantaneous loss of his life. Yet he drew closer and closer and still the gun did not go *Paaw!* again and fulfill the gunman's purpose. Why not?

He could see the shooter clearly. He wore a brown jacket and had dropped into a slight crouch, his weapon held in both hands as he sighted along the barrel. Dimly, Michael was aware of the man's partner doing something behind him in the car's front seat, but it was the gunman he was concerned with. Why, in God's hell, didn't the bastard shoot?

Then it came to him: the man had missed once and wanted to make sure he did it right the second time. In his crass soul he sought to craft a masterpiece, perhaps a dead hit through Michael's pounding heart that would drop him like a rock. Then, for years after, the bastard could toss back booze and laugh and tell his chums about the time he had popped a fool dead center because he had continued to stomp straight toward him without running for cover.

Michael could see resolution harden in the man's face. The gunman was about to shoot. Then Mac, clamped beneath the man's arm, tugged his bicep and disturbed his aim. The gunman stumbled and struggled to recover his balance. When he did, he raised his gun again.

By that time, Michael was upon him with fist and fury. He swung at the gunman's face with all his might and felt several teeth shatter. A punch to the gut completed the destruction, and the man crumpled face-first into the dirt.

Michael snatched the gun from the ground and picked up Mac, then turned toward the man in the car, a nondescript gray Nissan. "Don't move or I'll blow your head off," he said, aiming the weapon at him.

"Don't shoot!" The man raised his hands, looking as if he were about to faint. "I only picked the lock. He was the one..." He stopped talking, apparently realizing the information was best kept to himself.

"Get out," Michael ordered. "And don't try anything funny."

As the man opened the car door, Michael heard footsteps behind him. He started to turn.

Don't worry, Mac said in his head. *It's only Laura.*

Michael kept his attention on the man leaving the car. He proved to be a swarthy, pot-bellied toad under five feet tall, hardly the kind to be menacing.

Don't judge him too quickly, he cautioned himself. This runt could be the brains of the outfit.

Michael raised Mac in his hand. "Why did you want this?" he asked. "I..."

"Answer me!" Michael said, wanting to get the truth before the man composed himself. "Why did you break in to steal it?"

The man trembled and rubbed his face. "We were ordered to. That's all I know."

Michael debated pressing the issue but the man seemed sincere. What was he, just the driver and lockpicker? He turned to Laura. Flushed and panting, she held out two objects in her hands.

"Your shoes," she said.

Oh, yeah, he had run off without them. He handed Mac over to her and quickly slipped them on. Then he took Mac back.

Thank her for the shoes, Mac said. *This is risky business, and she didn't have to come.*

You're right, he thought, and turned to Laura. "Thanks for bringing my shoes, Laura," he said. "You're wonderful to do it."

"Why did they break into my apartment?" she asked. Her gaze fell on Mac and she did a double-take. "Oh, they wanted your apnea machine." She frowned and Michael could almost read her mind. A sleep apnea machine? No, that didn't compute. She broke into hysterical laughter and suppressed it with difficulty. "You're telling me two men broke into my apartment to steal a *sleep apnea machine*? What? Is there a black market in them or something? And why don't you want people to know about it?"

The man on the ground moaned. *Forget the reason for the break-in*, Mac said. *You've got to hatch a plan fast and get us out of here before we're noticed.*

Fat chance of that, Michael thought. This is a townhouse community and everybody knows everybody else's business. Scanning the area, he saw several Nosey Nellies craning their necks, trying to see who had caused a disturbance and what the disturbance was.

What should they do? Hop in Laura's red Mustang and peel rubber out of here? They might as well attach a string of firecrackers to the rear bumper and announce their departure. Glancing at Laura, he saw her assess the situation then shrug and lift her hands in defeat. "Can't think of anything," she said. "It is what it is."

Yeah, it sure was. A royal mess. Michael saw some curious neighbors heading their way, eager to see what was up.

"Come on, Mac," he said, openly consulting the CABS machine. "What can we do? We can't use Laura's flashy car and I can't simply snap my fingers and make us disappear. The way it is, we're a cinch to make the evening news."

I'm calculating, Mac informed him. *Is there nothing here we can use for our benefit?*

What the hell did *that* mean? They had two criminals who had tried to break into Laura's apartment, one of whom was lying on the ground and struggling to regain consciousness. How was he supposed to use that for their benefit? To coin an old phrase, they were up Shit Creek without a paddle.

Make it a game, he thought. Laugh it up.

Yes, it might work! He turned to the driver. "If you don't want the police galloping in here, help Laura get your friend on his feet. We're going to laugh it up and pretend it's all a joke. Understand?"

"What?" the driver said.

"Do you want the cops to arrest you? How will your employers feel about that?"

The short driver got the message. Together, he and Laura managed to get the other man vertical, though he swayed on his feet.

Michael said, "We'll pretend he got drunk, and we're all laughing at our friend. We're having a high old time, see?" He shot a look at the driver. "I'm going to call you Chester."

"Chester?"

"Yeah, you look like a Chester. And your friend's a Brad. Yeah, that will work. Okay, Laura, are you strong enough to hold Brad up and walk with him? Sure you are. I can see he's mad as hell but he doesn't want any publicity. He especially doesn't want his picture on the six o'clock news and the men who hired him to know he screwed up."

"You bastard," Brad said. "Look what you did to my mouth. Half my teeth—"

"Shut up, Brad," Michael said. "Okay, Laura, just use your shoulder to hold him up. And *Chester*," he said to the driver, "get your ass over here to me."

Chester shuffled over and Michael quickly searched him, just to make sure he wasn't armed. To his surprise, he liberated two knives, which he slipped into his pocket. Michael was also surprised to see that the bloody surface wound on his arm from Brad's gun had almost completely healed. He had barely a scratch now, though his shirt was spattered with blood.

"Let's go," Michael said. "We're all going to Laura's apartment and I want everybody to laugh and have a good time on the way. If either of you boys tries to escape, I'll shoot you in the legs and get you arrested."

Bold words, he thought, for a guy who hadn't shot a handgun in twenty-five years, and then at stationary targets.

They commenced their journey and Laura launched into a comic, one-sided conversation with her charge that was meant to be heard a mile away. "Hey, Brad, you really tied one on, didn't you? You're acting like a blind monkey and need to sleep it off. Hey, watch where you step! I'm just a girl and could never get you back up if you fell."

Such improvisation surprised Michael and gave him some hope. He'd never guess that Laura had a flair for acting and making it up on the spot. As Brad stumbled, he saw her rise on her toes and kiss him on the cheek, then head toward her townhouse. Once Brad dug in his heels and jerked around to stare at Michael. "I never had nobody hit me this hard in my fuckin' life. Who the hell are you?" he asked, clutching his bloody mouth. He spat out a tooth as if to emphasize the point.

Laura and Brad continued on, Laura propping up the much heavier man. Behind them, Michael had it easier, though his goal was the same. Be merry and act happy! The world is a wonderful place to be and you should crack jokes and laugh.

So he did, keeping an arm around his short, roly-poly companion. "Had yourself a great, wild time, didn't you?" Michael said. "Chugged a few drinks and got cute with some sexy girls." He broke into a rousing party song. Half his notes were off-key but he knew that everything depended on creating a drunken party atmosphere. People seldom questioned such scenes or peeked beneath the surface.

They were nearly at Laura's townhouse when several curious women stopped her. Michael saw shock and disbelief in their faces and read their thoughts easily. The prim, proper English teacher…look what she's doing, cavorting with a drunken man!

Laura met their stunned disapproval with smiles and laughter. "Oh, Brad's my cousin, and I happened to find him on a bender at a party. We're taking him and his frisky friend home now to sleep it off." She nodded back toward Chester.

"We should report this," a plump woman said. "There was a gunshot and I saw a man fall."

Laura laughed. "Nonsense. It was just a car backfiring and Brad passed out. Nothing to worry about."

They moved on. When they reached Laura's townhouse, Michael heaved a sigh of relief. Hopefully they'd fooled the onlookers and no one would call the cops. Now they could get inside and ask these boys some hard questions about who they were and what was going down. It was high time they got some helpful answers.

CHAPTER TWELVE
ELECTRICITY CAN BE A TRICKY THING

Once they were inside, it seemed at first that the men didn't know much and had few answers. They were just men who had been given an assignment on a need-to-know basis, with the only directive being to find Michael Windsor, get his CABS machine, and return it to a specified location. To Michael, that made sense. The more people who knew or suspected the truth, the greater the chance that it would get out.

Sitting against the wall beside Brad, Chester claimed to know nothing. All he'd been told was to drive Brad, whom he'd just met, to a building and pop the lock, then drive him wherever the hell he wanted. Chester seemed especially frank and convincing, but Michael didn't quite buy his act. At any rate, what could he do—beat or torture the guy to make him talk? Well, he'd think about it later.

Brad, the actual thief, also claimed to know nothing, or very little. He was bigger and taller than Michael and used his hands a lot to express himself. All he knew was that he was supposed to steal the machine and take it to... Well, here he grew secretive. "I ain't gonna be a snitch," he said. "If they know I told you where to take it, they'd fuckin' ice me."

After a little more grilling, Brad had almost convinced Michael of his ignorance. Then Brad leaned forward and asked a question. "What I can't figure," he said, "is how that thing screwed up my aim. It felt like it had hands. If it hadn't stopped me, you'd be dead and we'd be gone." His eyes widened. "Say, are you its handler?"

Feeling like it had hands was one thing. The word "handler," though, opened doors. Michael glanced at the battered door they had managed to close, weighing his words carefully.

"How could I control it?" he asked. "I must have been sixty feet away."

Brad was not bright but realized he'd made a slip. "I dunno." He tapped his head. "Maybe up here."

"Mind control?" Laura said. "Where do you get that?"

Keep this to one questioner, Mac advised, and Michael agreed. He flashed Laura a glance, hoping she'd get the message.

"It's just something I heard," Brad said, his gaze shifting to Laura. He smiled, evidently liking what he saw.

"Where did you hear it?" Michael asked, steering him back.

"Aw, it's just something a few guys said. I don't even know their names."

That was pretty lame. "Do you know who hired you?"

Brad snorted. "Naw, just where to drop the thing off."

Holy crap, these birds sure didn't know much. Brad's information seemed to be primarily anecdotal and speculative. "You seem to be talking about mind control," Michael said. "Explain what you mean." He gave the gun he'd taken from Chester a little bounce to remind them who was in control.

Brad shrugged his massive shoulders. "Somebody said you could talk to the ap machine up here." He tapped his head again. "Just a few words now and then."

"What do you mean?" Michael asked.

Brad struggled with the question. "Just what I said."

Chester spoke up. "He means just a few phrases, not complete sentences."

With Mac and me it's more than a few phrases, Michael thought with pleasure. "What else could it do?" he asked.

Brad touched his bloody mouth and winced. "It could make you strong, give you powers. Shit, there were even rumors the ap machine could think and heal itself too."

"'Heal itself'?"

"Yeah, you know, put itself back together if it was shot to pieces or had its teeth bashed in like I did." He moaned in pain, pressing a bloody handkerchief to his lips. "Some guy said the government would be interested in such a war toy for military purposes."

The *government*. *War toy*. The suggestion gave Michael a sick feeling. "I wonder how they created such a machine," he said.

"Machines," Brad said.

"Machines? More than one? How many?"

Brad shrugged. "I dunno."

Chester said, "Somebody said he'd heard there was an accident during production at a medical equipment company and something weird happened. Some of the machines were affected. They sent teams like us out to investigate promising reports." He shrugged. "Electricity can be a tricky thing and this time it caused a happy accident or two."

A happy accident and there was more than one just like Mac. Michael turned toward Mac, whom he'd put on a table. How he wished he could beam a question to this machine who loved him.

His stare compensated for his lack of telepathy. Mac responded: *I heard some techs speculate about duplicates. But I never saw another machine that could do what I do, I swear it.*

Another troubling inconsistency. How far indeed could he trust Mac? He thought of the correction marks Laura put on student papers. Any way you cut it, Mac's subject didn't match his verb or his verb didn't match his subject. He said he was alone in the universe and yet there were reports of duplicates. And he had never even mentioned them.

Michael was about to break the silence by speaking when Mac brought up a new subject. *For the record, they can never really capture me. If my situation becomes too precarious, like it almost did an hour ago, I can simply turn myself off for good. The machine will continue to run, but I'll be gone. I think you humans call it suicide.*

Mac could kill himself and he almost had? The possibility had never occurred to Michael, and it shocked and depressed him. The thought of being without Mac filled him with sadness.

His depression made him forget Brad and drop his guard, not long but long enough for Brad to sense an opening. Michael caught a glimpse of animal cunning in Brad's flat eyes and saw his thighs bunch as he prepared to rise.

"Don't even think it, Slick," Michael warned. He pointed the gun between the man's eyes. "Nothing would give me greater pleasure than to blast your fuckin' lights out."

Brad froze then settled back, subsiding like a wave. His eyes remained fixed on Michael as if waiting for the next opportunity.

Laura pulled out her cell. "I'd better call work and tell them I won't be in tomorrow. I'm sure they're already wondering what happened to me this afternoon."

Michael remembered Mac's warning. "Don't call," he said. "We don't know who's monitoring us and how they're doing it."

She gazed at him then put her phone back. "What are we going to do?"

Good question. To start with, what were they going to do with the two men? Threaten and hurt them to get more information? Perhaps stick Chester's pistol in their mouths and use a pillow to muffle the sound? No, it wasn't in his nature and would only create new problems. As for these men, Michael sensed he'd gotten everything useful out of them that he could. He didn't know how many teams had been sent out to investigate reports of unusual machines, but this particular team was not the best. Still, he couldn't just release these men into the wild. They'd report him and Laura and they might be killed.

And what about the police? Michael knew he was still a murder suspect, even more since the two cops who had followed him to the school had disappeared without a trace. Had that story hit the news yet, and what could he do about it?

Michael glanced at Laura and something clicked in his mind. "Quandary," he said.

She blinked. "What?"

"Remember the photograph of the spelling bee?" he said. "It's the word you spelled correctly in the third grade."

She stared back, then her mouth widened in shock. "Oh my God, you're right. I remember now. I almost misspelled it at the time." She paused. "How did you know?"

"It's part of the pattern." He looked at his arm, now completely healed. Laura had noticed it and been astonished. His shirt, though, had not fared so well and was still bloody. "Do you have a shirt I can wear?"

She nodded. "I'll get one of Stan's."

Michael watched her leave. The men did too. "Nice ass," Brad observed.

"To hell with her ass," Chester said. "Something weird's happening here."

"What do you mean?"

"The thing with the photograph. He said it's part of the pattern. What did he mean, and how did he know what word she spelled in the third grade?"

"Shut up," Michael said. Chester was obviously the more intelligent of the two, and he ought to watch what he said when he was around him. Seeing Laura return with a checkered shirt, he smiled happily.

Stan's shirt fit well except for the arms, which were three inches too long. "Reminds me of the long arms of the law," he said.

Laura smiled. "Just roll up the cuffs."

"I have another method." He turned Laura so their captives couldn't see, then held out his hands. "Watch."

He was foolish to believe it would work and it didn't. Nothing happened. Nothing at all.

"What is it?" Laura whispered.

Okay, one more try. He took a deep breath then focused on his hands, or more precisely, the sleeves of Stan's shirt. At first, nothing happened. Then, obedient to his will, the arms of the shirt shortened until they reached the tops of his hands and were precisely the right length.

Laura gasped. "My Lord!"

"How about that?" Michael said. "Some neat parlor trick, huh? Bet I'd make a great tailor."

Yes, one minor problem was solved. But what about the big ones, such as what he was going to do with their prisoners?

What are we going to do, Michael? Mac asked, echoing his thoughts.

Michael looked at Laura. "We can't kill these guys or even tie them up and run. Sooner or later, they'll get loose and report us. Not only that, the police are after me."

Forget the fuzz, Mac said. *You can't control them. The best thing you can do as far as they're concerned is stay out of sight, and you're doing it. As for the government, if these nincompoops had reported us, they'd already be here.*

Michael reached out and pulled Laura to him. "Whatever happens, I don't want Laura to get hurt."

"Don't worry about me," she said. "I can take it." She glared at the men on the floor. "I just don't want these bastards to cause us any more problems."

There might be a way, Mac said. *We can "neutralize" them without hurting them.*

"How?"

Ever hear of hypnosis?

Ah, he was right with him. "You want to hypnotize them and make them forget everything?"

Yes. Using you *to do it. It will tax my resources, but I think we should try.*

Michael felt himself smile. Or was it Mac smiling with his mouth? Either way, Laura was in on it too, fiercely grinning her approval.

In contrast, their captives looked worried and concerned. "The hell you're gonna hypnotize us," Chester said. He started to rise.

"Stay right where you are," Michael said, gliding forward. He raised a finger, feeling Mac's power pour into him in a sweet flow of electricity, filling him to the brim. It was like Wi-Fi, a strictly wireless connection, and he was the receiver.

Chester had said it himself: *Electricity can be a tricky thing.* Perhaps Mac could not only build up Michael's body and improve his tennis game from a distance but could use Michael's subconscious desire to

100

repair his car and give Mr. Starret a deadly heave-ho. Son of a bitch, if that was so, what couldn't his little machine buddy do?

Michael took a deep breath. "I want you both to look right at my finger," he told the two men softly. "Look at it very closely."

CHAPTER THIRTEEN
TRINITY

Working together, Mike and Mac molded the two criminals to their will. First Mike spoke, then Mac, communicating through Mike. To Michael, it was a revelation, a delightful, fulfilling synergy. As he spoke and as he listened, he felt he was not just one person but two.

Mike: "You will forget who hired you…"

Mac: *and your original purpose for coming here.*

Mike: "You will rise now and leave…"

Mac: *without looking back and you will go…*

Mike: "to the car you came in and you will remember…"

Mac: *Nothing. You will remember absolutely nothing…*

Mike: "of your experience here, not a single damn thing."

As Brad and Chester left Laura's townhouse, the three of them followed. Michael held Mac against him as they descended the steps and emerged onto the front sidewalk. They stood watching the two men walk to the car they had come in and get in. Before he did, Brad gazed back in their direction with a vacant, bloody smile, clearly not bothered at all by his broken teeth.

Laura spoke with concern: "What if your hypnotic spell wears off? They could come back here with a platoon, guns blazing."

"I don't think so," Michael said.

"How can you be sure?"

Press me against her, Mac said.

Michael obeyed, pressing Mac against Laura's chest. She gasped and clutched the machine.

"Oh, yes," she said after several seconds. "I see. You both erased their memory. It's as if they never came here." She stiffened. "But what if you missed something? A notecard they wrote or something else?"

Remind her that we searched them, Mac advised.

"We searched both of them carefully," Michael said, hoping it was carefully enough. "I think it'll be all right."

Brad opened the door on the passenger side and slipped in. They watched him fasten his seatbelt and nod at Chester. The Nissan drove off, a small, ordinary car on an ordinary afternoon.

Laura checked her watch. "It's 2:30," she said. "Officials at the school will wonder what happened to me."

"Go ahead, call them," Michael said.

"Are you sure?" She glanced up and around. "The bad guys could trace my call here."

Michael laughed. "So what? The boys in charge must know we're here." Yet he wasn't so sure. "What do you think?" he asked Mac. "Is there any danger if she calls?"

Mac was uncharacteristically silent.

"Mac?" He shook him to get his attention.

If she must call, Mac replied, *have her drive at least three miles away and do it. We don't want to call any more attention to our presence here than necessary.*

It made sense, but Mac sounded different. "Hey, Mac, are you all right?" Michael asked.

Silence. Then: *Feel a bit tired. Our hypnosis session drained me a little.*

"Why?" Vaguely he remembered Mac saying it would "tax my resources."

"I don't know. Probably because I'm a *machine*, Michael."

Oh, right. Despite their closeness, Michael realized they were still different in certain ways.

"Okay," Laura said, "I'll go for a spin. Want to come with me?"

"Think I'll stay here with Mac," Michael said. "Hope you don't mind."

"Nope, not at all. I should be back in fifteen or twenty minutes." She started to leave then laughed. "The place is yours. You can raid my refrigerator all you like. I think you'll find interesting exotic things in it."

Michael smacked his lips. "Yum yum. I can hardly wait."

He watched Laura get into her red Mustang and drive off. *Here I am!* the flamboyant vehicle seemed to shout. *You can't miss me!*

They watched until the car disappeared, then Michael checked his cell phone for any news about the two missing policemen. He found nothing, not even a ghost of a whisper. But what did he expect? Only a few hours had passed and Matthews's and Sanchez's bodies had dissolved into thin air, leaving not a trace behind.

Michael gave Mac a nudge. "Let's go raid that fridge," he said. "I'm positively famished."

I neither eat nor drink, Mac reminded him.

"Do you miss it?"

It's hard to miss what you've never had. For consolation, I keep reminding myself that I can never be hungry or thirsty.

"Good points," Michael said. To him, Mac still sounded off, strangely tired and sluggish. Not quite there.

In the kitchen, he opened the refrigerator and surveyed his new domain. Yup, it looked like exotic dishes all right, since he couldn't name a single one. Well, he was a basic meat-and-potatoes guy, born and bred. When in doubt, throw in more gravy. One dish here, though, really caught his interest. It looked like yellow rice with dark, reddish chunks of meat.

"Wonder what this is," he mused.

Show it to me, Mac said from the kitchen table.

Michael took the dish from the refrigerator and removed the lid.

Lamb biryani with saffron, yogurt, and caramelized onions, Mac declaimed. *What you're holding contains fluffy grains of scented basmati rice and tender chunks of exquisitely spiced lamb. I bet it's absolutely delicious.*

"How can you tell what I'm holding?" Michael asked. "How do you know there's caramelized onions and basmati rice? And how do you know it's absolutely delicious?"

You ask too many questions, Mac said and faded away again.

Michael snagged a beer from the fridge and popped off the cap on an opener. Then he located a plate and utensils, and sat down to feast.

He took one bite and grinned with pleasure. On top of everything else, his new girlfriend could really cook. He was halfway through it when he realized he should have heated the dish up. Well, maybe next time. Of course, he realized, there might not be a next time. Things seldom remained the same. It seemed just yesterday that he, Muriel, and Andy had sat down to a meal almost as delicious as this one. Now his family had dissolved like Matthews and Sanchez, and Muriel was trying to steal his son.

Michael sighed and gripped his fork. He didn't miss Muriel much, but Andy was a chunk of his soul. While he'd seen his remarkable son just a few hours ago, it had only been for a few minutes. He felt cheated and already ached with longing.

You'll see Andy soon. I'm sure you will.

He gazed into Mac's screen. "How did you know what I was thinking?"

I don't have to read your mind to know.

Ah, this was important information to know. So Mac could know what he was thinking even though he couldn't actually read his mind. How comforting!

"Let's try it again," Michael said. "What am I thinking now?" He concentrated on Mac's waning vitality, his fading strength, and his concern for him.

I'm sorry we can't retrieve your car, Mac informed him. *They might be watching it closely even as we sit here.*

Michael smiled, feigning amazement at Mac's ability. "Right again! How the hell do you do it?" He shoveled another forkful of lamb into his mouth.

———————

Laura was late getting back and Michael sat worrying and checking his watch at the kitchen table. Now she was gone for an hour, now an hour and a half, now two hours. How long did it take to make a stupid phone call? How many time zones would she cross before doing it? And why had they been so stupid as to let her leave the townhouse? They had only made it easier for the "bad guys" to grab her.

At two hours and twelve minutes, Laura burst laughing through the broken front door with a massive smile on her face. "I'm sorry I didn't call, but when I contacted the school, they had wonderful news to tell me!"

What news could that be? "I've been granted amnesty?" Michael said.

Laura seemed to come down to Earth. "Oh, no. Marsha—she's the vice principal—told me I'd been selected to head the Dual Learning Program. That's English and Spanish."

"*Bueno, señorita. Felicidades!*" Michael said. "I didn't know you spoke Spanish. And of course, you had to go to the school to talk about it."

"I'm sorry," Laura said. "I left and didn't think to call. And you're in this terrible mess."

Michael waved it off. "That's okay, I'm happy for you. And I get the feeling that you've wanted this position for some time."

"Yes! It's a…"

"'consummation devoutly to be wished'?"

"Well, yes, though that's *Hamlet* and doesn't exactly fit. He was talking about death." She hesitated. "I won't let you down again."

"Forget it. You already apologized. Besides, you have the right to your own life. And like I said, I'm happy for you."

"Thank you." She sat down across from him. "How is it?" she asked, gazing at Mac.

106

"Not *it*," Michael said. "Mac's a *he*." He realized, though, that Laura was right. It was only he who saw Mac that way.

Laura reached out and touched Mac, stroking his surface. "Does he respond at all?"

"Only a little. It was the hypnosis that did it, though I'm not sure why."

I forced my will on others, Mac said. *And in so doing, I lost my own.*

Michael shivered. He didn't quite understand Mac's words, but he could tell that his friend was exhausted and depressed, and he had a terrible fear. He reached out and touched him.

"You love Mac, don't you?" Laura said.

He nodded, gazing at Mac's screen. "Yes, I do," he said.

———

Laura's apartment had two bedrooms, and she assigned him the other one. "If you get lonely tonight," she said, "you know where to find me."

He mulled over her words through a delicious chicken and rice dinner and into the evening. Perhaps I can just call you up for a date, he thought, and chuckled.

As it turned out, he didn't have to call her. While getting ready for bed, he heard a knock on the door. He answered it, finding Laura in a tiny, two-piece pair of pajamas. He noticed that the pattern was daisies, ripe for the picking.

"I thought I'd tuck you in," she said with a naughty look.

"You're a wonderful host," he replied.

Looking past him, she spotted Mac and a mask lying on a night table beside the bed. She entered and picked up the mask. "May I watch you put this on and use it?"

"Sure, but don't get turned on."

He took a bottle of distilled water from the bag, enough for one night, and poured it into the tub. He slid the tub into the end of the CABS machine.

"The water moistens the air I breathe," he explained. "Otherwise, my mouth would get awfully dry."

"Fascinating," she said. "I wouldn't want you with a dry mouth."

"I get the feeling we're talking about different things." He raised the mask. "After trying all three masks, I opted for the largest one." He swallowed, aware of her stare. "I prefer its snap-on clamps. Also, it has less air leakage."

"I'm glad. I don't want your air to leak," Laura said.

"I agree." Aware of her closeness, he turned the mask so she could see it from all sides. "Now there's an art and a science involved in putting this damn thing on. You've got to get the length of the straps just right and—"

"Can we kiss a little first? I get the feeling it'll be rather hard to do once you put that thing on."

"Uh—sure." He set the mask down and took her in his arms. Her own arms rose and slid around his head, pulling it down. For a long time he savored her lips, relearning their taste and texture. There was a little nub on her upper lip he found especially delicious.

Finally, she pulled back with an impish smile. "Can Mac join us?"

The thought stunned him. "You mean a threesome?"

"A naughty menage a trois."

He shrugged. "It might be a way to get him involved again." He patted the machine, surprised he wasn't jealous. "Mac, what do you say?"

No answer.

"Mac?"

Sounds delectable, Mac said in his head. But it sounded as if he had used all his strength to respond.

Michael put the mask on, careful to get the straps and clamps right, then attached the air tubing to the mask and inserted the other end into the machine. All that remained for him to do now was plug Mac in and hop in bed without tangling himself in the tubing or knocking Mac on the floor.

"I'd like you to lie on your back," Laura said.

His head snapped back in surprise. "Female dominant. What would your students say?"

"I know, I'm surprised at myself. You've put a world class spell on me, Mr. Masked Man."

No point in arguing. The view would be just as good from the bottom. He adjusted the mask a little and lay down in bed, hoping Mac would join them and not be just a passive observer.

"You know," he said, "we've come a long way from the beautiful young peasant girl and the middle-aged aristocrat. It's hard to believe we're still in the same book."

Laura giggled. "Señor Windsor, each of us plays many roles. For all we know, there may be more in store."

She knelt between his legs and nudged them apart. He felt her fingers glide into his pajama bottoms and play with the prize within. At first she was hesitant, and it only tickled. Then she grew bolder and the pleasure morphed into a different and more intense sensation.

She removed his mask and pajamas and kissed him. He reached out and paused the machine so air wouldn't continue to hiss from the tube. Then he kissed her back and freed her from her frilly, daisy-covered garments. As he did, Mac commented on the action for the first time. It was not precisely a moan, but if Michael didn't know better, he'd guess that it was the birth cry of a machine that was beginning to discover sexual pleasure.

Now that they were both naked, Michael replaced his mask and restarted the machine so Mac would receive the full effect of his attachments. Gently pushing Laura down, he began to caress every inch of her body, partly because he wanted to and partly because he thought it might be instructive for Mac. The latter proved to be true, as Mac began to keen in his mind and speak in a strange way. *Oh glorious day! Sweet mercy sublime! Ecstasy I never dreamed of, dimensions I never imagined!*

Michael pulled back and briefly lifted his mask so he could speak. "Did you—"

"Hear him in my mind?" Laura said. "Yes, I did. He said something about it being a glorious day and sweet mercy divine."

His suspicion confirmed, they both laughed, and Laura turned the tables on him, not only caressing but kissing every inch of his flesh. She was even more diligent than he had been, and Mac's commentary became something like a runaway train that had joyfully jumped the tracks and sailed into the clouds.

Michael and Laura got down to serious business. He entered her with a sob of pleasure and for an hour or more they swapped and sometimes shared orgasms. Again and again they changed positions or invented new ones. It was a symphony of desire and at times, Michael thought that Mac was their conductor, guiding and inspiring them, exhorting them to greater efforts. *Oh, what a lovely flower we three are*, Mac sang, *a Trinity of Wonder.*

On and on it went with Mac their loving companion. At times, Michael even felt his phantom touch, caressing and stroking their bodies. *We three*, Mac sang. *We three are every star and galaxy that ever existed. We three are the universe.*

At last, they parted. Exhausted, Michael closed his eyes and slept.

———————

He awoke next morning as Laura called him to breakfast.

Remembering the previous night's adventures, he laughed with joy. Laura and he together.

And Mac too! How wonderful it had been for them to share, to come together as one. What had Mac called them? *A Trinity of Wonder.*

Michael rose, put on his pajama bottom, and grinned at Mac on the night table. His smile faded though, as he saw him more clearly. Something was wrong. He went and picked Mac up, examined him carefully.

Mac was dead.

He had no doubt about it. There was no life, not even a whisper of energy in the machine. Last night's passion had destroyed his friend, robbed him of his life. Added to the hypnosis, it had been too much—far too much to bear. Mac wasn't human, and he wasn't built to tolerate such an experience. Michael should have known better.

Grief rose, and he sank down on the bed. In God's name, why had he done it?

"Michael!" Laura happily called. "Did you hear me? Breakfast is ready!"

He rose numbly and left the bedroom, heading toward the kitchen. Halfway there, he heard the bell ring and saw Laura cross the living room toward the front door. She reached out to open it.

A terrible fear rose. "No, Laura," he called. "Don't open it!"

Too late. She opened the door and two uniformed cops entered without being invited. One was a big man and the other a petite black woman. Their eyes found Michael at once.

"Michael Windsor?" the man asked.

He straightened, wanting to lie. "Yes," he said.

The man moved his hand to his holster. "We want you to come down to the precinct with us."

"Do you have a warrant?" he wanted to ask. But he knew it didn't matter.

"What is this about?" Laura asked in amazement.

"It's about two of our officers," the female cop said. "Lieutenant Matthews and Lieutenant Sanchez. We thought Mr. Windsor could tell us something about their whereabouts."

CHAPTER FOURTEEN
GREEN THUMBS

This time the cops were even more intense than the ones he'd had before. And the real kicker was their names. The mean little woman on the left was named Judge, and the mean big man on the right was named Striker. If he wasn't so sad and depressed, he might have laughed at that.

They brought him to the police station and to a boxed-in room containing a wooden desk, a small table, and three chairs. They snapped at his listlessness, but he didn't care. He kept thinking about Mac. He'd had no doubt his friend was gone for he'd felt the absence in his soul. Laura was sad too when he'd told her, but her sadness hadn't stopped them from arresting her also. Whoops, he meant detained for questioning, which they were doing to her now in another room. He wondered how that was going and if they were treating her as rudely as they were treating him. He sure hoped not.

"Sit down, Mr. Windsor," Lieutenant Striker said. He had a face like an axe, which in a way was appropriate. Officer Judge, two or three ranks below him, had the most precise, beautiful features he had ever seen. Michael sensed she was either Striker's protégé or lover. Perhaps both.

Reluctantly, he sat down in the chair behind the desk and they sat down across from him. One of them, the human axe Striker, lifted his chair and slid it six inches closer. Intimidation plain and simple.

Striker set a recorder down on the small table and turned it on. He identified himself and Officer Judge, then Michael, and gave the time, which was 9:27 a.m. After a pause, he continued. "Mr. Windsor, we'd like to ask you some questions and record your answers." He motioned at a window that Michael assumed was a one-way mirror. "Another officer will be watching to guarantee we have an accurate record. Is that all right with you?"

Michael hesitated. "Yes," he said reluctantly.

"Good. First, let's talk about yesterday afternoon. Why did you go to your son's school?"

"I wanted to see him."

"Were you aware that police officers were following you?"

"No."

"And you didn't see them on the school grounds?"

"No," he lied.

"This is strange," the tiny cop called Judge cut in. "Their patrol car was parked in the school lot."

"I can't help that," Michael said. "I didn't see that either."

"But the police were searching for you. How do you account for your claim that you didn't see them?"

"I don't account for it."

"Then how—"

"I'm just saying I didn't see them. So please don't *judge* me."

"I'm not judging you and don't try any funny stuff with my name. Your answers simply don't add up."

Don't add up? My whole damned life doesn't add up. Michael thought of Muriel telling him he was a loser and leaving him, taking Andy with her. Of Beverly hounding him at work and what it felt like to gasp for breath in his sleep so he wouldn't die. Then Mac, his incredible sleep apnea machine had taken over his life and people were clearly willing to kill him for it. Why? What did they want Mac for?

He gazed at Officer Judge and felt something build inside him. It grew and grew and when he could hold it no more, he fed it to her, just released it from his chest and let it go. Her head snapped back and he saw her begin to breathe heavily, her nostrils dilating with lust. Such a beautiful, sexy, desirable woman. If it weren't for Laura, he might want her. He found even more power and blasted her with it from top to bottom. Officer Judge swayed in her chair then leaned across the desk. Her lips parted to kiss him.

"Angela, what are you doing?" Striker snapped in shock.

Michael eased off her, and Officer Angela Judge—damn, what a name!—sank back in her chair, trembled and fought to regain control. It took a minute but eventually she moaned and rubbed her eyes.

"Please excuse me. I...felt faint for a minute."

"Of course." Relieved, Striker shot him a hard look as if the attack on his colleague were Michael's fault, which of course it was.

"No more questions," Michael said. He pushed his chair back and rose. "Look. Your questions have all been answered. I've cooperated with you guys as much as I could. I'm tired of being kicked around for no reason. Either arrest me or let me go. And while you're at it, release my girlfriend too."

The cops exchanged glances. "We can't release you," Officer Judge said.

"Why not?"

"Well, for one thing, there's paperwork that needs to be finalized."

"Fuck the paperwork. Fuck finalizing it." When his profanity produced no effect, Michael took another tack. "If you're going to charge me, I insist on having legal representation." Oh, right, and how would he pay for it, with the princely sum he had left? With his jar of pennies back home, he couldn't even afford a first-year law school dropout. Perhaps a public defender? They at least worked pro bono. And if he lawyered up, he'd have someone to advise him about all these damned questions.

He thought of what he'd said to the cops. Bold words for a nearly broke guy standing in a police station. He knew his problems had made him short-tempered, inclined to utter rash and self-destructive statements, and his grief over Mac's death had added to his instability. The cops, however, didn't look one bit offended by his outbursts. If anything, they appeared to be thoroughly unimpressed, as if they heard such prattle all the time.

"Sit down, Mr. Windsor," Lieutenant Striker said.

The hell I will. But he knew he had already run his mouth far too much. He raised his gaze and scanned the barren room. Three chairs and a wooden desk, plus the small table and a one-way mirror behind which some jerk was watching and listening to everything they said. Other than that, there was nothing else unless you counted the light fixtures, not even a picture or a single flower.

"Mr. Windsor…"

"All right," he said, and sat back down behind the desk.

"I'm Officer Angela Judge," the woman cop said, "and I'm turning the recorder off at 9:34 a.m." She did so then stared at Michael. "Before I ask you more questions, what did you just do to me?" She trembled a little.

Michael considered again his situation. Should he cooperate or ask for a lawyer? He opened his mouth, wondering what he was going to say.

Striker frowned and pointed at the desk. "Where the hell did that come from?"

When Michael saw the tiny rose, he knew the answer to Striker's question. The two-inch-high rose in its tiny pot came from the same place that had enabled him to shorten Stan's sleeves so they'd fit, only this time he'd done it subconsciously. Michael also found that he was not much surprised. Hadn't he felt this barren room needed something extra, perhaps a flower?

He reached out and carefully stroked the small stem and petals with his thumb. Several seconds passed, and he felt it begin to grow.

Judge leaned close. "It looks like a rose," she said.

"A *rose*?" Striker asked.

"Yes. And I could be wrong, but it seems to be...growing." She turned the recorder on again, identified herself and gave the time. Then she and Striker got up and approached the rose as if they were a swat team surrounding a building that contained public enemy number one. Clearly, they were puzzled. Michael backed away to give them room.

They stared at the rose, not getting it. But he was getting something. Suppose, just suppose, that when he had found Mac still and lifeless, he had stroked and caressed him, just as he had the rose, stroked and urged him back to life. Probably it wouldn't have worked, but was it possible he had given up too early, that he had pronounced his friend dead and beyond resurrection before he needed to? *Goddamn it, was it possible?*

Judge and Striker clearly didn't appreciate the magic of a growing flower appearing in their sterile, immaculate interrogation room, especially since it was now twice as large as it was before. Their eyes rose in unison to his.

"How did you do that?" Striker asked. "Is it a trick rose of some kind? A gimmick from a toy store?"

Michael laughed. "Yup, cost me all of $2.99."

"It's still growing," Judge observed. "How is that possible?"

Michael raised his thumbs and waggled them. "I have green thumbs," he said. "They can make *anything* grow." When that knee-slapper didn't bowl them over, he chose a different explanation. "It's like Lieutenant Striker says. It's a trick rose."

Striker reached out and grabbed the rose in his meaty fist. He squeezed it to a pulp. "Now it's a dead one."

As dead as Mac? Michael forced his friend out of his thoughts. "Have you found my car yet?" he asked, hoping to distract them.

"Your car?" Striker said.

"Yeah, I was driving down a country lane when the battery went dead. If you're as good at being detectives as you think you are, you should know where my car is."

Obviously, they didn't, and Judge shook her head in confirmation. "No, we don't. Where did you say—"

Striker's cell phone beeped, and he answered it. "Yeah," he said, then listened for a long moment.

When he put the phone away, he looked shaken and not one bit happy. "Uh, stay here. Officer Judge and I have to step outside for a call and some discussion."

A call and some discussion? Michael returned to the chair. What was coming down the pike now?

Ten minutes later the door opened and Striker and Judge returned. To Michael's surprise, Laura was with them and two men he had never seen before. The first man was very tall and removed a card from his pocket which he held up. "Good day, Mr. Windsor. I'm Special Agent Stanley Grimm of the FBI." He introduced his partner, a fellow agent, and Michael shook hands with them.

Afterward, Laura moved forward and took Michael's hand. The simple act filled him with joy and relief. Thank the Fates! He'd wondered if he'd ever see her again.

But wait, was that a smirk on her face? And why did she glance so coyly at the tall agent? Michael looked from one to the other, trying to put it together. Laura's previous boyfriend had been named Stan and had long arms. The Stan before him in the neat, tailored suit had long arms too. And before the cops had brought them here from Laura's apartment, Laura had begged them to let her use her bathroom for a moment. Was that a trick? Perhaps she had done it so she could make a quick call for help to an old lover, a guy with powerful connections.

Holy crap, Laura, he thought. Why didn't you tell me your ex-boyfriend was a special agent of the FBI? Didn't you think that fact was relevant? He looked Special Agent Stanley Grimm over closely. The guy was at least six feet four and handsome as hell. Plus, he had a dashing mustache. Laura hadn't said anything at all about him being tall and handsome. Of course, she'd neglected to mention the mustache too.

Laura looked at Michael and gave him a covert wink. No, it seemed to say, I didn't think my boyfriend's job was germane then. But I do *now*.

Agent Grimm smiled. "Officers, I understand Mr. Windsor and Miss Kurick are suspects in the deaths of two officers."

"Let's just say they are people of interest," Judge said.

"I see," Grimm said. "Tell me, do you have the two officers' bodies to present as evidence?"

"No, but—"

Agent Grimm glanced at his partner. "Officers, while I appreciate your diligence, I feel it is necessary to inform you of a more pressing matter."

"A more pressing matter?" Striker said. "What could be more pressing than two missing police officers?"

Stanley Grimm raised his eyebrows and looked at the shorter agent, who responded on cue. "The FBI has been following Mr. Windsor's activities for some time," he said.

"You have?" Judge asked.

"Yes," Grimm replied. "And my superiors and I have become convinced that he represents a serious threat to national security. Therefore, we have been directed to take him and Laura Kurick into custody."

A serious threat to national security? What the hell was he talking about? The only thing he could think of was the attempted theft of his CABS machine at Laura's apartment. Did they think a machine that blew air was a global game changer? Hell, did they even know what the machine could do, what it was capable of? He sure hoped Laura hadn't told them.

Striker asked, "What threat to national security? Sir, what are you talking about?"

Agent Grimm smiled and moved his hand as if shutting a door right in their face. "I'm sorry, officers, but I'm not at liberty to say."

CHAPTER FIFTEEN
A WILD GOOSE CHASE

Judge and Striker weren't happy about losing Michael and Laura to the FBI (especially Michael). Striker pointed out that local police often worked with the FBI on cases where they shared a mutual interest. Stanley Grimm agreed but emphasized that this time, national security made it different. In addition, because Laura had called them and asked them to intercede with the police, it was necessary to take her and Michael away. Out of compassion, Michael waved at his former jailers on their way out.

They were led to a generic blue sedan. Grimm and Laura got in the front and Michael took the back seat at the direction of Maddox, Grimm's partner. After he sat down, Maddox ordered him to turn sideways and put his hands behind him. When he did, the agent promptly slapped handcuffs on him.

"What if my nose itches," Michael said. "How do I scratch it?"

Maddox ignored him.

Grimm started the car and they rolled through the streets. Michael waited for someone to speak but it remained silent.

"You called them from the john, didn't you, Laura?" Michael said. "Did you talk to your ex-boyfriend directly or leave a message?"

"Don't answer," Grimm said, but Laura ignored him.

"I left a message," she said.

"Did you mention Mac?" Michael asked. "Did you tell him what the CABS machine could do and the people who were after him?"

"If you don't shut up, I'll muzzle you too," Maddox said.

"Really? If you do, then I'll have to return these to you." Michael squirmed and removed his handcuffs, which he handed to Maddox.

Maddox gasped. "What is it?" Grimm asked, peering into the rearview mirror.

"He removed the cuffs," Maddox answered, his voice hoarse. "He just took them off like there was nothing to it and gave them to me."

"I can do other things too," Michael said. "I have a lot of tricks. I'll be glad to show you some."

Laura had turned completely around in her seat and was gazing at him with glassy eyes. "Believe what he says, Stan," she said. "And please believe me. I wasn't lying about the things Mac can do or the people who want to grab him."

Grimm was silent, apparently thinking it over. "This machine—"

"Mac," Laura stressed.

"Yes, Mac," Grimm said reluctantly. "You say it's at your apartment?"

"Yes, but he's…"

"Unresponsive," Michael supplied. "Possibly dead. And I'm the only person who might be able to revive him."

Grimm emitted a dry laugh. "A thinking AI who just happens to be a sleep apnea machine—it's rather hard to swallow, but we'll go to your place." He flicked on his turn signal. "But Mr. Windsor, please remain quiet until we arrive. This is an FBI investigation and certain rules of procedure apply."

Michael didn't give a damn about rules of procedure. What he did care about was whether Mac could be raised from the dead. He couldn't forget the bastards who had tried to steal his friend. How did he know that another team hadn't raided Laura's apartment in their absence and snatched him?

Grimm drove efficiently, but it still seemed to take forever to reach their destination. When they did, Laura hurriedly unlocked the front door and they all entered. After they'd climbed to the second floor, Grimm noticed the broken door and pointed at it. "What's that?"

"That's where they broke in," Laura said.

"You'd better get it fixed," Agent Maddox said, stating the obvious. "It's a security risk."

Michael headed anxiously toward his bedroom. "He should be in here," he said, hoping against hope. Please let Mac be here and alive!

When he reached the bedroom where he'd slept, half his wish came true. Mac was indeed here and fully intact, his attachments snugly in place. No marauders had taken him. But Michael saw almost at once that Mac was still dead. A brief examination confirmed his diagnosis.

Laura jumped right in and said what he was about to. "Stan, I know it looks like nothing, but Mac really existed. He spoke and interacted with us just like a person. We even did things together!"

What about our cozy threesome in bed? Michael thought. Are you going to tell him about that too? For a moment, he was afraid that Laura would discuss how Mac had supplied some of the erotic energy in their encounter, but she wisely omitted that activity.

Grimm picked Mac up and turned him over a few times. He glanced at Maddox. "Want to examine it?" he asked.

Maddox shook his head. "What for? It's just an apnea machine. My mother has one just like it."

Grimm sniffed and placed Mac in Michael's hands. "Your story is getting harder and harder to believe," he said. "We got involved because Laura called me and said you were being arrested because some people were after an amazing machine in your possession. But this tops that all to hell. A thinking, *conscious* apnea machine pursued by a mysterious enemy." He shook his head. "You're both either lying or deranged."

Michael said, "But what if we're telling the truth? You need to call it in and have Mac protected, placed under a close guard."

"Oh, I don't think so." Grimm gazed down at Michael and stroked his neat mustache. "My partner and I don't want to be laughed at."

"You're right," Maddox said. "As it is, we've already stretched the rules. The police did have jurisdiction."

Grimm waved his hand. "If they file a complaint, Curtis will smooth it over."

Michael turned the CABS machine in his hands, trying to will some life into it. Come back, Mac, come back!

Grimm gave Laura a tight smile. "Laura, can we talk privately?"

Her face tightened. "I don't think so. You not only didn't believe me and Michael, you insulted both of us by saying we were either lying or deranged. Under the circumstances, I'm not inclined to grant you favors."

"Laura, if you would just—"

"I will not 'just' anything! Please remember that you suddenly 'just' announced one day after a two-year relationship that you didn't love me anymore and were leaving. You didn't show me any consideration at all. Why should *I*?"

In the short time he'd known her, Michael had never seen Laura so angry. God, she was furious. In turn, Agent Grimm looked embarrassed and taken aback. His FBI dignity and decorum had just taken a major hit, and he clearly didn't know how to respond.

Maddox tried to rescue him. "Agent Grimm," he said, "perhaps we should leave." He pointed at Michael, who was still holding Mac. "Despite their claims, this device lacks any valuable properties that might affect national security. I'm afraid we've been on a wild goose chase."

Grimm nodded. "You're right. There's no domestic terrorism or organized crime here." He started to leave then stopped and looked back. "There's one thing I have to say. Laura, I didn't leave you because I didn't love you anymore."

Her eyes widened. "You didn't?"

He bit his lip. "At least once a day, you always had a new project that you went so wild about that you didn't care about anything else. It was always something different, something that came out of nowhere, and after a while I realized that what your past boyfriends had said about you was true. To be brief, there just wasn't room for me in your life. You were always on the phone or heading out the door, as flighty as a wild bird. So one day I finally got up and left." He cast a look at Michael. "Perhaps you've already discovered this a little?"

Michael recalled Laura leaving to place an important call to her school. Instead of taking only a half hour, she had taken over two, and he'd been sick with worry. When Laura had finally returned, she at first hadn't been one bit concerned that she was late. Instead, she'd been ecstatic about being appointed head of the Dual Learning Project. It was as if she'd completely forgotten the crisis they faced.

Grimm searched his face and nodded. "I see that it's already happened. Well, good luck keeping up with her. She's a wonderful woman, but she comes with a warning label written by past boyfriends."

Laura went up to him, her face etched in pain. "Stanley, I never knew. You never told me. You never breathed one word."

Grimm sighed. "Honey, I tried, lord but I tried. You simply never heard me, or forgot that I'd even spoken. There was always some new project or interest on the horizon, some new shiny object that got in the way."

"But the new project, interest, or shiny object was *never* another man," Laura said. "It was always you and only you because I loved you and you were the only man I wanted to be with. I was only 'flighty' about other things. Can't you understand that?"

Michael could tell from Grimm's face that her words hadn't budged the needle or registered as much as a feather. Stan the Man with the great arm Span towered over them in his neat, custom-made suit, unfazed and untouched by Laura's tears and passion. He was so convinced of his righteousness, he actually seemed to preen.

Michael thought he should defend Laura, or at least try. "Ever consider the possibility that *you* were the one who needed to change or that you just weren't the right man for her? It sounds like you wanted her to focus only on you."

Stan Grimm gave him a bitter smile. "Well, perhaps you'll have time to test that tender theory. As for now, I agree with Agent Maddox concerning this useless device." He sneered at the machine in Michael's hands. "We've been on a wild goose chase long enough, and it's time to leave."

Nodding at Maddox, Agent Grimm started to walk out. Maddox promptly followed him.

That was when Michael felt the machine stir in his hands and cough as if clearing its throat. The agents stopped in surprise and turned back. "What was that?" Grimm asked.

"I don't know," Michael answered.

The machine coughed again and shuddered. Then, slowly, it seemed to take a long, deep breath. Michael gazed in amazement as it swelled to twice its original size in his hands. Finally, it spoke.

"Hello, gentlemen," Mac said in a strong, clear voice. "Both of you have said that you're on a wild goose chase. You are indeed correct, and I'm delighted to inform you that an updated, improved, far more powerful version of myself is back with a fully expanded personality matrix to boot. Just call me Mac 2.0, at your service. Anyway, it seems that despite all your incompetence and skepticism, you have actually managed to find the wild goose."

Stunned, they all stared at the creature in Michael's hands. Despite his wonder, Michael noticed that Mac was twice as heavy as before.

"I know my resurrection comes as a surprise," Mac continued. "No doubt you considered me to be the equivalent of a useless tin pot. But I assure you I'm much, much more than that and we must act at once. Why? you ask. For one extremely good reason." Mac paused, his screen gleaming. "Gentlemen," he said, "my Dark Opposite has discovered my existence, and we are about to be attacked."

CHAPTER SIXTEEN
MY DARK OPPOSITE

The two FBI agents stood stunned. It was not just that a "tin pot" had suddenly addressed them in refined, arrogant tones, but that it had referred to a Dark Opposite who was about to attack them. Dazed himself, Michael could sympathize with their distress. Perhaps they doubted their sanity or thought they were dreaming. As for Laura, her lips curled in a bitter smile as if she had expected this all along.

"How is it possible?" Stan finally asked, thereby boosting Michael's opinion of him. Laura's former boyfriend was at least coming around and trying to cope.

Mac quickly explained. "A company producing sleep apnea machines accidentally upgraded two, making them truly exceptional. Until a few minutes ago, I thought I was the only one and that I was unique. I just found out I was wrong though. My Dark Opposite is the other. Evidence points to a non-standard configuration of three sub-circuits due to a freakish burst of electricity."

"T-That's impossible," Maddox said. "You're—"

Mac cut him off. "I don't have time to argue. My dark twin and his handler want to capture me and control my power, combine it with his and achieve an exponential upgrade. Unlike me, they want only to rule. Come on, let's get out of here. He could be here any minute along with his supporters."

Supporters? Who were they? Michael pressed Mac against him. "Where do we go, Mac?" he said, trying to keep his voice calm. "What do we do?"

Stan raised his cell to his ear. "We must get backup. I can have thirty men here in fifteen minutes."

"Too late," Michael said, speaking for Mac, "we've got to act *now*."

But how would they escape? He blinked then remembered the open manhole cover he'd seen from Laura's window and how he'd worried that some kid could fall in. "The sewer, doesn't it pass behind the townhouse?"

Laura frowned. "Yes, it's old and abandoned. We've tried to get the city to board it up, but kids keep breaking in."

"How far does it go?"

"I heard it goes a long way. Why..." Laura stopped. "That's only rumors. You can't mean—"

"You got a better idea?" Michael pointed over his shoulder. "The bad guys probably don't know about it."

"At least we hope they don't," Mac said. "Let's go!"

They headed toward the living room. As they went, Michael saw that Stan was talking intently into his cell phone. Maddox, by contrast, looked stricken, his eyes frozen. They went downstairs and Laura led them to a door in back. She pulled a keyring from her pocket.

"We seldom go this way," she said. "It's utility."

"That means useful," Mac said. "Well, let's use it."

Michael glanced out the opposite window just in time to see cars speed into the parking lot and stop. The doors opened and men burst out holding weapons.

"They're here," Stan Grimm said, following Michael's gaze. "And they don't look peaceful."

"They'll kill us and snatch Mac," Michael said. He hefted his friend's increased weight. "Come on," he snapped. "Let's go!"

126

Laura opened the door and they rushed outside. Bees buzzed in the air and Michael swatted a fly away. Craning his neck, he spotted the manhole cover. Yeah, there it was, sixty feet away and still partly open. It was an Underground Railroad if ever there was one and would take them all to freedom. He headed toward it.

After crossing the grass, he reconsidered his judgment. Christ, who was he kidding? This sewer was a dark, disgusting shithole where they would be trapped like rats. Maybe they should surrender before they were hunted down and shot to pieces.

"This is crazy," Maddox affirmed, peering down into the pit. "It's an effin' grave. They'll come after us and root us out."

Stan Grimm pressed his phone against his ear. "Brannon's building support now. Yes," he said into the phone. "The old sewer behind the Steinway Townhouses. We're going down into it. Get here fast!"

He pocketed his cell then jabbed Maddox. "We're going down," he ordered.

"Follow me," Michael said. Straining, he pushed the manhole cover aside and squeezed through, clutching Mac with one arm. His feet found a metal ladder and he started down, swaying precariously. "Watch out," he called, "it's shaky!" He imagined rusty bolts coming loose from the wall and the whole ladder falling off, carrying him and Mac with it.

Step after step he went. Five, six, seven. Even with his enhanced abilities, it was difficult. The ladder shook from side to side and once he almost lost his grip on the rung above. He caught himself though and continued downward. Eight steps, nine, ten...

Finally, his feet struck the floor and he slipped, dropping Mac. He heard Mac bounce away with a scrape of metal. Looking around, he searched the sewer for him, or tried to. Shit, it was dark and hard to see. To his left, the tunnel looked caved in, filled with earth and debris. To his right, the tunnel stretched away. It seemed clear and passable, but he couldn't be sure. Damn it, why hadn't he even thought to bring a flashlight? So much for advance planning!

The others came down after him and he went to help them. He felt Laura's soft thighs and Maddox's muscular butt. There was a clank of metal above as Stan closed the heavy manhole cover. Half a minute later, he stumbled off the ladder and joined them with a bright light that blinded Michael.

"Are your men coming?" Michael asked.

"Soon," Stan replied.

Good. But would it be soon enough? With the aid of Stan's flashlight, he located Mac and picked him up, brushing off some dirt. Glancing about, he found he could see the sewer to his right more clearly. It was about eight feet wide and indeed unobstructed, arching high overhead. Once, foul water filled with human waste had passed down its tubes in a swift, gurgling steam, perhaps a foot deep. It was not a pleasant thought.

"Let's go this way," he said, pointing down the tunnel.

"Wait a minute," Stan Grimm said. "Where are we going?"

Michael pointed again. "That-a-way."

"Why? What's your plan? Do you know what you're doing?" Grimm pointed up. "From this position we control an entrance. If they try to enter, we can shoot them."

Mac spoke up. "It's just one entrance, sir, and there are others. If you look around, you'll see that the tunnel behind us has largely caved in, making travel difficult. If they attack from below, we have nowhere to run." He paused as a piece of the ladder fell off. It landed with an almost musical ring, as if they were at a party.

Mac continued. "That shaky old ladder's dangerous. I'm not sure anyone's dumb enough to come down it anytime soon. Or try going up it for that matter."

Mac's voice and logic visibly stunned Stan Grimm. He looked at the ladder and wall, then at Mac, who was, after all, a machine.

"What are you?" Grimm asked. "A lot of people are after you. *Why?*"

Mac nudged Michael. "Lift me higher so I can see him better."

"Sure." Michael lifted Mac and moved closer to Grimm.

"To answer your first question *again*," Mac said, "I'm a manufacturing accident that happened in a nanosecond. As for the second, I have power they want."

"This is bullshit," Agent Maddox said. "This thing is some kind of trick."

"It is *not*," Laura said in outrage. She reached out and touched Mac. "Mac is real. I've seen him do amazing things."

"*Him?*" Grimm said. "Did you just give this machine a *gender*?"

"We don't have time for this," Mac said. "In a very short while, my enemy is going to come in here. And you don't want to be here when it does, because it's more terrible than anything you can imagine."

"How do you know this?" Michael had to ask. "Until today you thought you were the only machine that was different and had no idea why all this was happening to you."

Mac's screen displayed a rainbow of colors. "As I told you before, it's something I've begun to sense in the last few hours. My Dark Opposite is coming because he knows that together, our power will increase a thousandfold. Together, we can control the world, or try to."

"More rot!" Maddox said. "Did you hear what it said? 'Dark Opposite.'"

Maddox didn't say more because Laura slapped him. Hefty as he was, Maddox staggered back.

"Okay," Michael said, "I want to head down the tunnel. Mac, you agree?"

"Yeah. Sounds like a plan."

"Then let's go." Michael moved forward.

For a moment he felt like a little child again when he'd been terrified of the dark, especially at night when he'd been left alone in his room. This sewer was even worse, for the system was vast and unknown and he was trapped beneath the earth where the darkness would crawl down his throat and smother him.

Fortunately, Grimm and Maddox followed with their flashlights so he could both breathe and see. The tunnel wasn't very scenic, though. It arched above them, a round barrel with grimy white concrete walls. The air was dead and stale, hostile to life forms, yet Michael had taken only ten steps before he saw a pack of rats scurry away from them and encountered a small puddle. Where had it come from? A crack in the structure probably, or the water had oozed up through the ground.

The question was, where should they go, and where was the enemy? Back at the entrance, he had acted confident, but his certainty ebbed with each step. Glancing behind him, he saw Maddox and Laura following him. They depended on his judgment and he had no doubt they were now questioning it. What, after all, were they doing groping their way through a cold, subterranean sewer in the first place?

Would you like to see a schematic of this system? Mac whispered in his mind.

He had forgotten about their psychic communication. *Yes!* he answered, determined for the first time, to make it two-way. *Show me what you've got, bro.*

Okay, here it is. Prepare for a super visual.

Ah, it worked! "Stop," Michael ordered the others. "Mac is going to show us something."

They all obeyed him, including Stan, a man of authority who had probably experienced much nonsense in his career. Yet it was Maddox who snorted. "What crap is he pulling now? I—"

Maddox stopped when a large image appeared in the air before them. It looked like a blueprint of the sewer system through which they were traveling, only it was incomplete. Parts of it were missing, but Michael could guess at the sizable extent of this long-abandoned network. In a way, it reminded him of the confusing hallway arrangement at Dr. Turner's office where he had gotten lost. The main difference was that he could actually *die* down here.

Mac spoke so they all could hear. "I sorted through the files in over nineteen thousand databases and combined the clearest and most accurate parts I could find. This is my best synthesis of what this system looked like forty-two years ago when it was abandoned. As you can see, it is most incomplete to the north where the river is."

"Jesus," Maddox said. "You can do this? Just pluck this stuff from the air?"

"Of course he can," Laura said. "I told you Mac was special." She stroked Mac's sides, and Michael heard Mac sigh with pleasure.

"Let's head to the right," Michael said, indicating a side tunnel in the blueprint they were approaching. He nudged Stan Grimm. "You agree, Agent?"

"It's your call," Grimm said. He gripped his phone, desperately trying to get through. "Where the hell are you? We haven't even reached the first turn. It can't be that hard to find us."

Mac snorted. "Your phone won't work underground, Agent Grimm. You'll have more success sucking frozen molasses through a straw than receiving a message from your men. In addition, my dark twin has disrupted your radar. That's why they haven't located you yet."

"It's all right," Stan said. "They should be here soon."

God, I hope so. The blueprint now reminded Michael of a maze. Perhaps they'd meet the Minotaur soon, and it would devour them all. Even if no monster awaited them, he was beginning to doubt there was an exit.

They entered the side tunnel and after a few steps, Grimm motioned for them to stop. He took Laura's hand and drew her aside.

"Listen," he said in a low voice, "we may not get out of this and I have to say something to you."

Grimm was obviously trying not to be heard. Whatever deficiencies this sewer had, though, its acoustics were excellent.

"Okay," Laura answered. She shot a tense glance at Michael.

Grimm hesitated. "I want to apologize to you. I was wrong." He reached out and touched Laura's cheek. "I realize now you had the right to have a lot of interests, and I was fortunate enough to be one of them. It was your nature to be so complex."

Laura touched his hand and squeezed it. "You were the only man."

He nodded, sealing their mutual understanding. Michael waited a moment then slipped back to the corner and peered around it, back in the direction they had come from. He saw nothing, no invaders. Had they miraculously escaped detection and gotten away? If so, it made sense to stay here for a while rather than be caught elsewhere.

Michael noticed something on the wall near his elbow and squinted to read it. It was a fading red heart with an arrow through it. *Willy loves Lucy*, it said, and it reminded him of the pledge of love he and Muriel had etched on the white rock and revisited for years as a sacred ritual. But who had drawn this? Ah, a kid probably. Though faded, it had a childish feel.

For some reason, the heart reminded him of Andy. Would he ever see his brilliant son again? God, how he missed him. He remembered seeing Andy at the school, where he had said something "weird" had happened to him after he picked up Michael's machine. For a moment, Andy had looked haunted and fearful, unlike his son at all. What had the machine—what had *Mac*—done to him?

A faint scent of perfume. Michael turned to see Laura standing beside him, her face half-lit by the men's flashlights. "Are you going to put *this* adventure in our romantic novel?" she asked. Her voice cracked with tension.

He swallowed. "Funny how the plot changed. The lovers seem to have gotten themselves in one hell of a fix." Michael started to say more but felt an icy premonition. He slipped to the corner with Mac and peered around it again—just in time to see several men climb down the ladder at the far end. They had powerful flashlights.

He turned to the others. "They're coming," he whispered. "Let's get out of here."

"My men should be here soon," Stan said. He swung his flashlight as if looking for them.

"We don't have time to wait," Michael said. "Let's go!"

He took Laura's hand and ran, pulling her with him down the sewer they had just entered, leaving the others behind. But not for long. Maddox quickly caught up and passed them. Other footsteps followed in hot pursuit. Soon Michael felt a tug and saw Stan grab Laura's other arm. Michael glanced at Laura in the dim light and then across her at Stan. For a moment, the agent met his eyes and Michael thought he caught a message. Perhaps it was *She's mine!* or *Let her go!* Either way, Agent Stanley Grimm immediately dropped her arm and turned his head to the front.

Shouts and jeers suddenly rang behind them, echoing off the walls. "Why are you running?" a man taunted. "We want you to stop. If you don't, we'll kill you." At that moment the glare of their pursuers' flashlights struck them from behind. Michael gasped, able to see better but terrified by the implications. The enemy had turned the corner and was snapping at their heels!

Surprisingly, Agent Maddox led their pack. He was already ten yards ahead, his massive, muscular buttocks bunching with effort. Glancing over his shoulder, Michael saw the enemy coming after them with their flashlights and yelling at them to stop. Despite their anger, they seemed to be in no hurry, and that deeply bothered him. As they neared the end of the tunnel, he saw another one leading off to the left. But Maddox surprised him again by scuttling up a ladder like a nimble ogre. Please, let him find a manhole at the top and be able to open it easily! After a few bangs, though, Maddox scuttled down the ladder again.

"Can't get out," Maddox barked. "It's stuck!"

And we're locked in, Michael thought. Though the walls of the sewer remained about eight feet apart, they seemed to draw closer and closer in a tight, suffocating embrace. He doubted he'd ever see the sun again or draw a breath of fresh air.

Michael, Laura, and Stan passed Maddox and headed down the next tunnel. Maddox soon passed them again, his massive hindquarters chewing up the terrain. Musclebound or not, the guy seemed to have been born to run.

When Michael glanced behind him again, their pursuers had edged only slightly closer. They were toying with them, savoring the taste of their blood in advance! As if that weren't bad enough, Laura staggered and fell to the ground. "I...twisted my leg," she gasped.

He and Stan exchanged glances. What should they do? Who was the hero? Since Michael was carrying Mac, Stan bent down and lifted Laura in his arms. They continued on through air that grew ever colder, gasping puffs of steam as they went. Finally, they reached a point where the tunnel had partially caved in. It was blocked like the one where they'd started, and it was almost impossible to go any farther. Stan set Laura down and they all turned, facing their pursuers.

The enemy was now only twenty-five feet away, and they seemed to fill the tunnel. Michael scanned their ranks and heard a shrill burst of fear from Mac as they both found his Dark Opposite at the same time. An odious toad of a man in the middle carried a machine that looked much like Mac, but there was something different about it too. Eerie light moved across the screen, colors Michael had never seen before.

Soft fingers squeezed his. He looked down to see Laura's hand holding his own.

"What's going to happen?" she asked.

"Nothing good, I'm afraid," he answered. Looking sideways, he saw that Stan Grimm and Maddox held their weapons ready, just like good G-men should.

All at once, he realized something. "They aren't likely to take chances with Mac around," he said. "No gunplay. Mac's the one they want, and they don't want to risk damaging or destroying him with a stray bullet." He remembered something Mac had told him. "For all they know, Mac could self-destruct, turn himself off for good if they pressed him too close."

"Are you sure they wouldn't take the risk anyway?" Maddox said.

No, he wasn't, not completely. It made sense, though, that you didn't kill the Golden Goose. "Hold those peashooters ready," he told Stan and Maddox, "but don't provoke them. We don't want ricochets."

As battle strategy, it wasn't great, but Stan Grimm nodded. Maddox simply ignored him. *I'll shoot if I want to,* he seemed to say. *You're just a civilian.*

Laura squeezed his hand more urgently and he turned to her.

She nodded toward their attackers, who pressed closer in the narrow sewer. "Look at the person in the middle," she said.

"The one with the machine?" he asked.

"No, I mean the boy standing beside him." Her voice went airy with panic. "Oh, Jesus, Michael, please tell me I'm wrong. Tell me it's not who I think it is."

Michael looked and saw what she meant. He looked for a long time.

His son's hair was as disheveled as ever. He stood next to the man with the sleep apnea machine and kept one hand on top of it as if it belonged there.

Andy.

A chill tore through Michael. How had he missed him and what in hell was his son doing here? Despite his shock, the answer seemed obvious. The twisted little man who carried Mac's Dark Opposite had deliberately brought Andy here to drive the knife in deeper and make it plain who was in control. *If you want to save your boy,* he might have said, *give up the device you call Mac.*

Directly across from Michael and his companions, part of the wall had collapsed, leaving an alcove or recess. Roughly five feet wide and deep, it was only ten feet away and caught the eye of the little man. He laughed and walked away from their pursuers, steering Andy toward the recess. As they went, Michael's son gave him no sign of recognition. Was Andy hypnotized, drugged, or something else? Had Andy's vile captor stolen his soul?

He cleared his throat. "Hello, Andy," Michael called.

Michael waited but there was no response. Perhaps Andy hadn't heard?

He tried again, raising his voice. "Hello, Andy!"

Still nothing in return. Andy didn't even blink. Michael felt a terrible weight descend upon his heart.

The little man positioned himself and Andy in the alcove as if it were a stage. He grinned at Michael. "I'm Edgar P. Delgata," he said. When Michael didn't respond, he cackled. "Wouldn't you like to know why your son is with me?"

Michael clutched Mac, feeling he was going mad. Where was the goddamn FBI when you needed it? He looked at his son and wondered how he could save him from this monster, assuming there was anything left to be saved and any way to put some life back into those flat, dead eyes.

Michael stepped toward them, carrying Mac. "Yes," he said, after a moment. "Tell me."

CHAPTER SEVENTEEN
A FAIR TRADE

"I'll keep it simple," the little man said. "You give me your CABS machine for your son. Is that a fair enough trade for you?"

Michael ducked his head to enter the alcove, kicking aside a few rocks. He looked at Andy. "What have you done to him? Why didn't he answer when I spoke to him? Why doesn't he even recognize me now?"

The man waved a claw-like hand. "Just a mild sedative to keep Andy dandy," he replied. "In an hour or two, it will wear right off." He nodded at Mac and placed his bony hand on Andy's tousled hair, petting him like he would a dog. "Is it a deal?" he asked. "Your machine in exchange for your son?"

Could he trust this bastard? What if he'd given Andy a lethal dose and his son never came out of his coma, or whatever it was? How could he believe anything this foul creature said?

The man removed his hand from Andy's head and reached out, stabbing the air inches from Michael's face. *"Is it a deal?"* he said.

Michael sucked in his breath. If this bony bastard touched Andy again, he'd reach right down his throat and tear out his heart, then throw it in his fanatical supporters' faces.

"*Is it a deal?*" Delgata repeated.

Michael shuddered. Striving for control, he gazed down at the machine he was holding. "Mac, what do you think of this proposed swap?"

"Don't ask the friggin' air blower!" the man almost screamed. "What you're holding is not a person. It's only something I created."

"Something you created?"

A pleased smirk. To Michael, this man resembled a slimy little weasel, smug and sure of himself. He wore a poor hairpiece and had rotten teeth. "You don't think it made itself, do you?" Delgata said. "Or that it's an accidental anomaly? The only thing that's accidental is that some fool at the company shipped it without my knowledge and I had to hunt for it long and hard. And now I've finally found it." He slapped his chest with pride. "Let me be clear. *I, Edgar P. Delgata* designed and programmed the prototype. I and I alone brought it all the way through production and enabled it to achieve independent thought."

Michael felt a wave of surprise come from Mac and shared his friend's astonishment. Ah, this crazy narcissist hadn't lied or bragged without justification. Though he seemed pathetic, he had actually designed and programmed Mac, so Mac's intelligence was not accidental as the two of them had thought. What had Mac said before? *Evidence points to a non-standard configuration of three sub-circuits due to a freakish burst of electricity.* Nonsense! He and Mac had missed a crucial fact. Mac's intelligence was planned and deliberate!

Still, did even Mac's mad creator know how amazing his creation was? Did he know the powers Mac not only possessed but had electronically transmitted to Michael such as his growing physical strength and skills? Even more, did he suspect that Mac had also transmitted other abilities which could be used either for good or for bad? Good when Michael had subconsciously renovated his car, but bad when he had just as subconsciously caused Mr. Starret's death?

Most of all, did Edgar P. Delgata suspect Mac's ability to love and inspire love in others, as he'd done with Laura and himself? No, of course he didn't. Nor would the man care.

Michael smiled, wanting to slip the needle into this smug, arrogant bastard. "But despite all your brilliance, Mr. Delgata, you could only create two breakthroughs, isn't that right? And you need *both* of them to achieve your goal. That explains why you followed us down here."

Delgata hissed in anger. "And now I've caught you."

If you're so sure you've caught us, why are you talking so much? Michael wondered. He tapped Mac's screen. "Mac, I asked you a question. What do you think of me swapping you for my son?"

"I'm a CABS machine with profoundly destructive potential," Mac responded promptly. "I realize that you love and miss your son, but it is terribly wrong to engage in such a transaction."

Edgar P. Delgata stiffened in disgust, but before he could respond, another voice grated like steel, filling the tunnel. "*I* will answer the question."

Before Michael, the machine in Delgata's arms came alive. Black depths swirled on its screen, along with jagged red lightning bolts. "As a machine, I am so much worthier and more capable than a human child could ever be. And if I'm paired with my reluctant twin before me, our powers will exponentially increase. If he will only listen to reason and cooperate, we can rule the world together."

Not bloody likely, Mac said in Michael's mind. *The last thing I want is to be a tyrant.*

Delgata's supporters, however, felt differently. They shouted in agreement with Delgata's machine and waved their guns. "Hell, yeah," one man said. "That's why we're here. To rule!" Another cried, "The Age of the Machine has come, and Edgar P. Delgata is its prophet!"

The Age of the Machine. Michael gazed at Andy, silently imploring him to resist Delgata's control and come alive, even take part in the discussion. But Andy continued to show no awareness of what was happening. Michael felt sure his son didn't even know he was here.

"Do you agree to the exchange?" Edgar P. Delgata asked. "Your machine for your son?"

The atmosphere in the tunnel grew even more tense. Michael knew that the slightest mishap or misstep could trigger mutual destruction on both sides. Mac could die and so could Andy, not to mention Delgata, Mac's Dark Opposite, and most of the others. Yes, they were outnumbered by Delgata's men, but Grimm and Maddox were trained professionals who would make every bullet count, especially since Delgata's men were lined up in the tunnel like ducks in a row.

Michael heard Grimm speak behind him, emphasizing this very point. "Mr. Delgata, I urge you to exercise caution. If even one of us fires a shot, there will be a bloodbath. And if that happens, the machine you seek will perish too. Is that what you want?"

Michael risked a glance at Grimm. The tall, impeccably dressed special agent stared down at Delgata, his weapon held at his side.

Delgata fell silent. For once, it seemed, he had nothing to say. After a moment, it was his machine that responded. "What do you propose?" Mac's Dark Opposite asked.

A damn good question! Michael could almost hear Grimm's mental wheels turning. Everything hung suspended as they did. He wanted to turn around and give Laura one last look in case it was all he would ever have. How was she bearing up under all this, and was she sorry she had ever met him? He also wondered how the two machines felt about each other. They were only a few feet apart and practically bathed in each other's essence. Though they both possessed an amazing potential synergy and might be able to conquer the world together, Michael wondered how they would get along.

We wouldn't, Mac told him. *Why do you think I call him my Dark Opposite? It's because he hates life and wants only to conquer and destroy. If we came together, there would be war, and he would probably win. He would seize all my energy and I would be lost forever. Perhaps it would be better if...*

If what? Michael asked mentally, determined to keep their communication a secret.

If I turned myself off, Mac replied. *You remember I said I could do it if we got in another "precarious situation." Well, this certainly qualifies.*

Michael remembered how stunned he'd been when Mac had told him he could commit suicide. *But what would that accomplish?* he said to

139

Mac. *You'd be gone and Delgata would feel cheated of his sick dream. There's no telling what violence he would cause.*

Maybe not, Mac replied. *Maybe he'd just give up.*

Michael considered the possibility. *No. He'd want revenge.* He deliberately changed the subject. *Tell me, Mac. Why is Delgata's machine so mean anyway?*

Look at his handler, Mac answered. *Delgata created my Opposite in his psychic image. Both of them hate life and want to destroy, and both need the other to achieve their goal.*

So Delgata had devised a machine that embodied his worst traits. But what had caused Mac's good traits, such as his loyalty and ability to love? There was much to consider here, but Michael's son came first. Could Andy be saved, or was he doomed with the rest of them?

Finally, Grimm broke the silence. "Mr. Delgata, you were impatient and made a stupid mistake in following us down here. You should have waited and caught us in the open when we least expected. As it is, we are at an impasse, a stalemate. I suggest that both sides quietly withdraw and go their separate ways."

It made sense, but Michael realized it was a nonstarter. Even if everyone could get out of here safely, a draw was not what Delgata or his obsessed men wanted. They wouldn't settle for a retreat under any circumstances but would try to take Mac with them by force.

One of the men in the crowd sneezed. It was a funny sounding sneeze, and it ignited a series of piping squeaks. Michael knew that in other circumstances, most if not all in the tunnel would have laughed or smiled. But the man's sneezes continued without mirth or commentary, adding to the tension instead of alleviating it. When the sneezes finally stopped, the sewer was silent again. Would the sounds of bullets and screams soon follow?

Michael's fingers tingled, a strange sensation. He remembered how they had tingled this way the very first time he had held Mac, even when he had felt him through the nylon of the carrying bag. And ever since acquiring Mac, he had developed enhanced abilities. Just a few minutes ago, he had managed to carry him down a tall, shaky ladder into this dark place, sometimes using just one hand.

Yes, but how could his new abilities help him now? He looked at Andy's vacant face and at Edgar P. Delgata's sinister smile. The man was in charge, but didn't he realize how delicate the balance was here and that if any of their prisoners resorted to violence, he too would likely perish? Hell, just one more sneeze could set things off. Stan Grimm was right. The man had made a "stupid mistake" in following them down here.

Or had he? Perhaps Delgata had calculated his attack as carefully as he had planned his two deviant machines. These narrow underground tunnels might seem a foolish gamble, but he wasn't in this man's twisted but brilliant mind. He studied Delgata's cruel expression and the whirling, slashing, red and black patterns on the machine he held, which were aimed directly at Mac. Michael had no difficulty interpreting what they meant. They screamed *Hate, Hate, Hate* at Mac, its virtuous opposite, and Michael saw the patterns on the screen change into a hideous monster with gaping jaws, hungry to swallow Mac whole and devour his essence.

The beast roared and charged toward Mac!

Mac screamed and lashed out, delivering a psychic punch that threw the other back, head over lethal claws until it crashed against an inner wall. Mac's Dark Opposite recovered, though, and counter-attacked, smashing Mac's screen right down the middle. The blow staggered Michael and made him almost drop the machine. He knew neither of them could take another attack. Unless he found a weakness, he would have to accept Delgata's terms and surrender Mac. If he didn't, they would all die anyway, including Andy and Laura.

Delgata's grin widened as he read Michael's expression. What the hell could he do? There was no way out.

His fingers tingled again.

Michael gestured at Andy, feeling an odd impulse. "Do you mind if I touch him first?"

"Touch him?"

"Yes, just once to make sure he's all right." He felt the tingling increase, cover his entire hand.

Delgata considered, then nodded. "Be my guest," he said.

"Thank you." Michael reached out and touched Andy's arm.

Andy didn't react, but Michael was not surprised. After all, his boy must be heavily sedated. He increased the pressure then reached up and stroked Andy's shoulder, hoping to see some glimmer of a response. But there was nothing.

"I'm waiting," Delgata said.

Michael sighed in despair and started to remove his hand. At that moment, his son opened his eyes and smiled.

"Hello, Daddy. I knew you would come."

His son was awake and recognized him! He felt a burst of joy even greater than he'd had when he'd scaled the fence at Andy's school and given him a hug. Shortly after, though, he felt confusion. How could Andy have known he'd come here? It didn't make sense.

Delgata's eyes widened in disbelief as Andy's hand slowly rose. Up it went, and then it descended until it rested again on top of Delgata's machine.

"H-how the h-hell are you awake?" Delgata sputtered. "I gave you enough juice to keep you comatose for a week!"

Andy ignored him. Instead, he stared directly at Michael and began to tap Delgata's machine as if he were entering code. "Daddy, after I touched your sleeping machine that day," he said, "I changed. I felt different in here." He touched his head.

"I remember," Michael said. "And you soon knew some fancy words."

"Yeah, I've forgotten most of them, but I've learned something else, something Mr. Smarty Pants here didn't consider." Andy's face filled with the awe and fear Michael had seen on it before, at the school. His son started tapping Delgata's CABS machine again. "Somehow, Daddy, your sleeping machine changed me even more. It taught me how to be brave and how to do...*this.*"

A sound rose from inside Mac's Dark Opposite. At first it was slight, but soon it became a vicious grinding as if the machine's guts were being torn apart. Glancing away, Michael saw that the eyes of Delgata's followers were riveted on the machine and their leader, who stared at the device he held in horrified disbelief.

Get ready, Mac said in his head. *You must prepare to act.*

Prepare—how? Michael asked.

Prepare to kill.

At that moment the machine began to crack and come apart. *It's dying*, Michael thought as a panel came off. *Andy is killing it.* Behind him, he heard men gasp in amazement, their commitment to violence derailed by this stunning and inexplicable development. But how long would it be before someone recovered his senses and opened fire?

The front of Delgata's machine now resembled a savage face screaming in torment. It shook and trembled, and a part from inside shot upward. Michael didn't know what it was, only that it was long and sharp and somehow part of Andy's plan. As the part rose, he and Delgata watched, and when it came down, they leaped for it together. To Michael's surprise, Delgata not only caught it first but struck him with savage strength. Delgata might be little more than a skeleton, but a preternatural force animated his body.

He must not let this monster win! Seizing the metal part, Michael wrenched it from the man's hands and drove it as hard as he could into his stomach. Blood spurted over Michael's hands, and he carved upward, seeking to rip his adversary's entrails apart. Pulling him close in a tight embrace, Michael glared into Delgata's eyes as the men's first shots rang out in the tunnel.

"You took my son!" Michael snarled, and saw the light fade and then go out in Delgata's eyes.

Michael dropped the corpse and pushed Andy to the ground. "Stay down!" he shouted. He glanced around for Mac but couldn't find him. Where was he? He called Mac's name in his mind but there was no reply. Their psychic connection was gone. God help him, was Mac still alive? Perhaps he'd been shot to pieces and blown away.

No time to search. Michael pushed Delgata's corpse aside and moved toward the back of the alcove with Andy. The strategy provided only scant protection. Bullets whizzed above them, ricocheting off the walls of the recess. Turning, Michael saw Grimm move to shield Laura with his body and return fire along with Maddox. Their shots were effective and Michael saw several men scream and fall. Still, the contest was not as close as Michael had hoped, for Grimm and Maddox were not only outnumbered but had no cover. Bullets struck their bodies and they jerked and twisted like dolls before falling, leaving half a dozen of Delgata's supporters still standing.

Where was Laura? Was she still alive?

He leaned forward for a better view but almost got his head shot off. Even worse, the remainder of Delgata's little army was heading their way, hell-bent on revenge for what he'd done to their leader. Since he and his son Andy had nothing to defend themselves with, they would soon be dead.

Hoarse shouts and angry faces. One woman with blue-dyed hair even waved two pistols as if to celebrate the fact that she could kill them with either hand. Michael glanced at Andy, who looked terrified.

"What are we gonna do, Daddy?"

"I don't know." He glanced behind him, but there was nowhere to go. His enhanced abilities did not include burrowing through concrete walls like they were butter.

A crash somewhere, then another. The men coming toward them stopped and turned. What were they staring at?

Another crash. It seemed to come from the section of the tunnel that had partly collapsed. Earlier, he and the others had stopped fleeing because the cave-in would slow them down and make them targets. What could be causing the crashes?

Wait, he remembered Mac saying the enemy's radar had interfered with FBI agents locating their underground position. It sounded crazy, but could they have finally found another way to reach them?

Michael turned to get a better look.

There was another crash, and several armed men and women emerged from the direction of the caved-in tunnel. It looked like a SWAT unit, complete with helmets, bulletproof vests, and submachine guns. When the agents spotted the occupants of the new tunnel, they did not hesitate or say hello. They opened fire at once in a deadly stream of bullets. Michael saw some of Delgata's followers scream and fall. Several others, including the woman who had waved two guns, turned tail and scampered back down the tunnel, but FBI agents quickly pursued and captured them.

Within ten seconds, over a dozen agents packed the tunnel, efficiently taking charge of the situation. Michael weighed his chances and rose, lifting his hands as he stepped out of the alcove. "Please don't shoot!" he said.

For a moment Michael feared both he and Andy would be shot, but after a quick search, he was handcuffed instead. They were taken to where Stan Grimm's and Maddox's riddled bodies lay sprawled. Grimm's eyes were closed, his mission honorably completed, though he had paid a heavy price. In contrast, Maddox's eyes were wide open, as if looking for a place to run or another ladder to climb. Perhaps this time, Michael thought, he'll find a friendly manhole cover, one he can easily open so he can escape this hellhole.

Hearing a moan, Michael looked down and saw Laura lying on the ground.

Ignoring a barked order, he knelt beside his son's favorite teacher. An agent grabbed him from behind to pull him up, but Andy cried out, "Don't, she's my teacher!"

The agent hesitated, then released him. Michael knelt again beside Laura, who had several bullet wounds and was covered with blood. Andy knelt too and took Laura's hand in his. The agents spoke softly to each other then withdrew a few feet.

Laura's eyes fluttered open. She saw them both and smiled. "My two favorite guys."

"Oh, Miss Kurick," Andy sobbed. "I'm so sorry!"

"Me too," Michael said. "You would have been much better off if you'd never met me."

"I know," Laura said. She blinked, and even in the dim light, Michael could see she was going fast. "Where's M-Mac? Isn't he with you?"

He started to say no then heard an agent stumble over something to his left. He turned to see Mac bounce over the floor. Reaching out, Michael caught Mac before he passed him and pulled him in. To his surprise, Mac was intact, having succeeded in healing his slashed screen.

What's more, for the first time, his friend actually showed a face on it, one that looked anxious and full of concern as he noticed Laura.

"Mac's right by your side," he told Laura. "We're all here for you."

She coughed, her eyes wet with tears. When she spoke again, he had to lean down to hear her. "A shootout in an old sewer, with the feds arriving just a l-little too late. One thing's for sure, Michael. You've g-given our romance one hell of a final chapter."

She was trying to be brave, and he loved her for it. Her voice sank into him, and he felt his fingers begin to tingle, even stronger than before. It reminded him of a feeling he'd had in his apartment, when he'd stood before a mirror admiring his growing muscles. At the time he'd felt his body was building toward something, *becoming* something that had been trapped within his DNA. He had not known what it was, only that it was something greater, a power even larger than the ones he'd already demonstrated.

Now, for the first time, he felt he knew what that power was.

Slowly, Michael bent down and kissed her cheek. "Laura," he said. "What makes you think our story's over?"

She gasped for breath, her face twisting in pain. "Well, look at me. I-I've run out of adventures."

Michael deftly removed his handcuffs so the agents wouldn't see and set them aside. Then he began stroking her face with his fingers, feeding her his strength. "You might be wrong," he said. "In fact, I think we're due for a sequel."

CHAPTER EIGHTEEN
FOR THE FIRST TIME

Five minutes later, Michael could actually see Laura's wounds start to heal. Thank God, it looked like she was getting better and might even be all right! For the first time, he wondered how such a change was possible. Somehow, Mac must have transferred his amazing healing power to him, perhaps by activating some dormant potential in his own body.

Michael reached out and touched an agent. "Hey," he said, "I think she's still alive." He nodded down at Laura.

The man knelt in the tunnel and examined Laura, then grunted in surprise. He called to someone and a few moments later, two more agents bent over her, administering aid.

Another agent put Michael in handcuffs again, then gripped his arm so he wouldn't move. Mac himself received special treatment. A man slipped a nylon case over him and gently picked him up. Together, Michael and the two agents marched off, their footsteps echoing off the surrounding walls.

Michael soon lost track of Mac and Laura. He tried to turn and search for them, but his escort had an iron grip and pushed him onward. Divide

147

and conquer, he thought. They want to get us in different rooms and interrogate us separately so they can compare our stories.

First, though, they had to get out of this damned sewer. The easiest way would probably be to retrace the steps Michael had taken to get here, but the FBI seemed impatient. Their leader barked an order and an agent climbed a ladder to open the manhole cover at the top. Michael recognized the place and the ladder, which Maddox had climbed with much greater efficiency. As it turned out, the manhole cover showed the agent the same disdain it had shown Maddox, and the agent in charge barked another order. The man scuttled down the ladder and another agent—a specialist, judging from the odd instrument he carried—climbed up.

Michael waited, fretting about Mac and Laura. Mac had been all right, his smashed screen healed, and Laura's wounds were on the mend. He knew it had been a near thing with her and was deeply grateful for his ability to heal.

A blast came from the top of the ladder as the cover was blown off. The sound made Michael's ears ring, and dust and bits of concrete rained down. Michael saw several agents climb up and after a few seconds, the agent holding him gave him a nudge. Michael headed for the ladder and two agents assisted him up it until he stepped out onto the grass.

The first thing he saw was a gray helicopter standing nearby. The Night Hawk was about forty feet long and its four rotor blades were turning slightly in the breeze. Two men sat in the cockpit and another man sat behind the pilot. All were staring directly at him.

No thank you, I don't need a ride.

A shove from behind reminded him that he had no choice. He took a few steps forward then turned. To his surprise, the townhouse complex looked far away. How surreal! He felt like he had entered a different dimension. Had they really come so far in the tunnel? The agent who'd pushed him seemed uninterested in his sense of dislocation and spoke a single word.

"Walk."

Michael turned back and obeyed. When he reached the helicopter, the agent started to assist him into the vacant seat behind the co-pilot's, but the pilot stopped him.

"Wait. We heard he removed those cuffs earlier without any trouble. We've got something a little more difficult for him to slip out of." He nodded at the other two men. "Bring it out."

Michael watched the agents get out of the helicopter. The man who sat behind the pilot held a bright-red straitjacket in his hands, and the co-pilot slipped behind Michael and removed his handcuffs. They then commenced to put the damned thing on him. The device had more straps and buckles than he could count, and they trussed him up as tight as a turkey on a table. Houdini in his prime wouldn't have been able to escape. When they finished the procedure, he could barely breathe, let alone move.

The co-pilot smiled at him. "We hope you aren't too uncomfortable."

Michael looked down at himself. "Not at all, but did you have to make this thing so red?"

The co-pilot stopped smiling. "This way it will be difficult to lose you in a snowstorm," he said. "We have some questions to ask you, and we wouldn't want that to happen."

Difficult to lose you in a snowstorm. The bastard at least had a sense of humor, though it wasn't the kind that made you laugh.

The men assisted him up into the seat behind the co-pilot and buckled him up, connecting the lap and shoulder seat belts so he was trussed up even tighter than before. It was a difficult operation, and the straitjacket forced them to fold the chair back and seat him at a slant. Then they themselves sat down so that there was a pilot and co-pilot in front, and an agent and himself a couple of feet behind them.

"You guys don't trust me very much, do you?" Michael asked.

The pilot said, "Mr. Windsor, you're a valuable man and we have a lot of questions to ask you. We just want to make sure you don't get away."

A lot of questions. Well, hell, he had some of his own. *Where's Mac? And how's Laura?* But he didn't ask them.

Michael had never been in a helicopter before but from where he sat, preparing to fly was a complicated procedure. The pilot pulled this, coaxed that, fiddled with something else. What wasn't complicated was the shrill, rising whine of the twin engines behind Michael's back, toward the rear of the copter just before the tail. It soon became all he could hear except for the occasional *whop whop whop* of the rotor blades as they spun and picked up speed.

Michael stared at the colorful displays on the instrument panel and out through the windscreen, wondering where they would be taking him. Probably to some isolated, top-secret facility that specialized in interrogating and breaking war criminals, enemy scientists, and assorted enemies of the state. And with Mac in tow somewhere, an ordinary sleep apnea machine mysteriously upgraded to AI status, their leaders must feel all their efforts to track them down were worth it. Surely, by now, he and his machine buddy had sprinkled enough tantalizing clues along the way to make it a good investment.

What methods would they use to extract his and Mac's secrets? Would they inject him with truth serum or pull off his fingernails, subject him to excruciating physical and psychic pain? If so, how long would he be able to hold them off and keep what he knew? Ah, but what he knew paled before Mac himself, for he was the real prize. He was, after all, what Edgar P. Delgata had been after. Of course, Mac could always turn himself off like a light switch and commit suicide. But would he do it and leave Michael behind and all alone? Or would he cooperate and give them what they wanted? Yes, this time he might, since he'd reason that as questionable as the FBI's actions were, the organization and the government it served were not as bad as an insane maniac bent upon worldwide domination.

Or were they? In the final analysis, perhaps there was little difference between the two, especially if you were on the receiving end.

The pilot completed a lengthy checklist and then lifted a lever, causing the helicopter to rise. In just seconds, everything became smaller and Michael found himself staring down at a stretch of uncut grass. Amazing! He watched the progression and soon realized they were heading toward the townhouses. From way up here, they looked like tiny blocks and the people like proverbial ants. It was hard to believe they mattered.

His nose itched and he needed to scratch it. But he couldn't because they'd put him in a fucking straitjacket and he couldn't even move his hand. The itch intensified and became maddening. To distract himself, he shifted his weight and asked a question.

"Where are you taking me?"

No one answered. To make it worse, Michael could barely see the pilot and co-pilot. Glancing to his left, he saw that the agent who sat behind the pilot was black and wore sunglasses. Other than that, his abductors seemed faceless and without identity.

He tried again. "What crime have I committed?" he asked. "What are you going to do to me?"

Silence. Then the co-pilot spoke. "Please be patient, Mr. Windsor."

That was it. Just five words. If they weren't going to talk to him, why didn't they put him back in storage where no one had to look at him, perhaps stick him in a locked box with tiny airholes? Wouldn't that be safer and better for security? Ah, he had it. The order had come down: Use the silent treatment. It would piss him off and make him drop his guard, reveal something important. *Loose lips sink ships,* and he had no doubt that everything in this cabin was being carefully recorded. Michael strained against the straitjacket, thinking of how he'd run for his life from Delgata's bloodthirsty army and how Laura had almost gotten killed. "Goddamn it, let me out of this thing," he snarled. "Take it off me!"

For a long moment, he received no reply. Then the agent to his left leaned toward him.

"It won't be long," the man said in a deep voice. "Sit still or we'll have to sedate you."

He wanted to scream but closed his eyes instead, thinking of the men who had died to protect him and Mac. He saw Special Agent Grimm again, shielding Laura with his body as he died on his feet. And even Maddox, mean-tempered and initially skeptical, had climbed up ladders to find a way out of the tunnel and ultimately died right beside Grimm, like him filled with bullets. And for what? What good had all Michael's clever running and hiding accomplished? In the end he had gotten captured anyway and would be forced to cooperate.

The helicopter tilted slightly in the wind and Michael got a clearer view of the earth below. It looked like they were leaving the last buildings of the city behind. Where to now? The Pentagon? Guantanamo Bay? Damn it, he'd appreciate a little information.

A little flash of light to his right made him blink. He started to raise his hand to block it out, but of course his hand was buried deep beneath the folds of the straitjacket. Even if he'd wanted, he couldn't scratch his balls. He shifted his weight and it seemed to work. But no, there it was again, far off to the side of the helicopter, about as high in the air as they were. It was shaped like a tiny bug and something spinning at the top reminded him of...rotor blades.

He blinked again, telling himself he was imagining things. The object was an atmospheric fluke and must be miles away, too far to see clearly. It could be anything. But just think now. Having captured Mac, the FBI would probably take him in a helicopter to the same place they took him, right? He felt a tingling run throughout his body. And as an electrical device, Mac had powers, an amazing ability to communicate and affect things at a distance. What had Michael called it before? *A kind of psychic Wi-Fi.* Mac was the transmitter and would use radio waves or frequencies to carry data or instructions through the air to another device. And what would be that device?

Ah! *He* would be the device that received Mac's signals. After all, weren't he and Mac already one in so many ways? He had felt Mac's tube coil about him at night and breathed his air. And he had probably inhaled microscopic particles from Mac that were embedded deep inside him, particles that would function as receivers.

The thought filled him with a warm thrill of kinship. Yes, he could *feel* Mac now. He knew Mac was in the other helicopter. Listening, he heard his friend whisper ever so softly to him. By some strange wizardry, Mac must be in charge of the other copter by now, but what was his plan? As hard as Michael listened, he couldn't quite make out Mac's words.

"That's funny," the agent in back said. "My watch has stopped working." Michael saw him tap it. "Carl, what time do you have?"

"Let me see," the co-pilot said. "Hmm, mine's gone south too."

Both men then checked their cell phones, which weren't working either. Michael felt a rush of joy because he knew the source of the disruptions. While he couldn't anticipate Mac's next moves, he felt certain that Mac was working through him to shut off these men's devices. And like a good electrical relay, he would continue to carry out his friend's orders.

Michael felt the two men's growing concern as they examined other devices. It was the same deal. Dead as a doornail.

The co-pilot turned toward the pilot. "Sir, we have a problem."

"I've heard." The pilot looked at his watch. "Well, mine seems all right. It works fine." He paused. "What the hell. It just stopped." Michael heard him tap his watch a few times.

"It won't start again," Michael said.

"Why not?" the pilot asked.

"For the same reason the other devices won't start," Michael said. "My friend and I have taken them over. We've commandeered them."

"Command-what?" the co-pilot asked.

The pilot waved him off. "Who is your friend?"

Michael hesitated, wishing he had Mac's guidance. "He's my partner," he finally said. "And he controls the copter over there just as I do this one."

Such bluster and bragging! Had he gone too far? For the first time, Michael felt doubt. How could he be sure Mac was in charge of the other copter, let alone interfering in this one? For all he knew, Mac wasn't in the other copter at all, and it was just his imagination. Still, he'd made his play and had to act confident.

The agent beside him drew his pistol and cocked it. "I don't know what you're up to," he said. "But a bullet will settle you down."

"Put your gun away!" the pilot snapped. "Do you know what could happen if you discharge a weapon inside a copter ten thousand feet up?"

Michael felt something new—a surge of power from Mac. It rippled through his body and stunned him, then made him laugh in relief. Mac *was* present. He wasn't imagining it! "This trigger-happy cowboy won't have a chance to shoot," Michael said. He felt Mac direct his focus at the man and gave him an electric jolt, making him drop his weapon on the floor.

The pilot spoke into his radio. "Control, we have a situation up here—"

Michael cut his communication with a slight surge, courtesy of Mac. "Mister, you don't have anything up here. Everything's completely copacetic and peaceful. We're all taking the air, you might say. But unless you follow my orders, the 'situation' is going to deteriorate pretty fucking quickly."

The pilot turned toward him. For the first time, through the space between the front seats, Michael saw his face and managed to read his nametag. *Thomas T. Toosha.* Jesus.

Agent Thomas T. Toosha jutted his chin out. "I'm not following any orders you give. We're proceeding on and will rendezvous with our destination in fifty-five minutes, per my *official* orders."

Rendezvous with our destination. Christ, where did the FBI get such lingo? Michael realized he was dealing with a hard case, a higher order of primate than the other two.

The agent beside him bent down for his gun. "Don't!" Michael ordered. He glanced back at Toosha, who'd returned his attention to the front. "And don't *you* make me do anything we'll all regret."

"What else can you do?" Toosha asked over his shoulder. "You're sealed tight inside a straitjacket. You can't even take a piss."

Thanks for reminding me. It was a good jab but also a reckless one, one intended to provoke. Faintly, across a distance of miles, he caught Mac's counsel. This time he *could* make out the words. *Call his bluff.*

Yes, boss. He realized that for the first time, Mac was putting him in charge, probably because he was actually at the scene. Mac now expected him to be an active agent and not just a relay. But what could he do to justify his friend's trust? What did either of them, or both, have left to try? For all he knew, Mac hadn't achieved anything in the other copter.

Michael glanced desperately around and saw nothing. Just three men and a gun on the floor. Plus the bright displays of the instrument panel. Ah…

The lights began to flicker and go out. Then the engines faltered. How far did he dare to push it? Abruptly, he realized that what he knew about helicopters he could put on a Post-it slip.

"Damn it, the engines are cutting out on me," Toosha said. Michael heard him work the controls, trying various options. "They don't respond!"

Michael shifted his attention and the engines returned, or tried to. And Pilot Thomas T. Toosha tried with them. The co-pilot assisted wherever he could, but Michael hindered them both just enough so the copter continued to falter.

For nearly a minute, Michael heard Toosha do everything he could, his hands pressing levers, buttons, and God knows what else. As he struggled, the engines continued to sputter and the helicopter sank in the air. Beside him, the agent shouted. "Do something! For God's sake!"

In the end, it was not quite as close a call as it had been with Laura, who'd almost died. Michael, throbbing with fear, managed to stabilize the copter, but the steep fall—perhaps a thousand feet—made him sick. He might not be able to piss in this straitjacket, but he could certainly puke if he wasn't careful. After he let the pilot regain control and climb to his previous attitude, Michael swallowed and gave him an order.

"Okay. You saw what happened. Now pay attention."

"No."

"If you don't—"

"What are you going to do—trash a few cell phones, turn off the engines again? If you do that, we'll all be dead."

The man had a point. What else *could* he do? Michael reached out to Mac who told him what he already knew. No matter which direction they went, no matter how high or low they flew, the FBI would quickly find them. Radar would track them easily and there was no place to hide.

In the distance white lightning forked against the blue sky. It reminded him of Mac. Both were electrical systems, only the lightning was an electrical system writ large. He imagined hurling lightning bolts against the enemy and smashing them to pieces.

So do you want to surrender? Michael asked. *Let them torture us to make us talk?*

Mac's response came quickly. *You know the answer to that. What's the point of seizing these copters in the first place and trying to escape if we only surrender and go meekly to our slaughter? Dammit, Mike, once they get their hands on us again, they'll suck us dry and never let us go. We've got to at least try to be free!*

Michael had never heard Mac express himself so bluntly. *I agree completely*, he replied. *Live free or die hard.* Clumsily, he shifted his weight in the straitjacket to meet the pilot's eyes. Toosha was a tough hombre, all right, and he had an iron will. But so did he.

"We'd rather be dead," Michael said, "then have your sadists pick our brains apart like hunks of cheese. Since we're all on the same side, you guys should have come to me in peace and *asked* for my cooperation. If you had, I would have been glad to do it like a true-blue patriot. But you didn't."

Agent Toosha nodded. "You may have a point," he said, "but I have my orders, and an important part of them is not to endanger national security or under any circumstances let this aircraft fall into enemy hands."

Enemy hands? Did he just say *I* was the *enemy*? Choking with anger, Michael watched Toosha consult a gauge.

"It's a long way down," the man said. "But there's one good thing. It's open country down there and we won't hurt anybody."

We won't hurt anybody. As Michael chewed on the words, Toosha turned back and gave him a long measuring stare. Then he spoke to the other two men. "Gentlemen, it's been a privilege serving with you. Hold on tight."

A moment later, he jerked the stick and the helicopter swung and dived almost straight down. A bird shot past, squawking as it narrowly missed them. Michael strained against the rigid jacket, futilely trying to escape. It pressed so hard against his diaphragm that he barely managed to scream. His earlier threat to crash the copter had been scary but intended as a bluff. This looked like the real thing.

"Stop, you crazy bastard. You don't have to do this!"

Down they went, the wind howling about them. Far below, as if eager to meet them, the earth seemed to rush up.

CHAPTER NINETEEN
RISE AND FALL

The world went dark and his lungs shut down. He was thrown into the recent past when he suffered from sleep apnea and was still learning how deadly sleep could be because he could die in it.

Screaming inside, he strained to breathe, feeling himself approach the very edge of oblivion. As before, though, he wouldn't give in. No, he would fight to survive. He would escape this torment, no matter how overwhelming it seemed.

But to survive, he must escape this monster that held him and rise to his feet. He tore at it desperately, twisting and turning in its hungry grip. The world raged and howled. He couldn't breathe, and he knew he was about to die. But he fought on, caught between life and death.

Then his eyes opened and he gasped, drawing a deep, painful, but life-saving breath. His world returned and he saw that he had succeeded in climbing to his feet and that a man sat in a seat before him. The man gripped a lever on the left side of his seat and Michael realized he was pushing it down, forcing the copter toward the earth below.

No! The mad bastard (the pilot, he remembered) wanted to crash it and kill them all just so the copter wouldn't fall into enemy hands. What screwed-up, demented devotion to his orders! But what amazed Michael even more was that during his attack, he had squirmed and twisted and forced one arm free of the straitjacket. He had also managed to open the chair straps with his fingers, which stung and were bloody. As an escape artist he was no Houdini, but thanks to Mac, his strength was still growing and had just reached new heights, enabling him to break partly loose from his canvas prison.

He only hoped it would be enough to save the helicopter and their lives.

The copter lurched and he struggled not to fall. Leaning over Toosha's seat from behind, Michael reached down and seized the man's hand, trying to pull the lever up so the aircraft would slow in its descent and then rise. Not only did Toosha resist, but there were other problems with Michael's plan.

The first was that the copter swung, bounced, and vibrated in a stiff wind, making it difficult for Michael to keep his balance and get any traction. Another was that the man behind him had unsnapped his seatbelt and grabbed his gun from the floor. Michael felt him press the barrel against his head.

"Let him go or I'll kill you!" the agent screamed.

Michael braced himself and lashed out with his elbow, catching the man in the face. He shot back across his chair and hit the floor, his gun flying in the air.

Fortunately, the gun flew in Michael's direction and disappeared. Michael turned and saw the man rush into the bay or transport area of the copter, possibly because there were weapons there. Damn, he'd have to watch his back!

Turning back, he noticed the co-pilot. The man sat frozen in his seat, staring at the pilot.

"Help me!" Michael screamed. "You're a pilot too! Don't let this thing crash!"

The man did not react.

Michael returned his attention to Toosha, who was hell-bent on committing patriotic suicide. Straining, Michael found that having only one arm free of a cumbersome straitjacket was another handicap in stopping him. It made it difficult to move and get a good grip on the lever, especially since Toosha was already holding it. Desperately, he started to strike the pilot's hand.

Let go, dammit! Let go!

Despite Michael's increased strength, Toosha did not release the lever. "Stop it!" he screamed. "Carl, help me!" His co-pilot did not reply.

Michael glanced out the windscreen, which was tilted at a sharp angle toward the earth below. Shit, in just seconds they had fallen so far, probably hundreds of feet. His stomach clenched, bracing for the impact.

No, don't give up, you still have time! Michael raised his fist and began to strike the pilot again. This time he focused not on Toosha's hand but on his helmeted skull. Rattle his brains. Rattle his brains to hell. The helmet was hard and hurt his knuckles, but he persisted. Finally Toosha went limp and his hand fell from the lever.

As it did, Michael noticed another lever. It rose from beneath the front of Toosha's seat and looked different. Could the first lever be for changing altitude and the other for changing directions? There were pedals too, by the floor. With a gasp, he realized how difficult and complicated it was to fly this aircraft. Even if he were qualified, he would have to sit where Toosha sat and have both hands free to operate the controls. With the helicopter bucking like a wild mustang, replacing Toosha was impossible. He didn't have the time or ability to do it!

He glanced again at the co-pilot, who looked like he'd just seen Medusa. No hope there. And he suddenly knew why, like a blow to the gut. The man was dead, possibly due to a heart attack or something he had sustained during the steep fall. And Michael had thought *he* had suffered from it!

He decided to take a chance. Grabbing the lever, he raised it. The copter vibrated in the wind and fought him tooth and nail as if it had a mind of its own. Finally, Michael felt its descent begin to slow — and then they began to rise. He trembled in relief and continued to raise the lever.

Toosha had said they were ten thousand feet up. Was that how high he should be, or did it make any difference? Assuming it was the right figure, how did he determine when they had climbed that high? There must be an altimeter somewhere on the display panel, but he didn't have time to search for it.

Of course, if he somehow reached the right altitude, he would have other problems. What did he do with the pilot when he regained consciousness, and how did he get the rest of his hide out of this damned straitjacket? Most of all, how did he go about flying this thing with no experience and only one arm?

Shit. Who was he kidding? The copter had already started to wobble and veer dangerously. Michael realized that nothing he did would make any difference. Even if he miraculously regained control and avoided a crash, the feds had radar and would scoop him up like a piece of lint. For that matter, they were probably sniffing at his tail right now.

He looked out the co-pilot's side to see. Nope, nothing important, only another jagged white bolt of lightning, a bit closer than before. However, he glanced to his left just in time to see a military helicopter draw up right beside him. The copter looked similar to his except for a slightly different design and a different name: *Anaconda*. And there was one other detail.

Mac was pressed against a window and grinning directly at him.

CHAPTER TWENTY
A SUDDEN FEAR

W hy was the bright, broad face etched on Mac's screen grinning at him and popping its lips from the other helicopter? And how was Mac, who seemed bigger and taller, moving about when he didn't have any legs? For that matter, why had Mac's captors permitted him such freedom? These and other questions bombarded Michael as he strained to see more clearly into the other cockpit, which was thirty feet away. He opened his mouth to speak, but Mac's voice came through in his head as it had on other occasions, most recently when they had faced Edgar P. Delgata and the Dark Opposite in the tunnel. Only now it crackled with tension.

Go back to your cargo area. I'll fly above you and drop a rope ladder down.

Fly above me and drop a rope ladder? he thought. *Are you crazy? You don't have any arms!*

Bruno will do it for me. I'll also have to tilt your chopper sideways so the ladder can enter it. I ran an inventory and you don't have one.

Isn't there another way to do it? Michael asked.

Nope, there isn't. Mike, just slide the cargo door open, then hold on to something so you won't fall when your chopper tilts. Be ready to grab the ladder

162

when it comes down. Get on it fast and climb out carefully. Keep yourself centered to maintain your balance.

It sounds crazy, Michael thought. *I'm not sure I can do this.*

If you don't, your chopper will crash.

Climb up into the *other* copter while this one fell through space? It was madness! As Michael's copter bucked and threatened to keel over, though, he realized Mac was right. He didn't have any choice. Rising, he lurched around and stumbled toward the cargo and troop transport area amidships. As he entered it, he tripped over a trunk and almost fell. Catching his balance, he turned toward the door to his left. It looked like a sliding door about five feet high with two windows, and through them he caught a glimpse of Mac's copter. He'd heard somewhere that its rotors' disc span was nearly sixty feet. How the hell could Mac handle that? He had no hands or legs and no experience flying, but Michael remembered something Mac had said in the tunnel. He'd *sorted through the files in over nineteen thousand databases* to find what he needed.

Hell yeah, Mac was many things, but he was primarily a computer, an AI that could manipulate and guide any machine. With Mac's ability to electronically access blueprints and other files from computers near and far, who could say what he was capable of? And judging from the darkness and lightning Michael saw through the door's windows, Mac would need every facet of such skill, because it looked like a storm was brewing.

The door...even if he could open it, how could he possibly climb anything in this fuckin' jacket? It not only restricted his torso but part of his thighs as well. He imagined himself trying to climb the first rung of the ladder and dropping straight down like a stone.

Michael felt a familiar tingle course through his body. *We need to get you out of that monkey suit now!*

Mac. He kept forgetting they had a telepathic connection. *How do we do that?* he asked.

Let me help you. We'll do it together.

The tingling increased, became a fire in his blood. Michael found himself merging with Mac, straining against the straitjacket together. The copter bounced and tilted. There was no one in charge of the controls and Michael knew the aircraft could fall end over end at any moment. After all, he'd knocked out the pilot and the co-pilot was probably dead.

Why don't you control this thing? Michael cried. *How can you tilt it sideways when you can't even prevent it from crashing?*

I'm trying, Mac replied. *The ship is damaged and resists me.*

Damaged? Had *he* done it earlier when he had frozen the copter's engines? It didn't matter. Michael knew he must get out of this straitjacket now!

He and Mac drove against the jacket from inside, and from the outside, they tore at the device with Michael's free hand. No matter how hard they struggled, though, they were getting nowhere.

A ripping sound! They strained more, staggering across the deck, which was slanted downward because of the helicopter's descent. Then they heard another ripping sound. Again they tried…

The jacket abruptly parted and they shook free of it. It fell to the deck and Michael tottered to the door, found the handle, and pulled. Oh, shit, it didn't move. He tried again, using all his strength. This time the door slid sideways and he forced it all the way to the other end where it hit with a bang.

Wind lashed him, and he almost fell again. Then, miraculously, the copter's descent began to slow and the deck became level. Mac, he realized, had succeeded in controlling its fall.

Mac suddenly screamed in his mind. *Behind you!*

Michael swung around and saw a familiar face. Shit, how had he forgotten him? It was the agent who'd dropped his gun and run into the cargo area. He had found another gun, and its barrel was pointing directly at him.

"You bastard," the man said. "I was just nine days from getting my pension!"

"I'm sorry," Michael said. He knew it wasn't good enough. The agent's face hardened. He was about to fire! Then the copter lurched and they both fought for balance. Michael recovered first. Reaching out, he seized the man's arm and pulled, launching him toward the door. The man screamed and dug in his heels, but he ran out of deck and went airborne. For a moment he hung suspended in space, a stricken look on his face. Then he dropped from sight, his sunglasses falling after him.

I'm sorry, Mac said. *I somehow missed him.*

Michael trembled. *It's okay. Nobody's perfect.*

Peering up, Michael saw the blades of Mac's copter whirling around just twenty feet above. A moment later, he felt his copter's descent stop.

Mac said, *As best I can, I've put both our choppers in a hovering position. Now I'm going to tilt you back at a 45-degree angle. Hold on tight. When your chopper's stable again, Bruno's going to drop the ladder to you. I may not be able to hold your chopper more than a minute, so you'd better catch it quickly.*

Soon after, the helicopter began to revolve. Michael braced himself opposite the door and watched it turn with him as he slid down the wall. Lighting flashed beyond the door, and he heard the powerful sound of wake turbulence caused by Mac's rotors.

When the tilting stopped, the ladder fell through the open door and hit him in the chest.

Grab it! Mac shouted.

Michael did so. *Got it!* he said.

Well, get on fast and climb out before I lose my position.

Michael got onto the ladder and climbed toward the door above. Damn it, why was he suddenly so scared? If he could face the Dark Opposite and everything else, he could certainly face this.

Still, all it would take was one slip and he'd share the black agent's fate. To his dismay, the ladder was wet and hard to hold. Why couldn't they simply lift him up to Mac's copter?

When he climbed out of the copter into open space, he felt his stomach fall toward Earth, dropping straight down and leaving him behind. But it was a false sensation, and he continued climbing. After a few more steps, though, he started to gasp and stopped, trying desperately to find air. It was like the times before he'd been diagnosed when he'd awoken during the night struggling to breathe.

Michael clung to the ladder, determined not to fall off. He resumed climbing but froze after three or four steps. Though he'd felt only a few raindrops, the rungs kept slipping away from his feet, threatening disaster with each step. He seemed to hang in space forever, a mile above the Earth, belonging nowhere. Then the universe exhaled a warm breath of air right in his face, stunning him. Was it trying to blow him off, scatter him to the winds? It should be easy since he was a poor climber and afraid of heights.

He glanced up at Mac's helicopter. *Anaconda* it said on the fuselage, and the image of a giant snake on the side made its militant message clear. To Michael, it was the most beautiful thing he'd ever seen. An anaconda was the biggest snake in the world, and it could swallow just about anything. Still, if this treacherous ladder didn't get him, the damned wind would. Or both would cash his check together.

At the moment his fate loomed clear. He was going to be blown off this ladder like a leaf and ride the winds to his eventual death. He wondered how long it would take and where he would come down. Perhaps he'd sail for miles and could enjoy the view on the way. The thought fueled a perverse desire to look down, to confront what he most feared. He resisted it.

The worst part was that he'd never again see the people he loved the most. He'd never watch Andy grow up or know where his brilliance led him. And Laura...even as the wind tore at him, he ached for her. Ever since she had followed him onto the trail that day, she had been a constant source of wonder. Grimm had felt she changed too often and was too flighty, lured by too many interests. He welcomed those interests and would have liked to explore them with her, as well as to kiss her lips one last time.

And Mac, perhaps the most amazing creature in creation. He'd never see him again either.

No! He wouldn't give up without a fight! Gathering his resolve, Michael started climbing the ladder again. Up and up, moving his opposite foot and hand each time, just as he'd seen soldiers doing it in a video. Left foot, right hand. Right foot, left hand.

Then he ran out of ladder and someone caught his arm and pulled him into the cargo area of Mac's copter. Exhausted, he lay on his back, just inches from the edge.

After a minute he recovered a little and peered carefully out and then down at the ground. There was no sign anywhere of the other helicopter.

Had it already crashed to earth with its two passengers, one of whom had still been alive when he'd left? Yes, he felt it had. Perhaps Thomas T. Toosha had regained consciousness before they struck and received pleasure in knowing that his patriotic sacrifice had been completed.

Michael rolled away and crawled deeper into the cargo hold where it was safer. Hallelujah, he was alive! His whole body sang with joy and the expectation of seeing Mac again. Where was his bright metal buddy, and how did Mac get around in this thing without any legs? He laughed and crawled on, eager to see him.

After a few feet though, Michael encountered a disturbing anomaly. It looked like a pair of shiny black shoes, planted directly before him on the deck.

Michael retreated quickly and looked up. Oh, shit. He had forgotten the guy who had pulled him in here. Above, an FBI agent stood looking down, his face twisted in rage.

CHAPTER TWENTY-ONE
BEHAVIOR MODIFICATION

The agent hated him, that he could clearly see. The man's face practically boiled over with it, and Michael knew he was in imminent peril. When it came to danger, his climbing up into another helicopter high above the Earth in a blustery wind was merely a 5 on a scale of 10 compared to this because he was about to die.

The agent lowered himself to crouch beside him. As he did, he brought his hate with him. Michael tried to rise but the man pushed him down with a giant hand and shoved his meaty, malevolent countenance close. Michael waited for the worst. Where the hell was Mac?

The agent's lips opened in a massive, goofy grin. "Hiiiii," he said.

"Uh, hi," Michael replied, feeling suspicion rise. Good God, was this Bruno, the one who had pulled him in? If so, he had looked like he wanted to murder him.

"Will you be my friend?" the agent pleaded.

"Sure. I'll be anything you like." *Where the hell is Mac? What in God's sublime orchards is happening here?* The only answer he received was the vibration of the copter's walls as the wind struck them.

The agent opened a ham-sized fist and stroked Michael's cheek. He endured it for a few seconds, then shoved the hand away and sat up.

Michael heard something roll toward them. He had no idea what it was but he did recognize a familiar sound. It sounded like…a squeaky wheel.

The object rolled closer and closer. Finally, it entered the cargo hold and Michael stared at it, his mouth falling open.

"Hello, Mike," Mac said in a deep, rich baritone. "I'm sorry I wasn't here, but I had an issue in the cockpit."

Michael didn't respond. Mac had grown again since that day in Laura's apartment when he had swollen to twice his original size in Michael's hands. In addition, his friend now perched on top of a motorized suitcase or travel bag with four wheels on the bottom. Some crewman, perhaps the pilot, had brought this rolling piece of luggage onboard, and it featured flaps, pockets, flashy travel stickers, a handle, and straps, the last of which had been used to secure him on top. The question was, how had Mac tied them?

Since the suitcase was motorized, Michael knew that Mac could easily control it and guide it about. He studied Mac's screen and the large dial beside it. Once the dial had been small and Michael had used it to navigate the machine's menu and select options. Everything from Ramp Time and Humidity Level to Mask Fit and Sleep Report. He wondered what Mac was using it for now when he had no attachments, such as a mask, tubing, or water tub. Perhaps Mac had simply outgrown the dial and it was obsolete, or he had created his own options, which were as incredible as he was.

"You better oil that wheel," Michael offered.

"I know," Mac said. "It squeaks abominably. I've been searching for the right lubricant but resources are limited here." He rolled left, then right. "It's not too bad, once you get past the fact that you've got some guy's *luggage* for a body." Michael saw a sad face appear on Mac's screen. A simulated tear ran down its nose. "Even if it qualifies as a body, it has no arms and legs," Mac continued. "It would be nice to tie myself onto this thing rather than have Bruno do it for me. Also, it would be nice to scratch my ass now and then. Now that I think of it, though, I don't have that either."

Am I dreaming? Michael glanced out the door of the cargo area and saw that the weather had worsened still more. The sky was darker and lightning forked here and there.

A particularly bright flash illuminated the cargo bay and revealed what he had missed before. Two agents sat strapped against the far wall. They were humming softly to each other, a tuneless melody as vacant as their smiles.

Michael stiffened in surprise. "What's up with them?" he asked. "Why do they look that way?" *And who's flying this thing anyway, a computer or you? Come to think of it, though, you're a computer too. A most unique and amazing one.*

Mac's screen flashed red, white, and blue. "I couldn't tolerate strict jailers," he said. "It was necessary to make them more cooperative so I could move around freely."

I couldn't tolerate. Mac seemed to have changed.

"And how did you do that?" Michael asked. He rose to his feet and edged away from Bruno. He still crouched on the floor, viewing him with what looked like love. It occurred to Michael that the man would be happy to gaze at him that way forever, indifferent to his responsibilities or bodily needs. He looked like a lotus-eater enthralled by divine fruit.

"Being a prisoner forced me to think," Mac said. "And one of the first things that came to mind was helicopters. And why not? I was being detained in one against my will with no one caring a rat's ass about my wishes. So I accessed six or seven hundred files from thirty or forty different places, searching for a weakness, a way in. Or more accurately, a way *out*. And after a couple of minutes I found it. Can you guess what it was?"

Michael didn't have a clue, but he gave it a shot anyway. "A weakness in the helicopter's construction maybe? A design flaw?"

Mac's screen produced the image of an astonished face. It looked like someone's kindly uncle. "That's remarkably close, my dear Watson. It was *vibrations*."

"Vibrations?"

"Yes. Helicopters shake a lot more than airplanes due to asymmetrical aerodynamics. Perhaps you've noticed this?"

As a matter of fact, Michael had. "It's hardly a jet-smooth ride. The walls rattle and roll, especially in the cockpit. Does it have something to do with the rotor blades?"

"Indeed it does, though they're not the only cause. Rotors being out of track and blade tip alignment irregularities can ruin the ride in a hundred different ways. They can cause rattles and vibrations that endanger not only the aircraft but passengers and crew. As for the pilot, they can screw up his hands, feet, eyes and fuck up his spine, causing degenerative osteoarthritis and musculoskeletal damage. Take it from me, amigo, whole-body vibration can push you to the limits of human tolerance and cause severe physiological and pathological disorders."

The bland face on Mac's screen smiled and morphed comically into that of a wise old scientist with thick glasses and white hair hanging in wild disarray. "When I read that stuff, Michael, an absolutely brilliant idea came to me. Can you guess what it was?"

Michael shook his head. "Beats the hell out of me."

Mac laughed. "Okay, I'll tell you. The idea came like a flash from the sky. Eureka! I wondered if it was possible to use the rattles and vibrations to adjust the crew's moods in a different way, make them happy rather than irritable, docile rather than stern, compliant rather than strict."

Michael glanced at the three crewmen's peaceful faces. "How could you do that?"

Mac paused. "Look at me. I'm *evolving*, Michael. Evolving all the time. Master Avionics should be my new name. If an electrical system emits even minor vibrations or signals, I can tap into them, fine-tune their resonance to fit individual crewmen or passengers. I feel those vibrations in my core, and I can use them to change travelers' minds and psychology, their whole world view." Mac stared at the three men. "You see the result."

"Yeah, but why go to all that trouble? You've used telepathy with me. Why not simply brainwash your victims directly and make them do whatever you want them to do?"

Mac looked disappointed in him. "Mike, because we're so close, you're the only one I can share my thoughts with, and I'm not capable of controlling your mind or 'brainwashing' you. I wouldn't do it even if I could. You're not a thing, you're a person."

"Oh, sorry. I should have known that." Embarrassed, Michael eyed the huge agent who had pulled him inside the cargo hold. "You know, at first this guy seemed to hate me. I thought I was finished."

Mac laughed. "You mean Bruno here? I assure you, he's as gentle as a lamb and wouldn't hurt a fly. Unfortunately, like the other crewmen, he's so passive, I couldn't rely on him to pull you up, so you had to climb the ladder yourself. I apologize for that, but I knew you could do it. As for his demeanor, I promise you're completely safe, though occasionally, Bruno's facial expressions can be problematic."

Problematic. Michael thought it over. "Despite what you said, it sounds like mind control."

"Yes, though I prefer to call it behavior modification."

"Can you reverse the process, make them the way they were originally?"

"I won't know until I try, but I think I can."

I won't know until I try. And if they didn't recover, what would they be—smiling vegetables? Had Mac performed the equivalent of irreversible lobotomies on these men? Even if Mac had, who was he to judge? Michael thought of the three men on the other copter who had died because of him, including the agent who had fallen to his doom and would never get his pension. It might not be his fault, but if Michael hadn't been aboard, they'd still be alive.

Max continued. "As I said, if there's an electrical object or system, I can manipulate and control it by mind alone. I don't have to physically touch anything. Of course, I do have limitations, such as how many I can control and how far across space I can reach, but I hope to overcome them."

Wow. That explained a lot, like how he'd brought both helicopters to a hover and piloted this one while doing it. "You know what this means, don't you?" Michael said. "Your evolving abilities make you even more valuable to the bad guys. They'll raze heaven and hell to get their hands on you."

The wise old scientist on Mac's screen nodded. "And on you, too because of what you know and your attachment to me. Which is why we both have to escape."

"How do we manage that?"

Mac glanced at the passive crewmen with obvious regret. "Bruno, get up and strap yourself down next to your fellow crewmen so you'll be safe. In the meantime, Mike, you come with me."

As Bruno rose and obeyed Mac's order, Michael followed Mac to the cockpit where he found one more crewman, a handsome young man who looked barely twenty. He sat strapped in the pilot's chair, staring passively into space. Michael wondered if he saw anything.

Mac sighed. "Depending on your point of view, I was least successful or more harmful with the pilot. He appears to be completely nonresponsive."

Michael remembered that Mac had been busy in the cockpit with an "issue." "That's too bad," he replied, aware of how inadequate his words were. The truth was, this young pilot might be brain dead, all his hopes and dreams of a rich and fulfilling life lost almost at the beginning. And that meant Bruno, who had greeted Michael with what appeared to be homicidal hate, was actually the best of a bad lot. He was the only one of the four men Mac had "adjusted" who was minimally functional and still capable of acting.

Turning away, Michael focused on the digitalized instrument panel and the vibrations Mac had mentioned. Now that he was in the cockpit, he sure could hear and feel them. What impact would these sounds and vibrations have on a crew who sat confined here day after day, traveling through all kinds of weather? Did it depend on the individual or gender? Above them the main rotor blades whirled as did the tail rotors at the stern, contributing to the half-deafening effect.

Michael considered the fact that Mac was mentally keeping the copter in a hovering position while dealing with him and other matters. How mind-boggling crazy that was. He saw a lever move, making an adjustment in their position. A chill rippled through his body as questions rose.

Why was this helicopter still hovering? Why hadn't Mac moved it on?

The answer came quickly. Because there was no place to go. The enemy was close and all around them.

Michael peered through the windscreen. At first he saw only blue sky and white clouds. A flicker of lightning to the northwest hinted at the storm's exit point.

Then he saw the government aircraft. There were three of them, and they were so close he could make out individual features—wings, rotors, cockpits.

Mac said, "There are six altogether. They were about two hundred yards off when I left the cockpit. While we were chatting, I felt them draw closer on all sides. The closest are now only about eighty yards off."

I felt them draw closer. Michael experienced a burst of awe. Mac not only could fly this chopper when he wasn't in the cockpit, he could *feel* aircraft approach!

"Do they know you've taken over?" Michael asked.

"Uh-huh. One of the crew radioed a report as I was seizing control. Say, would you like to see the overall picture of our situation?"

Michael nodded.

"Okay," Mac replied. "Just watch."

A section of the instrument panel lit up. Michael saw six white lights, all of them surrounding a flashing red light in the middle.

"Yup, you guessed it," Mac said. "The red light is us. The others are choppers like ours—Night Hawks, Chinooks, you name it."

Michael frowned. "Looks like overkill. Six against one. Compared to them, our firepower is puny."

"Most of it's show," Mac said, "designed to scare and intimidate us. They don't really want to use their guns. What they want…"

"What they want is *you*," Michael said. "They want you to surrender rather than fight. You're so valuable they don't even want to risk mussing your hair. They don't know how far your powers go or what you're fully capable of, but the hints you've scattered in your wake are very hard to resist. If handled right, you might become their Dark Opposite—and more."

Mac rolled toward him and Michael saw the wild-haired scientist on his screen beam. "Very astute, my dear boy."

Michael pointed at the instrument panel. "Each of those lights represents an electrical system. Can't you use your power to 'modify' their 'behavior' from here, give them a long-distance whammy so to speak. Or wait till they get closer?"

"I'm afraid not. As I mentioned, I do have my limitations. Our guests would still be too far away, and there's too many of them."

Oh, sure. He should have known that. "It's like a crazy, hopelessly lopsided game," Michael said. "That whole army is arrayed against you."

"Against *us*," Mac said. "We're a team."

"*You're* the one they want," Michael insisted. "If they had to choose, they'd take you in a heartbeat and throw me to the wolves."

"Not quite so fast as that," Mac said. "They find you interesting, too. But you know, I like your calling this a game. From one point of view, that's what war always is. It's like a chess match in which you always have to make the right moves. Come to think of it, didn't you play a game of chess with Mr. Starret?"

Mac had changed subjects so fast, Michael had to hurry to catch up. Of course. He'd forgotten that he was also an "electrical system." Mac must have followed his signal or trail to the hardware store, so he would know about the chess game.

"Yeah, and I beat him." Michael waved at the helicopters surrounding them. "But we can't beat them. There's too many."

Mac's screen brightened with excitement. "Ah, lad, where's your competitive spirit? View this as another chess game. The greatest chess game in history! A colossal confrontation. One ship against a vast and mighty fleet in the sea of space."

Michael stared at him. "Hyperboles aside, we'd have to make awfully good moves."

"Haven't you seen the ones I've already made? As when I lowered the ladder and hovered exactly above your chopper while the wind blew? You can only imagine the enormous number of precise, lightning-fast calculations I had to make."

"I know that," Michael replied. "But still, even with your abilities, do you think we could possibly win?"

"It's doubtful," Mac conceded. "Not only do they outnumber us, but they have fast, long-range aircraft monitoring the situation from a distance. Plus, we only have about three hours of fuel left. And where would we go and hide if we succeeded? I know some places below us in Kentucky, but getting there without being spotted will be difficult." He gazed out at the enemy. "Ah, but wouldn't it be glorious for us to try? Just think of it, compadre. The two of us have gathered here in dubious battle against merciless marauders who seek only to conquer us and drain our brains, suck them dry. Truly, our cause is just. What endeavor could be more epic and noble?"

Yes, Mac *has* changed, Michael thought. He sounds mad and hyper now, downright deranged. But then, such growing powers as he possesses must be a difficult burden to bear. Just a few weeks ago, Mac was no more than an appliance I plugged into a socket. Now he has half the government hot on his heels, desperate to catch him and suck out his secrets. Under the same circumstances, how would *I* have coped?

"We do have one big ace in the hole," Mac said, his rich baritone filling the cockpit.

"Oh? And what would that be?"

"They don't want to hurt me or kill the golden goose. I'm an unknown quantity, Michael, and as you suggested earlier, they'll be very afraid of doing something accidentally that would render me useless to them. That's why they're going to intimidate us up close from hovercraft rather than use premium jet fighters. For all they know, I'm a bomb that could explode right in their faces if they're not careful."

Michael had harbored the same thought. "Yet they can't and won't let you go."

"Nope." Mac was briefly silent. "You know," he said, "I miss Laura."

Another stunning change of subject. "So do I," he said.

Mac rolled closer, bringing the image of a sad pilgrim on his screen. "You remember when the three of us joined—how wonderful it was?"

"Yes."

Mac continued. "It was the most transcendent experience of my short life. I never knew what intimacy and sharing was until we came together. If only we could return to it."

Michael ached with the memory. "I'd like to see my son, too."

A long silence fell. Then Mac rolled back a foot, his faulty wheel squeaking. "Well, what's it going to be, mon ami? Do we attack and try to escape, with you as my second-in-command and trusting my brilliant tactics, or do we do something else?"

Michael gazed at the instrument panel, focusing on one red light surrounded by a rapacious and hungry army. No sir, you didn't have to be a genius to see how that would go.

"Perhaps we could try something else first," he said.

"A different strategy? Name it."

"Well, we could try talking to them." He pointed at the instruments. "I assume there's a radio hidden there somewhere."

Mac laughed. "Talk to them. Do you really think you'll get anywhere?"

"We could at least try," Michael said. "Maybe we could learn something about them. Something we can exploit."

"Well, we won't. They're inflexible. The only thing they want is for us to surrender immediately."

Michael was undeterred. "Maybe you could use your knowledge of electrical systems to connect us directly with their leader. And once you home in on the bastard, he and I could, uh, chew the fat, wheel and deal. Hammer out a compromise."

"Really?" Mac sounded amused. "What would you say? What golden-tongued words would you pour into his ear?"

"You won't know until you hear them."

The image of an orator appeared on Mac's screen. He was speaking into a microphone and making wild, dramatic gestures.

"Not like that," Michael said. "I'd be more subtle." *I hope.*

"Ah, *excelente, señor*! Subtle as a bubble on the double. But for safety's sake, I suggest we sit down and buckle up first."

Michael hesitated. "I'll take the co-pilot's seat."

"Fine." Mac slid off his travel bag and Michael buckled him into the seat behind the pilot. After sitting down in front, Michael heard a switch click on the instrument panel and saw a headset float through the air. It settled onto his head with the microphone positioned just before his mouth.

"Go ahead," Mac said after a moment. "*Speak.*"

CHAPTER TWENTY-TWO
A WHIM OF NATURE

Michael opened his mouth to speak but nothing came out. He had acted like a smart ass in convincing Mac to let him talk to their pursuers, but now that he'd succeeded, the only thing that came to mind was "How is my son?" and, "How is Laura?" Plus, "What have you done with them?"

But saying such personal stuff would expose his weakness and vulnerability. He must not do it.

Michael glanced at Mac whose screen projected a single word. *SPEAK!*

Michael turned back to the instrument panel. "Hello," he said. Ah, so brilliant!

"Hello," came the deep-voiced, rough-burred reply. "This is Major Terrence Hammer, USAF. To whom am I speaking?"

Ah, a *major*! Unless there was someone who outranked Hammer, it seemed that Mac had managed to find the man in charge. On the instrument panel, the white light directly before their copter was flashing. That must be Hammer, who had an appropriate name for a guy you were about to meet in battle.

"My name is Michael Windsor," Michael replied. "Major, why are you chasing us?"

"Is the entity we call the Anomaly with you? I want to speak to it."

It was a straight order, and Major Hammer had not only ignored his name and amenities but his question too as if they were of no consequence. Michael realized if he didn't stand firm now, it would be game, set, and match, with him on the losing side.

"Please answer my question, Major Hammer," Michael said. "Why have you chased us here with all these aircraft? Do you intend to shoot at us?"

This time he had asked two questions instead of one. Perhaps it weakened his position still more. Major Hammer would probably double down on his contempt and ignore both of them.

Which he did. "Mr. Windsor, on the authority of the President of the United States, you are hereby ordered to stay in place as our forces approach and escort you to Williams Air Force Base. Do not resist in any way or—"

Michael was getting pissed. "Or what, Major? Or you'll blast us from the sky? Reduce us to dust? Is that what you're saying? Because if it is, we have a few tricks and weapons of our own. We have..." He remembered the name Major Hammer had given Mac and tried to utter it as ominously as possible. "We have the *Anomaly*. You know hostile operatives tried to capture it, and you must also know about the Anomaly's Dark Opposite. We managed to destroy it, and the FBI killed or captured all of the enemy present in the tunnel. But world domination remains the enemy's goal and they will continue to seek the Anomaly's powers. Powers which I'm sure you know can be turned against you, the FBI, and the entire government if you attack us."

The not-so-veiled threat had its effect. Major Hammer was silent, and Michael heard low voices counseling him. Had he gone too far? Babbled his way into even deeper trouble? If so, Hammer's advisors might urge him to attack no matter how much they wanted Mac. Michael turned around to see how Mac was taking his daring insolence. The image on Mac's screen gave him a thumbs up and mouthed four words. "I'm not an 'it.'"

Returning his attention to the front, Michael noticed the storm was not gone after all but had swung back. Unless they had flown in a circle, lightning and darkness had reversed direction and were in play again. Perhaps the storm had run into a warm front, or a cold front. Who could say?

"If you fire on us," Major Hammer said, "we will be forced to retaliate."

"If you attack," Michael said, "you will risk losing powers you haven't even dreamed of."

On the instrument panel, Michael could see the six enemy aircraft were drawing closer on all sides, perhaps just sixty yards away. If he wasn't careful, they'd soon be caught in a noose. Hammer's manner made Michael try to imagine what he looked like. He'd bet he was a lean, hard man who seldom smiled.

"Major," Michael said, "have you heard how the Anomaly helped me to create new life?"

"To create new *life*?"

"Yes. I was being interrogated by two cops, and thanks to my closeness to Mac, who you call the Anomaly, I was able to create a rose from nothing, from my subconscious. Boom! It just appeared out of thin air. Then when I touched it, the rose started to grow until it was more than twice its original size."

"Striker," Hammer said.

"Yes," Michael said, "he was the cop in charge! The Anomaly gave me the power of God, which means you'll fuckin' lose if you push me any further. So back off!"

Tense minutes passed. The Hammer Squadron (as Michael thought of it) didn't drop back but neither did it advance farther. Behind Michael, Mac killed the audio long enough to privately render his opinion. "Excellent bluff, and a darn good chess move! I'm beginning to think you're a budding grand master. You've stopped this entire group in its tracks. Major Hammer doesn't want to risk killing me but if he doesn't take chances, he and his men will just be sitting ducks."

Michael demurred. "It might seem like we have an advantage but time's on his side. In three hours we'll run out of petrol and will have to land. He, on the other hand, can order a refill from backup." He glanced in Hammer's direction. "I think they've been ordered to fire on us—and on the Anomaly—only as a last resort, only if intimidation doesn't work and they have no chance at all of capturing you. In the end, if they can't have the Anomaly, no one can. But Hammer hopes it won't go that far. He wants to wait us out because he knows their fuel supply is greater than ours. Rather than risk harming you, he'll bide his time and scoop us up after we've landed."

The face on Mac's screen frowned. "I didn't think of that."

No, Mac hadn't, and Michael found it troubling. Lightning flashed nearby and the sound of thunder struck the copter broadside. Talk about vibrations! His head rattled to beat the band. What would Mac do with vibrations like these if he could just focus them on the intruders, fine-tune them to fit their psyches? Mac could make those airmen gentle as sheep who would accede to his every wish.

Michael said, "A chess player has to keep his eye out for opportunities."

"How true," Mac said. "If his opponent makes an error, he has to jump on it."

"Or if the game unexpectedly heads in a new direction," Michael said. "A whim of nature, for example."

"A whim of nature?" Mac pondered the phrase as lightning flashed again, making them blink. Outside, rain sheeted down, striking the windscreen and obscuring their escort.

Michael was surprised Mac didn't get it, and he felt the beginning of dread. He raised his finger and pointed out at the growing storm.

Mac stared at it. After a few seconds, Michael saw him finally make the connection. "Oh, we'll use the storm to escape!"

"Do you feel all right, Mac?" Michael asked.

The face on Mac's screen swirled and came apart, like dust in the wind. "D-Don't worry about me," Mac said after a moment. "We've got something important to do. We have to beat an army."

"And I think I've thought of just the right move," Michael replied, trying to sound confident. "You were wrong, Mac. Chatting with the enemy was not a waste of time. It did serve a purpose. We learned something strategically important."

"We did? What is it?"

"We learned that they want you so much, we might even be able to hit them a couple times before they react. And this wild storm improves our chances even more. It's like a sign. It's too good to waste."

"You're right," Max said. "It's an unexpected event that should unsettle them. Plus, it makes it harder to pick their targets." He paused. "And you may also be right about chatting with him."

"What do you mean?"

"Did you hear the way Hammer's voice sounded after you told him I helped you to create new life? Their commanding officers must have told him to get me or else, especially if they learned of a new power I possessed. And you can't do much better than the ability to create new life. It's really upped the stakes."

"Right," Michael said. "Just think of the military applications. They could create an army of Frankensteins, super soldiers who would be nearly invincible in battle." He nodded toward the instrument panel. "Please activate the radio so Hammer can hear me again. When he answers me, start moving the copter toward him. And remember, I don't know how to fly this thing, so you'll have to do everything." He stared at Mac. "That means we'll have to merge again as we did before only closer, as close as we can get. My plan is to approach Hammer's chopper and use his reluctance to hurt you, to surprise him. Use your computational ability and lightning-fast reflexes to choose the exact right moment and fire right past him, using the machine guns mounted on each side of the cockpit and any other pistols and popguns we have. Don't hit him but stun him so we can make a break for it and use this storm to hide somewhere, maybe in the clouds. Later we can land somewhere. *Capische?*"

"Yes, Mike. *Capische.* I'm ready to rumble. You can count on me."

I sure as hell hope so. Michael turned around and gripped the arms of the chair. As if this "game" wouldn't be hard enough, now he had to worry about Mac who suddenly seemed to be losing it. Hell's bells, could he still rely on him?

Michael opened his mouth. "Major Hammer!" he said.

Lightning flashed; thunder boomed; rain lashed the windscreen. Michael gazed at the storm with a calculating eye and felt Mac's hunger for battle throb through his veins even though Mac had agreed not to attack.

"Major Hammer!" he repeated, this time shouting.

A burst of static. "Yes, Mr. Windsor, we can hear you," Hammer replied.

Michael felt Mac begin to move the chopper forward. *That's good, Major Hammer*, Michael wanted to shout. *I've got a trick I want to show you.*

But he didn't say that. He'd shouted Hammer's name to startle him a bit and throw him off balance. Call it the element of surprise before he and Mac broke and ran.

Mac had called this contest a chess game or chess match. The question was, no matter how brilliantly they moved, did a lone piece like the *Anaconda* stand the slightest chance of escaping Hammer's Squadron without a fight?

CHAPTER TWENTY-THREE
A STROKE OF LUCK

Even before they fired the first shot, the storm changed. Within seconds it grew much worse, the lightning, darkness, and wind creating chaos all around them. Unless you used the instrument panel, it was hard to home in on targets, especially when they surrounded you.

To Michael, the storm's intensification was a blessing. It was just what the doctor ordered.

Okay, he said, *shoot past the leader and then make a run for it.* He felt Mac aim slightly above Hammer's helicopter, which featured a bright flamethrower on its nose.

Aye, aye, Captain, Mac responded. *Here we go.*

Their weapons management system was fully integrated with the digital flight controls, which meant it did much of the work for them. It calculated the range and the complex ballistics required for pilot gunners to hit targets. In addition, Michael found that Mac didn't even have to physically press a trigger. He did it with his *mind,* launching a burst of machine gun bullets past Hammer's copter.

To Michael's horror, a couple of bullets hit Hammer's chopper head-on, one of them close to the cockpit.

What happened? Michael asked. *You were supposed to miss Hammer's chopper.*

I...don't know why I hit him, Mac replied. *Must be the storm or the launch program.*

But Michael knew the problem wasn't the storm or the launch program. The problem was in Mac. He remembered Mac's hunger for battle. Yes, something *was* definitely wrong with him.

No time to dwell on it, though. Michael felt Mac swing the copter and try to fly between an Argo and a Night Hawk just like their copter. But he was as stunned as Michael was by his bad shooting and had hesitated just long enough for the Night Hawk to move into his path and block him. Michael's only hope was that the worsening storm would discourage combat or make it ineffective. With all the turbulence, it was hard to see anything, though the enemy was clearer on the instrument panel.

The Night Hawk fired, narrowly missing them. Mac swung the Anaconda, searching for an escape route. No good. All the other aircraft had slipped closer, boxing them in.

The Night Hawk fired again. Despite the poor visibility, Michael heard bullets strike their cargo area. He knew that at any moment, the others would open fire as well.

I have to shoot at them, Mac said.

I know, Michael answered.

Thunder crashed and wind pummeled the Anaconda. Michael felt Mac focus on the Night Hawk. Despite the wind, his aim was better this time, free of accident. He concentrated on knocking out the tail rotor, which counteracted the main rotor's torque and kept the copter from spinning. Michael saw him hit the rotor multiple times. The chopper lurched and lost control. Spinning around and around, it descended toward Kentucky's hilly terrain far below.

They swung again and Michael saw a huge wall of dense black clouds only a hundred yards away. Where had it come from? How could it come together so fast? Regardless of the reason, its presence was welcome. If they could reach the heart of the thunderstorm, they could hide and try to escape. Mac not only shared his idea but was already heading toward the clouds.

They had barely entered it though when an Apache chopper with a painted Indian on its fuselage appeared. Not only that, but it sent a volley of missiles their way. Any one of them could have destroyed their craft at once, reduced it to a fireball. Mac's mind worked the controls with masterful precision. He made their craft dive and spin, swoop and turn in a dazzling aerial ballet. His superior maneuverability outwitted and outflanked their merely human opponent. They flew upside down and strafed the other aircraft while suffering minor damage in return. Still, the Apache hung on.

Once again, they had no choice. They had to go for the kill. Michael felt it was his hands along with Mac's that worked the 50-caliber machine guns in the windows. *Rat-a-tat-tat. Rat-a-tat-tat.* The Fed gunner fired back in futility. Then the Apache cockpit windows blew and spewed fragments into space.

Let's get out of here, Michael said. *They're finished.*

Mac agreed. *Yeah, they're headed to the Happy Hunting Grounds!*

Missiles flew past them. The other copters had decided to join the party. They were going to fight back, which meant it was kill or be killed.

Fortunately, there was another option. They headed toward the clouds again, hoping to hide. Strong winds bashed the hull along with rain and hail as they entered it. Bright lightning stitched down from the sky, and one clap of thunder was so loud, that Michael thought the helicopter might shatter into pieces from the sound.

All about them the wind howled, a ferocious cauldron that was miles high and deep. They worked the controls, determined to put distance between them and their pursuers. But how far should they go into the clouds? They only had a couple of hours of fuel left and would use much of it battling these winds. Hell, if the feds didn't catch and kill them, this storm could.

Michael said, *Let's drop five hundred feet then head southwest for a half hour. We can poke our nose out then and see if we have company.*

Sounds like a plan to me, Mac said.

Thirty-three minutes later they emerged warily from the clouds. They peered about and consulted their gauges.

The coast seems clear, Mac said. *Thanks to the storm, we lost them.*

Michael wasn't so sure. *They could have followed us into the clouds.*

That would be pretty stupid, wouldn't it?

Michael thought about it. Yeah, dumb as hell. The clouds were a colossal death trap that could kill a pilot at any moment. The only reason they'd gotten through it was Mac, who could navigate the highways of hell with his eyes closed.

You're right, Michael said. He glanced around. *The borders of this storm are ragged and uneven, though. It's easy to miss them.*

But minutes passed, and they saw no sign of the four surviving Federal aircraft. Their adversaries were gone, probably searching for them elsewhere.

Michael was just starting to smile when their instrument panel beeped, showing a green blip approaching from behind. Glancing at the rearview mirror, he saw a familiar object bearing down on them. The flamethrower emblem on its hull promised retribution rather than a truce.

"Clever boy," Michael said softly.

Instead of running, they leveled off and waited. Lightning flashed and rain sheeted down. Outside the cloud, visibility was still wretched, but Michael could swear he saw something sleek and long emerge from the Flamethrower's side after it slowed and hovered in place eighty yards away.

He heard a boom, and something shot overhead. They lowered the copter as heavy rounds continued to pass above them.

"What the hell's that?" Michael asked.

"Sounds like a 20 mm cannon," Mac said. "Let's make tracks!"

They promptly did so, darting away and using evasive maneuvers. Hammer's copter chased them, but he was handicapped by the storm, and they were faster and cagier. The major was persistent though, and his continued pursuit, though hopeless, worried Mac. After another cannon burst, he reached a sudden decision.

"We're going back and take care of Major Hammer."

The pronouncement stunned Michael. "Why? He's no longer a problem. The man can't catch us."

The face on Mac's screen was resolute. "Just a feeling. If we don't stop him now, Major Hammer will never let us go. He'll hound us forever, like the police inspector who hounds Jean Valjean in *Les Miserables* for stealing a loaf of bread."

Why was Mac talking this way? He sounded irrational. "Mac, don't do it," he said. "Let's go and escape like we planned to. Okay?"

But Mac swung the chopper around and went back. He attacked Hammer, shooting rockets and machine guns. Though he opposed Mac's decision, Michael's connection to him remained close. He could still feel the weapons respond. It was as if he held them in his hands.

The hull over Major Hammer's engines exploded and came off. In return, the enemy's fire smashed into the pilot's side of the cockpit, jolting the aircraft. Michael bit his lip so hard he tasted blood.

"Dammit, I gotta admit this Hammer's good," he said. "There goes a bishop!"

"Eh?"

"Talkin' chess, Mac. Remember, it's *your* analogy. You know, some folks say chess was modeled after war, the oldest game of all. And this is one hell of a war we've got ourselves in." He gasped as more shots narrowly missed them. In response, Mac released two missiles that caught Hammer's craft amidships.

"Got him!" Mac crowed. "I've really pulled his cork now."

"Maybe," Michael shouted. "But we're losing altitude!"

"How fast?"

Can't you tell? Forgetting his fear of heights, Michael peered down through the window. "Not as fast as he is!" he shouted. "Look, it's checkmate!"

Together, they watched Major Hammer's aircraft plunge toward the green hills and mountains of Kentucky. Over an hour before, Michael had tried to imagine what his foe looked like. He still didn't know and would always wonder. All he knew was that the man and his crew were finished.

As for their own prospects, that remained to be seen. The blow to the cockpit had dislodged Michael from Mac and returned him to his separate consciousness. Now he watched from a respectful distance as Mac struggled to restore power and reverse their freefall. Since the Anaconda had an electrical system, it was a task he was uniquely qualified for. Despite his talents, though, the outcome was in doubt. If Mac couldn't do it, they were screwed. Well, it served him right. Next time he'd take an airplane when he wanted to fly somewhere. If he were in a plane, he'd be strapping on a parachute about now and getting ready to jump.

The cockpit vibrated and the chopper groaned as Mac tried to power up again. Miraculously, he succeeded, and the instrument panel lit up, as beautiful as a Christmas tree. The young man sitting in the pilot's chair, though, gazed at the lights without expression.

Michael sighed in relief as their speed of descent slowed. "Good work! It looks like we're going to be all right," he said as thunder boomed above them.

"What?" Mac shouted. "Speak louder, I can't hear you."

He turned around in his seat so Mac could see him. "I said we're going to be all—"

That was when lightning struck the Anaconda. Behind Mac, the crewmembers screamed as they fell through a hole in the cargo hold. An instant later, air rushed into what remained of the cockpit.

"Oh, Mike," Mac screamed in horror. "What do we do NOW?"

CHAPTER TWENTY-FOUR
SKYBORNE

The storm tossed the copter like a fragile ball that was about to come apart. Time seemed to slow down, to acquire a dreamlike quality. Michael felt he was in the other cockpit again with Thomas T. Toosha, only this time their aircraft was a plaything of the gods. The wind heaved them up and down as he struggled to breathe.

Mac, of course, lacked lungs and had no such problem. *Hang in there, Mike!*

Easy for you to say.

The copter lurched and plummeted straight down, making his stomach sick. God, how he hated heights. This was even worse than climbing the rope ladder.

Can't you fix the copter? he asked.

Lightning shorted out the engine, Mac replied. *I can't do a thing with it. Fortunately, I have a chute stowed in my travel bag.*

Michael remembered the luggage covered with travel stickers that Mac rode on. But he wasn't sure about the chute. *Do you mean a parachute?*

Of course. You don't think I'd go up in a chopper without one, do you? Hop up and put it on so we can jump out.

Mac was sounding crazy again, but if he didn't act, the storm would ram them right down into the earth. When the feds finally found them, they'd need a giant spatula to scrape up their remains.

Michael unbuckled himself, then struggled up and lurched to the seat behind him. With Mac's guidance, he opened the travel bag Mac sat on, pulled out the parachute, then strapped it on his back with the harness. He placed Mac under his shirt against his chest, fastening him with a couple of straps from the bag.

Mac said, *It'll open automatically after you jump out. Just duck down so you'll miss the rotary blades.*

The cockpit tilted. Before he slid down toward the pilot, Michael managed to open the door on the co-pilot's side. The wind slammed it shut. He tried again, leaning into it. C'mon, damn you, open!

The wind granted his wish and opened the door, sucking them out. They dropped through space like a stone.

Far below the whole world lay waiting. It was dark, ravaged by storm, and it stretched forever. It emptied his mind the moment he saw it. He couldn't breathe and he wanted to die.

Down he fell. Down, down, down. Then he felt a powerful jolt and their descent abruptly slowed. Stunned, Michael peered up and saw the rectangular canopy fanned out above him. He reached up and grabbed the thick straps on both sides, then gazed in wonder at the world below. God, he thought, blinking against the rain, I'm riding the wind.

You sure are, my boy, a voice said against his chest. *I'm proud of you!*

Michael gasped. *Mac, how ya doing, pal?*

Mac laughed and Michael laughed with him. They both howled, glad to be alive. Mac said, *I'm half-mad but happy to be aboard. Now we need to get down in one piece.*

I don't know, Michael said. *This storm could kill us.*

Naw, it doesn't stand a chance. It's just a collection of mindless forces, Mike.

Yeah, Mac was still crazy. Mindless forces could kill you in a heartbeat if you weren't careful. Michael sucked in air, trying not to be overwhelmed by sensory overload. Stay focused, he told himself. Don't lose it!

They had fallen far but were still so high. Staring at the distant ground, Michael felt his lungs suddenly shut down. *Eeeeeeeeeee!*

Relax, Mike! Just breathe naturally.

He tried to obey but his lungs resisted. Then, to his relief, he felt them inflate, bringing air into his body again. Such a blessed feeling! He relaxed, remembering how it felt to breathe with a CABS machine as he became one with the process. Inhale, exhale, inhale, exhale…

He concentrated on watching the ground, seeing trees, hills, a farmhouse, and a pond. Where will we land? he thought. And how will I do it?

As they drifted southwest, he spotted two haystacks and gave Mac a mental nudge. *How about a haystack, Mac? It'll be soft.*

Nope, not my style, Mike. Plus, the wind is carrying us past them.

Something passed overhead at that moment. *Thought I saw a shadow,* Michael said.

You did, two actually. One's a Jupiter Sentinel, a surveillance aircraft. The other's a Republic X-305 fighter jet. Looks like the feds are keeping tabs on you, Mike, trying to find out where we are.

Michael didn't find this news reassuring. However, the fact that Mac had provided it was. His friend was still sane and functioning, at least part of the time.

He rubbed his chest against Mac. *I'm glad you're with me, buddy.*

That makes two of us. A warm, mutually shared feeling flooded Michael.

Pummeled by wind, lashed by rain, they continued to descend. Only now he found that none of it terrified him the way it had. Even his fear of heights was gone.

About a minute before they reached the ground, he spotted the complex from seven hundred feet up. Even as the storm intensified, Michael could make out the buildings along with parked cars.

What is it, Mac? he asked.

It's Mammoth Cave National Park. There's a Visitor Center and other buildings.

The name rang dim bells. *It's a pretty big cave, right?*

Yes. It's the world's largest cave system by far, nearly 500 miles long. Land near the small building to the right. It's our destination. Use the toggles by your sides.

Toggles?

Yeah, circular straps. Just slip your hands through them. Turn the left one to go left; the right one to go right.

Michael found the toggles and followed Mac's directions. Though the storm made it difficult, they worked. When he turned the right toggle to the right, their rig headed in that direction. Michael saw the building approach. Hallelujah!

Then something went wrong. The parachute twisted sideways as if stricken. Michael struggled for control.

What's wrong? he said.

I think it's the suspension lines. They got snarled.

Wind buffeted them, and they continued to descend. Only now it was too fast, and they were heading down toward the building's roof.

Michael frantically worked the controls, but they didn't respond. Squinting against the rain, he saw the roof just fifty feet below. There was a red spot in the center that looked just like a target.

Mac said, *Land on the balls of your feet, then the side of your calf. Fall sideways.*

Once more, Michael planned to follow instructions. But just before he hit, he knew they both were about to die.

CHAPTER TWENTY-FIVE
BLIND SEEING

He crashed through the roof like it was cardboard, falling to the floor where he lay stunned. While his upper body felt all right, his legs and feet hurt like hell. Even without examining them, he knew they were scraped raw. It was possible they were broken.

Are we just going to lie here? Mac asked.

Gingerly he moved his limbs. *I'm in pain. Give me a moment.*

We don't have a moment. Get your arse up!

He obeyed, his foot throbbing as he looked carefully about him. The place looked dark, but he could see well enough to tell that most of the parachute had come through the ceiling and dangled to the floor. The harness had broken on impact and come off, not even leaving a bruise. Still, he had left one hell of a spoor for anyone following his trail.

As for the store, they might have turned out the lights and left because of the storm, which he could hear raging outside. Either that, or the storm had taken out the electricity. As well as he could tell, this was some kind of gift shop.

Belatedly, he remembered his manners and took Mac out from under his shirt. *Mac, are you all right?*

It's so good of you to ask.

Sorry. I've been distracted lately.

Mac actually laughed at that. It was a whispery, old man's cackle. *I'm fine. Thanks for falling sideways to protect me.*

Had he fallen sideways to protect Mac? Michael doubted it. He'd been absorbed by other matters at the time. He tested his legs. Yep, they were sore, but his right foot was the real problem. It really hurt and he couldn't put much weight on it. Shit, he needed a cane.

Forget about your foot, Mac said. *Let's count our blessings. We're still alive!*

Mac's reminder was an excellent mood adjuster and directed Michael's thoughts to what really counted. Hell yes, they *were* still alive! Though he hadn't intended on going through the roof, he had apparently absorbed Mac's instructions and managed to fall with a damaged parachute in such a way that they both survived.

Now don't get too pleased with yourself, Mac said. *I did some research and directed us here for an important reason.*

Don't tell me, Michael said. *How many files in how many data bases did you sniff through this time?*

Only three, Mac replied. *There should be an old, locked door in back that leads into the cave system. All we must do is open it and we have an escape route.*

I left my lockpick at home.

No need to fret. Fortunately, lad, you've got me.

They moved toward the back of the shop, Michael limping painfully on his probably broken foot. He was dripping wet from the storm, and he wiped the rain out of his eyes to see. Despite the dim light, he made out trinkets and memorabilia associated with the world's largest cave system. Mammoth Cave postcards and bracelets, books and videos, coffee cups and T-shirts and other souvenirs. Limping forward, he reached out to touch something on a counter and a titanic clap of thunder made him jerk back. *Hands off! Burglars not allowed!*

The door's in back, Mac reminded him. *This-a-way.*

Right. He returned the spurned body part to Mac, holding him with both hands against his chest. Mac had grown in size and weight since the days when he'd been merely an obstructive sleep apnea machine, and Michael needed both hands anyway. He reminded himself to get serious and stop acting like a tourist.

As they neared their destination, they encountered a problem. They saw the door, but someone sat before it.

They stopped short. The shadows made it hard to see, but to Michael, it looked like a little girl in a chair. Mac concurred, after he got over his initial astonishment. *She can't be more than seven or eight*, he said.

Her age isn't the problem, Mac, Michael replied. *It's that she's here at all.*

Right. It's a complication we don't need. Didn't she hear us when we came through the roof and fell on the floor? The storm must have covered the noise we made.

Michael leaned forward. *What's she doing?*

Reading.

In this *light?* Michael glanced around. Not only had his eyes failed to adapt to the poor light, but he saw even less clearly than before. When he turned back to the girl, though, he could see that her fingers were moving on something in her lap. What was it?

It's Braille, Mac said. *She's blind.*

Of course. He could "see" that now. Mac had excellent intuition where such things were concerned. But the need to open the door and enter the cave trumped this kid's ability to read in the dark. If necessary, they could take her with them to hush her up. They needed to act *now*, though.

Mac agreed. *Yeah, we can't leave any loose ends behind, so we'll have to take her with us. Okay, grab her and open the door.*

The only thing wrong with Mac's instructions was that they created more problems than they solved. Yes, they had to take the girl with them so she didn't tell people where they'd gone. But what if she screamed and resisted? Thinking of Andy, he remembered how difficult he could be at times. Man, he could kick up one hell of a fuss. Not only that, how long could they keep this child with them? There were nearly five hundred miles in the cave system for Chrissake. On top of that, how could he open a locked door in the first place? Michael knew he was hardly a locksmith with a full set of keys ready to go. Pick a lock? He could barely pick his nose.

Still, they must act. He'd cross the bridge named HOW when he came to it. Michael took a painful step forward.

As he did, the little girl looked up at him and smiled. "Hello," she said.

She had the sweetest voice he'd ever heard, and it stopped him cold. He stared back at her. "Uh, hello," he said.

"Are you looking for my Aunt Cho? She'll be back soon to close the shop."

Uh-oh. Her aunt would be returning soon. "No, we're not," Michael said, thinking that she hadn't heard him crash through the roof. "I, uh, see you've already turned out the lights."

"Aunt Cho turned them out when she left. She pinches pennies like a pauper and likes to save. Fortunately, I'm blind and don't need light to read." She flapped the book in her lap. "See?" she said and laughed.

Fortunately, I'm blind. Under other circumstances, Michael would have liked to contemplate those words, but Mac reminded him they had a pressing matter. *Auntie could be here any moment, Mike. Let's get that friggin' door open! If necessary, I'll show you how.*

"Is someone with you?" the girl asked.

"Why do you ask?"

"It's strange. I heard you fall through the ceiling in front and then get up and limp toward me. I counted only one set of footsteps, but I feel two people. You're carrying something, but it's some kind of a machine."

Be careful with her, Mac advised. *None of this is normal.*

Mac was right. A little girl should be afraid of being alone with a strange man. But then, she shouldn't talk this way either and sounded much older than seven or eight. And being blind, how could she tell that Mac was "some kind of a machine"?

"What's your name?" Michael asked.

"It's too long to pronounce. It would take a year to say."

He leaned forward to see her better and discovered that her face was a perfect oval and looked as sweet as her voice. It was also Asian and ageless.

"Could you do me a favor?" Michael asked. "Move your chair aside so I can open the door?"

"You and your friend want to go into the cave."

"Uh, yes."

"I'll be glad to."

She rose quickly, put her book on the chair, and pulled it aside. As she did, Michael felt Mac flinch against him. *How can she move so fast?* he said. *She's blind.*

She knows this place a lot better than we do, Michael answered and went to the door.

As soon as he tried to open it, he knew he was in trouble. After ten seconds, Mac pitched in with his advice. For all Mac's confidence, though, his instructions proved useless, and the productive harmony they'd enjoyed before broke down. Michael pulled, then pushed where Mac indicated. Next, he twisted and when that didn't work, pressed where Mac told him to. They were pitted against an old, sturdy door, and the rusty, recalcitrant lock refused to cooperate. Finally, Michael shoved his shoulder against the door and pounded the knob, then searched his pockets in vain for something to pick it with.

The girl touched his arm. "Would you like me to open it for you?"

"Yes. Please."

She raised a slender hand and found the doorknob as if it were part of her. It turned obediently, and she opened the door a few inches.

He reached for it, but her hand caught his. Michael gasped in amazement. How had she done that? It was as if she used radar. Altogether, this girl with the endless name was the most unusual child he had ever met.

"Before you and your friend go," she said, "may I touch your right foot?"

"My right foot?"

"Yes, I think you hurt it."

He hesitated, but Mac prodded him. *Better do what she says.*

"Sure," Michael said. "Go ahead."

She knelt and removed his right shoe, then took his foot in both her hands. He felt her start to knead it.

"What are you do—" Michael began and stopped. The pain was already receding.

"What is your friend's name?" she asked.

"My friend?"

She means me, Mac said.

"It's Mac," he said.

"I hope he feels better soon," she said. "He's too much like me."

She put his foot down and inserted it into his shoe, then tied the laces. "Feel better?"

Michael took a few steps. "Good as new. How did you—"

"I'll open the door for you," she said. She reached for it then froze as they heard the front door opening.

"Aunt Cho, she's come back!"

The jig is up! Mac said. *She's going to see us!*

But their luck held. They heard Aunt Cho flick the switch a few times without success. "Oh, dear. The lights must have just gone out. I can't see anything. Why is there a draft in here?"

The girl motioned to them to get down behind the chair. Then she rushed toward her aunt in the front of the store.

"Watch where you step, Aunt Cho. I heard lightning strike the roof just a few minutes ago. There's shingles and stuff on the floor."

"Lightning? Oh, dear. It was such a bad storm. Thank heaven you weren't hurt! You could have been killed."

"I'm fine, Aunt Cho. I just sat here reading about Don Quixote and all the adventures he had on his fabulous quest."

"You're so brave, Cassandra. If your parents were alive, they'd be proud of you."

Crouched behind the chair, Michael and Mac heard Aunt Cho fuss over her niece to make sure she was all right. "There were some awful booms before," Aunt Cho said. "Real ear-splitters."

"I liked them," the girl said. "They were heaven's orchestra." They heard her being kissed and giggling in response.

"Cassandra, did you remember to take your meds? You know what happens when you go off them. Dr. Scott doesn't want you to have another incident."

"I know, Aunt Cho, but I feel so flat when I take them. Like a tire that's lost its air."

Open the door, Mac said. *Let's get out of here.*

I was just about to. Michael slowly rose. Bent over, he tiptoed to the door and found the knob, only to stumble and almost fall.

Aunt Cho spoke up sharply. "What was that sound back there?"

"I didn't hear anything, Aunt Cho."

"Well, I did. It was in the back room."

Michael returned to the chair and crouched behind it, clutching Mac to his chest. He could see better now and couldn't miss Aunt Cho's approach. Aunt Cho turned out to be a woman over six feet tall who reminded him of Heavenly Beverly except for the fact that her plentiful muscles hadn't turned to fat yet. There were two other differences as well.

Aunt Cho was wearing a policeman's uniform, and she was pointing a bright flashlight in his direction. "There's someone here."

Michael got as low as he could. The chair had separate slats, so the flashlight's blinding rays went right through them. Peering up, he could see Aunt Cho's suspicious glare piercing the area behind the chair. She looked fired up and determined to apprehend public enemy number one.

We're done for, Mac said. *We should never have come in here.*

Aunt Cho's massive nostrils sniffed. She pulled her revolver and started to move around the chair. Just one more step…

Cassandra rushed up and tugged Aunt Cho's arm. "Come back, Aunt Cho. There's nobody. I want to show you something."

Her aunt resisted but she had lost the scent. Reluctantly, she accompanied her niece back to the front of the store while talking about how T-storms always gave her the jitters. A minute later, Michael and Mac were relieved to see Cassandra return alone. She reached out and touched the doorknob.

"It's a magic door," she said. "A *portal*. I learned that a long time ago when I was young. You just have to discover its secret."

"Secret?"

She opened the door wide. "Yes. And there are twelve magic realms out there, each one more wonderful and amazing than the last. You just have to know how to look."

Michael hesitated, then stepped through the door.

"Wait," Cassandra whispered. "May I see him?"

Michael stopped. *What about it, Mac?*

Go ahead. I wouldn't miss this for anything.

Michael hesitated, then held Mac out. Cassandra smiled and touched him. "I know what you're going through," she whispered.

How could she? Only *I* do, Michael thought. He wanted to say that, but Cassandra grabbed his hand. "Let me go with you," she said. "I can be your guide."

Michael had a son about her age, and he'd bet they'd get along fine. But it wasn't in the cards. "You have to stay here," he said. "Your aunt loves you."

"I know," she said reluctantly.

"And try to take your meds even if they do make you feel flat." He freed his hand from hers and stroked her cheek.

"I know you're on a secret mission and bad men are after you," Cassandra said. "I promise not to tell anyone you were here or where you've gone."

Where did she get the "secret mission" and "bad men" from? At the moment, she seemed more like an oracle than a child.

Cassandra leaned close. "Watch out for windmills," she said. "They can deceive you and lead you astray." She smiled, then withdrew like a shadow. Puzzled by her words, he pulled the door shut, not sure at all that he had given her the best advice concerning her meds.

Darkness pounced and swallowed them in a single bite.

CHAPTER TWENTY-SIX
TWELVE MAGIC REALMS

The darkness was so intense, the only things Michael could see were tiny firings in his eyeballs. He clung to them for comfort.

Are you sure this is our best course of action? he thought.

Yes.

Since we don't have any food or other provisions, did you commission a feasibility study?

Nothing so elaborate, Mac replied. *I just went with my gut, though technically, I don't have one. Plus, I have a complete diagram of the cave system in my head.*

Michael rubbed his eyes, wishing he could see something. *So, it's like the sewer system all over again. We've come full circle.*

Yes, except this time we don't have that maniac Delgata chasing us.

Only the government. They're out there, you know.

There was no need for Mac to answer. Michael gazed out into blackness. Cassandra had said there were twelve magic realms out there. He'd be so relieved to see just one.

They couldn't just stay here. Michael held his hand out for protection from obstacles and started to walk, alert for sensorial cues or clues. After a minute, Mac broke into his concentration.

I can guide you, you know. Just like when we flew the chopper.

Go ahead.

Michael felt Mac gently take over. It was like a warm psychic massage or having a friendly hand on the tiller or a wise skipper at the helm. Synergy. Yes, Michael thought, we both add to each other and are worth far more together than when we're apart.

Mac asked, *Do you think we can trust Cassandra not to tell about us?*

I think so, Michael said. *She's quite a girl. She cured my foot just by touching it.*

Or she convinced you to heal yourself. That's magic, too.

Maybe there was magic on both sides. Mac, something she said has been nagging at me. What did she mean when she said both of you were alike and she knew how you felt?

She meant we were kindred souls.

Kindred souls. It was a nice phrase, but it didn't tell him much. So he guessed: *She meant you both have some of the same emotional problems.*

That about sums it up, Mac said. *Oh, hey, look at those bones.*

What bones? Christ, Mac, I can't see.

I think I can remedy that. Mac's head lit up, projecting a beam down at the ground.

Michael jerked in surprise. *How'd you do that, Mac? I know you're a machine, but there's nothing to plug into here to juice you back up. Not a single socket or power source in the joint.*

Au contraire, mon ami. There's a nearby generator I tapped into. It's strictly self-serve.

Holding Mac with one hand, Michael bent and picked up what looked like an old femur.

Hmmm, could be Cherokee or Shawnee, Mac said. *They were active in these parts. Or perhaps Chickasaw. Judging from its age, my guess is that some Indian—whoops, I mean Native American—was exploring these caves a few centuries back and ran into trouble or couldn't find his way out. It happened sometimes, you know.*

Michael put the bone down. *Let's get moving! I know you have a map in your head, so where do we go?*

Mac said, *This cave comes to a dead-end about five miles from here. Fortunately, there's a narrow passage to a larger cave before then, one with guided tours, lights, and handrails.*

Michael asked, *Will anyone be there right now, while a storm's blowing? It's most unlikely.*

Michael hesitated. *Mac, something's happened to you lately. You're not the same.*

Mac sighed. *I'm like that blind girl, Cassandra. Sometimes I feel all alone like a motherless child. I love you, Michael, but please remember I'm a machine. I was never meant to be quasi-human. I'm running down, sputtering out, operating on residual power.*

N-nonsense, Michael said. *You're much more than a machine. There's so much you can do that I never could. You're light-years beyond me.*

N-nonsense in return, Mac gently mocked. *Oh, buddy, from the beginning you've been far beyond me. Don't you know that? You fill me with awe and envy. Sometimes I've almost hated you because you can have a mate, friends, and a child, a place in the natural world, while I can only run on residual power that wanes with every second.*

Michael started to dispute Mac's claims, but his friend squirmed against his chest. "Come on," Mac said aloud, "let's go. On the way I'll educate you about this cave system."

As Michael walked, Mac told him more than he wanted to know about the Mammoth Cave system. It was nearly three hundred and fifty million years old and consisted primarily of limestone topped by a layer of sandstone. The most interesting fact was that the system was still being explored and still growing as rainwater continued to enter it and enlarge the caverns and passageways. It was a living thing, and it was possible the neglected, mostly forgotten, self-enclosed little vein they traveled now would one day become part of it.

Maybe, but to Michael, it was a boring, tedious vein. Dirt floor, dull brown and gray walls. Once Mac pointed out the rustle of bats near the ceiling and some stalactites pointing down. It failed to impress him. Where was even one of Cassandra's twelve magical realms? *That* would merit his interest. He imagined the blind girl exploring the dark cave with sure-footed confidence and conjuring up all sorts of wonders. Beautiful, fantastic fairytale lands beyond description. How could her imagination have been so rich when it had so little to work with? And how could she have cured his foot with just a touch? Or convinced him to heal himself? Either way or both, wasn't that magic, too?

He dismissed such thoughts and focused on what worried him most, which was Mac and two words he had used.

Residual power.

The words made him think of a battery running down, which was what Mac essentially was. He tried to guard his thoughts, but Mac stirred with outrage in his hands. *Concentrate on walking. Don't bury me yet!*

Michael might have been comforted were it not for the tone of bravado in Mac's voice. It also didn't help that Mac's light flickered and went out, plunging them into darkness again.

Don't worry, Mac told him. *It'll return soon.*

Before he could respond, he heard a sound about ten feet in front of him. It seemed to be near the ground, though he couldn't be sure. He heard a harsh snarl and tensed, instantly stopping. Various sounds ensued as the creature, whatever it was, displayed its repertoire. A loud purr, a grunt, even a whistle. In the dark, it was hard to tell where the thing actually was, but he had the feeling it was threatening him and perhaps about to attack. Since the last thing he wanted to do was to challenge phantoms in the dark, he backed off a few steps.

No need to do that, Mac said. *Here, I've just about got it.*

Mac's light flickered, went out, and flickered on again. Michael blinked, trying to see his challenger. In the meantime, he imagined all sorts of mythical and fabulous beasts, some with multiple heads and hissing fangs. Perhaps it was even hideous Edgar P. Delgata, returned from the grave for round two. Or the family of Major Hammer had prepared a gruesome surprise for him in payment for his mistreatment of their illustrious head. For a moment, before he could see, Michael was positive that the last explanation was the right one.

The light stabilized, and he beheld the creature. It was neither a legendary beast, Edgar P. Delgata, nor a horrible monster sent by Major Hammer's family. Instead, it was a medium-sized mammal with dense fur and a masked-bandit appearance. Black fur around its eyes contrasted with a white face. What really caught his attention, though, were the dozen or so small white babies that clung to the mother's back and sides, babies that Michael realized she had wanted to protect.

Procyon lotor, Mac said. *Say hello to Mrs. Raccoon.*

She has quite a family, Michael observed.

It's probably not her first. Life goes on here, my boy. More than two hundred species inhabit Mammoth Cave. White-tailed deer, foxes, finches, rabbits, owls, even my favorite, a tiny, pygmy shrew.

Michael didn't need another lecture, and he noticed that the raccoon was not giving up any ground. She dug into the dirt with her claws, and her bright eyes bored into his. For that matter, so did the eyes of all the babies clinging to her body. *Do we need to worry about you?* they seemed to ask.

I come in peace, Michael thought. He moved around them to the left. He didn't know if all those eyes watched him, but he assumed they did.

He'd gone only a little way when he discerned something in the shadows. It looked like a square object against the wall, and when he went there, he discovered a large cardboard box. Mac produced a feeble light that enabled him to see that the top flaps were taped shut, as if to thwart thieves. But tape would be a weak deterrent, and this dark cave was a foolish place to keep anything of value. It made no sense.

He pulled off the tape, attaching one end to the box so he wouldn't lose it, and opened the flaps. Bending down, he peered in, pointing Mac carefully so he could see better. After a moment, he reached down and picked up one of the objects he saw so they could both examine it.

It was a knight on a brown plastic horse, about three inches high.

What's it for? Mac said.

Mac's ignorance was another sign of his decline. *Can't you guess? It's a toy knight on a horse.*

Bingo. And the box was taped shut so rats and other critters wouldn't get in. Michael bent down, picked up a few more toys and sat down. *Here, let me show you.*

He placed the knight on the ground. Next came two serfs or farmers, which he placed nearby. The fourth piece looked like a lovely princess in a gossamer gown. The fifth piece was the biggest of the lot and a real surprise. Even in Mac's feeble glow, Michael could tell it was a fiery red dragon with outstretched wings and open jaws.

The girl, Mac whispered in his mind. *She put them here. She said something about...*

Magical realms, Michael finished. He imagined Cassandra coming out here to her own secret, private place and sitting exactly where he sat now to lay these and other pieces out. Alone, with no one to disturb her, she would create her own worlds, each filled with its own cast of heroic and monstrous characters. Knights and dragons, princes and princesses, wizards and witches. Good would battle with evil, and from time to time, she would bring new toys, perhaps some which she had made with her own hands. The possibilities were endless.

He could feel Mac's wonder now. *How did I miss it?* he said.

It's easy to do, Michael said. *We all miss connections.*

Well, hey, say, I didn't miss this. You dropped something when you took the toys out of the box.

Dropped something? Where?

Right next to the box.

Michael peered down and found another piece right where Mac said it was. Only it wasn't a piece exactly. It was a familiar tube twenty-six inches long from his childhood.

It's a flute, Mac said. *A magic flute. C'mon, Mike. Play something for us. Pipe me a ditty of no tone.*

I'll have to pass on that. Playing the flute had been one of many failures in his life. In the seventh grade, he had wanted to join the school orchestra, only to find he had no talent.

Why don't you want to play it, Mike? Oh wait, I see. You weren't very good on it.

Michael remembered how they had laughed at his audition. *That's putting it mildly. I sucked big-time. Mangled the notes and had no breath control. Bad as I was, though, I was practically a master on the flute compared to what I did on the trumpet.*

He raised the flute to his lips and blew. To his surprise, he produced delicate notes of haunting beauty. Below, on the ground, the knight seemed to respond. He nudged his mount with his spurs and advanced toward the dragon, which blew fire from its nostrils in response. The princess and two serfs cheered, urging their hero on.

Michael felt a wave of dizziness and closed his eyes. When he opened them, he was sitting in a saddle upon a horse. The saddle was uncomfortable, and so was the suit of heavy armor he wore. It had a helmet with narrow eye-slits that made it hard to see.

That was not the worst thing about his new situation. The worst thing was that even though the eye-slits were narrow, he could clearly see a monstrous dragon waiting before him. It had mighty, arabesque wings, a glittering, scaly body, and a barbed tail. Plus, it was blowing flames from its cavernous nostrils as if in anticipation. Though the dragon was at least a hundred feet away, it possessed a terrible, terrifying beauty. He could also feel the heat of the flames and smell their sweet stench, which made him think of babies being roasted alive.

This couldn't be happening! He must be dreaming! He glanced about and received another shock. He was in a vast arena or coliseum with tens of thousands of spectators cheering for him in the stands. Multicolored banners and pennants waved in the wind, which was filled with exotic scents. Unless he was mistaken, the tiny toy princess he had set on the ground was now a full-sized woman sitting next to the mayor or king, her eyes glistening with excitement.

Michael wanted to scream that this was all a mistake. He wasn't a knight and couldn't even ride a horse. Hell, his armor weighed a ton, and it was hard to hold up the lance. Before him, the dragon crept closer, acquiring greater significance with each step. It was not only a fearsome beast, but it reminded him of the mighty federal government itself. The connection between the two seemed so close that it made his task even more impossible. To defeat one he must destroy both, beast and bureaucracy entwined. He hefted the lance under his right arm. To vanquish such a foe, his aim must be absolutely true. He must impale the creature in its most vital spot. But how could he do that when he didn't even know where that spot was?

He glanced again at the princess, who now looked exactly like Laura. What a welcome change, but what was Laura doing here, in this strange and dangerous place he found himself in? He wanted Laura very much, wanted her lips, body, and company in every way imaginable, but what he wanted most was guidance as to what he should do. His horse stomped the ground, eager for battle, and he reached down and stroked its muscular brown hide, admiring its strength and its flowing mane. How beautiful and warm his mount was in the sun! He could feel the sinews move in readiness beneath his fingers.

Looking up, he beheld the dragon's most vulnerable spot. Yes, there it was waiting for him at the base of the massive throat. Somehow he knew it was the one place where this monster could be killed. His aim just had to be exact, and he had to hit it true. He lifted the lance, sick with dread but firm with resolve. He could do this. He could!

Trumpets blared in bright, powerful bursts—a call to battle! Time to joust against a dragon! He nudged his steed with his knees, and it instantly responded. At the same time, the dragon charged toward him, its wings beating the air and its breath a raging furnace. And its eyes—oh, Christ, its eyes! They blazed with hate and hellfire, capable of searing the soul with the slightest glance. He saw the dragon raise its head again, exposing its single weakness, and he charged directly at it, knowing he would only have a few seconds to strike.

At the last instant, the dragon roared and leaped over him, raking his cheek with a talon as it passed. Michael continued on, then reined his horse around. To his chagrin, he discovered that his adversary had changed places with him and now waited where he had begun. As the crowd screamed, his guts twisted in shame. How cleverly the dragon had tricked and toyed with him as it swept by! Now it stood mocking him and laughing, delighted by his disgrace.

Enraged, Michael touched his cheek, which was ripped to the bone and bleeding profusely on his armor. It hurt like hell, and he was lucky the dragon hadn't torn out an eye. By all that was holy, this cursed and vile creature would not live to celebrate a second victory! Driving his spurs into his steed's sides, he set forth again, hearing the excited spectators cheer him on. Once again his horse's hoofs pounded the ground, and he prepared his lance for a killing thrust. The dragon was clever, but this time Michael read his foe's sly plan in the facets of its demonic eyes. As it rose above him, he drove his pointed lance skyward, puncturing one of its beautiful, ornately patterned wings. Continuing on, he heard the dragon's shrieks of pain, mingled with rage and hunger for vengeance.

Michael reined his mount in and swung it around. *Very well, my enemy. You shall have your third chance.* For a moment he hesitated, then he dug in his spurs and galloped back, every atom of his being focused on a single point. The dragon, in turn, charged directly at him, clearly determined to devour him whole. As it drew close, though, Michael saw it make its signature mistake. It raised its head slightly, and yep, there it was—its Achilles' heel! He grinned in anticipation, carefully adjusting his lance. At the moment of contact, he felt a most satisfying sensation. The dragon's flesh yielded, and the lance slid in. Ah, yes. This time he would not fail…

The dragon vanished, along with the cheering multitude. Stunned, Michael found himself sitting on the ground before a few toys. He held a flute in his hands.

"Michael," Mac said, "are you all right?"

Michael lowered the flute and touched his cheek, finding it unharmed. Talk about magical realms, he had just entered one! "I wish I'd had a chance to know that little girl better," he said. "All we had were a few minutes."

"I know," Mac said. "She's special and has an old soul."

Michael rose. Oddly, though the dream was over, his mouth was still filled with fear and blood-lust. He could also still feel the saddle, and his ass was sore. He rubbed it, wondering where the dragon had gone and if his dream-self had managed to kill it or if he had been killed instead.

He picked up the toys and returned them to the box, careful not to break any. He put the princess in last, kissing her as he did. Then he taped the flaps shut, just as he'd found them. Briefly, he considered telling Mac about his dream but decided not to. Let it be his one secret from his friend.

I have something rather interesting to show you, Mac said. *It's just a little farther on.*

CHAPTER TWENTY-SEVEN
RESIDUAL POWER

"Just a little farther on" turned out to be quite a distance. He walked and he walked, carrying Mac against his chest. The magic seemed to have drained from the cave, and in its place, he smelled the sour stench of his own sweat. And why not. He had come a long way in the last few days and experienced some hairy adventures. Jumping out of a chopper with a makeshift parachute of questionable quality on his back and meeting a magical girl with a gun-toting aunt were only the most recent.

Now and then, Mac emitted odd, discordant sounds. He tried not to think of a clock running down but it was difficult.

How much farther? he asked.

We're getting warm. Keep watching the wall to your right.

What are we looking for?

No answer. Michael obeyed Mac's instruction and kept a close watch. Even still, he almost missed the narrow passage in the wall.

We go through there?

You *go through there and follow the cave system to freedom. The passage is tight, especially when it approaches the next cave. You'll have to tuck in your belly and really squeeze onward.*

Michael held Mac up so they could see each other. On Mac's screen, his friend had chosen the face of a tired and ravaged old man. *It's not that bad, is it?* he asked.

Set me down, Mike.

He grunted, not wanting to obey. *How do you expect me to follow the caves without a map?*

Set me down and I'll show you.

Steeped in dread, Michael placed Mac near the entrance to the passageway. He stood up and waited.

The old man on Mac's screen smiled. *My race is run, and I've come to the end of my journey.*

Michael spread his arms. *What the hell are you talking about?*

You're a lousy actor, my boy. You know *what I'm talking about. During the last few days, you've observed my irrationality, my bouts with stupidity. I've been operating on residual power, the dregs of my energy. If I were human, the diagnosis would be Alzheimer's or something similar.*

But why has this happened? Mac asked.

The feds are right. I am an "anomaly." In short, I was never meant to be. I'm an accident, a perversion of the natural order and it's time for me to go.

Michael shook his head. *You can't leave me, Mac. You're too wonderful, able to do so many amazing things. If one of us has to go, it should be me.*

That's not the way things work. Mac paused. *You've never really understood me, Michael. I'm just a fancy air machine that used to have a hose. You* are *the one who's wonderful because you gave me real life. I would have no existence at all without you. Somehow your breath, your breathing the air from my hose summoned me into being and gave me sentience and a conscious mind. Somehow it taught me to love you.*

A tear ran down Michael's cheek. *What am I to do?*

Follow the passage and then the caves to freedom. Find Andy and Laura, who you love so much, and be sure to tell Laura I love her. I know it will be difficult because the government will track you like Indian scouts and try to capture you. But you are resourceful, Michael. I've seen it many times.

Michael started to speak but a three-dimensional image of the cave system suddenly appeared in his mind. It was vast and complex, and he gasped in wonder.

How did you do that? he asked.

You're an electrical system, Michael. I just downloaded a program into you. If you concentrate, you can find our exact location and the passage beside us. With a little practice, you can use this map to find just about anything and navigate anywhere.

Mac...

There's no time to chatter, Mike. I'm about done. I just wanted to thank you for giving me life and letting me love you. Thank you too for all our exciting adventures. The ancient face on the screen pressed closer. *My mind is fading. It made me forget. There's one more thing I must tell you before I go. It's the most important thing of all. You...*

Mac stopped talking. The face on the screen frothed in a wave of golden bubbles. He waited, hoping for some Delphic utterance that would make it all clear. Then the face faded and disappeared. After a moment, the CABS machine began to dissolve.

No! This can't happen! You can't die!

Michael glanced around, seeking a solution, anything to stop Mac's disintegration. But all he saw was dirt and barren walls, a rock formation off in the shadows. Fighting off tears, he bent over Mac. In just seconds the dissolution had spread like wildfire. Nearly a quarter of Mac was gone now, had just bubbled away in a golden froth. And he just knelt helplessly over the machine and watched it melt, unable to do anything. He reached out desperately and picked Mac up, but he saw at once that his touch only hastened the process. Feeling heartsick, he had no choice but to set the machine down.

Please don't die, Mac. I love you.

In less than a minute, though, there was nothing left.

Michael dried his eyes. "Goodbye, Mac," he said. "I want to thank you, too."

When he went to the passage, he found it looked even narrower than before. Now it resembled a hairline fracture, a mere slit in the rock. How was he expected to navigate such a slender channel without scraping the skin off his bones? Well, Mac had thought he could, and that was good enough for him.

He turned sideways and slipped inside, trying to forget about Mac, who he'd never see again. He hadn't realized before how much he'd liked it when Mac called him "my boy," or lapsed into profanity. And how would he get by without Mac's advice and instructions, and most of all, his selfless love? What was it Mac had said?

I just wanted to thank you for giving me life and letting me love you.

He bumped his knee against the wall and almost screamed in pain. Try not to think about Mac. Concentrate on your task. You can mourn later!

Michael continued on, sucking his belly in and sliding his back against the wall. Out in the cave, without Mac's light, it had been difficult to see. Now, in this dark, tight crevice, the only thing he could discern was the firings in his eyeballs again. He soldiered on, though, wishing he were thinner so he could make quicker progress. This close space reminded him of the iron maiden, another torture device, the major difference being that it didn't have spikes strategically placed to impale his eyes and other vital organs. He tried everything he could think of to find more room, including sliding down, but it was no wider close to the ground than it was higher up.

Then he got stuck.

He didn't know how he did it, only that he'd managed to wedge himself in tight. He felt like a cork stuck in a wine bottle. Squirming, flexing and reflexing his muscles had no appreciable effect. He could go neither forward nor back. Bad as his situation was, he suddenly had a thought that froze him cold.

Mac had made a mistake.

Only Mac didn't make mistakes, certainly not a mistake of this magnitude. And Mac had seemed so confident he could do this. He tried to remember what Mac had said about the passage but something else came to mind. It was the very last thing Mac had said. He'd said there was *one more thing I must tell you before I go.* And it had been *the most important thing of all.* But Mac had not been able to tell him what it was.

He tried to guess but something else occurred to him. It was the map or schematic of the cave system that Mac had implanted in his brain. He immediately called it up and examined it.

It took him only twenty seconds to zero in on the passageway he was stuck in. Yes, it was narrow all right, a mere capillary in the rock. He located a place, though, where it bulged just a little, and squeezed toward it. Nothing changed, though, and he felt his spirits sink in terror. Perhaps lately, the rock had shifted here, moved just a little. All it would take was a tiny change that wasn't recorded on his map to make it impossible to move. As it was, he could barely breathe in here, and if he tried to scream, it wouldn't be very loud. Nobody would hear him if he called for help.

One thing was for sure. This wasn't one of Cassandra's magical realms, filled with romance and excitement. Or maybe it was of the black magic kind, the close, suffocating kind he'd learned to fear as a little boy when his mother had locked him in a closet for being bad, though he never could remember what he'd done. The kind swarming with evil, creepy creatures that poured endlessly from his own imagination. The kind where you could scream and scream forever, and no one would ever come to let you out.

A ghastly image filled Michael's mind. One day in the distant future, archeologists would excavate these caves and find a dried-out skeleton trapped within this wall. They'd look at each other and smile, wondering who could be so stupid as to get caught here like a fly in amber. Perhaps they'd even laugh and crack jokes.

Michael tried to be calm and think rationally. Forget about never holding your son again or embracing Laura. You will! But his fate seemed sealed. Face it, he had only seen what he'd wanted to see in the map and had exaggerated the width of the passageway. Mac had made a mistake, that was all, a mistake that would cause his death. His friend had said it himself more than once. He was impaired and exhausted, operating on residual power.

Though it seemed certain he was doomed, something in Michael would not give up. He kept trying to move on, bruising and punishing his flesh with the effort. And gradually, to his relief, the walls parted a little, and he wormed his way through. At first progress was merely difficult; then, to his amazement, the crack widened, and it became easy. Soon, he staggered out into the next cave, and took a deep breath of the open air.

He could see better here. This cave was dim but doable. He dusted off his clothes, peering about, then consulted the map in his head for directions. Yep, that-a-way, to his left and straight ahead.

Before he could move, an acrid smell made him sneeze, then sneeze again. He covered his nose, trying to suppress a third sneeze. This was the big one, the earthshaker that would register on seismic scales halfway around the world. And even if it wasn't, what if a Mammoth Cave National Park employee happened to be here and heard it? How would he explain his presence? And surely he would then be caught and taken into custody.

Seconds passed, then a full minute. No, he was all alone. With a torrential T-storm coming, the park's employees would have retreated behind locked doors, or everyone would have gone home. In relief, he felt his titanic need to emit a third blast subside.

Michael started walking, holding the handrail fixed to the wall. The ground sloped gently down, making it easier to walk. He stopped once and looked back, fearing that someone was following him, but he didn't see anything. There were plenty of shadows, though, and he couldn't be sure. Perhaps a military unit was closing in on him, about to pounce.

About him, the cave's shadows pressed close, whispering secrets that had been old a hundred million years ago. Menace saturated the air, and he sensed that at any moment, ageless creatures could leap out and seize him by the throat. He recalled a horror movie he had once seen with just such a storyline, and what had happened to the foolish man who hadn't listened to warnings.

Stop worrying about it. You're all alone here, and it's just a cave.

He continued on. Though he was relieved to be alive, he had a heavy heart. Mac was gone, gone forever. He had vanished into the earth, probably leaving not even a microscopic trace. Unless you cremated them, people at least had bodies and something to bury. But Mac had left nothing, and therefore there was no reason even to put up a headstone. It was as if his friend had never existed, and as he walked, he found himself missing Mac's inner voice more and more. He had never realized how deeply he depended on it. Lately, it had always been there, always responding to his own thoughts and questions. It was like the beat of his second heart. Mac had been his other self, and in a way, Mac's voice had validated his existence and made him real. Now that Mac's voice was gone, he doubted his friend had ever existed in the first place. Perhaps he himself was an illusion.

No, that was nonsense. Mac *had* existed, and he too was real. Mac lived on in Michael's memories of him. From now on, though, he would have to carry on without him. The worst thing of all was that he had lost the loving companion and sidekick who had warmed his heart and shared his thoughts. Mac had been as close as his breath, his other soul, and he would never see him again.

Michael grew so depressed that he dropped his guard. He rounded a corner to find three young people lying on a blanket, two men and a woman, sharing a whiskey bottle and other things.

They saw him and rose quickly and came forward, "Hola!" said the man who took the lead. He pointed a flashlight at Michael, half-blinding him. "Where did you come from? How did you get in here?"

Michael stopped walking. "I might ask you the same question."

The other man pulled up his pants and then produced a gun, which he pointed at Michael's chest. "Answer his question, man. How the fuck did you get in here? The entrance is locked tight."

What kind of mess did I get myself into this time? "It's a long story," Michael said, hating himself for being so careless. He had a bad feeling this wasn't going to end well.

CHAPTER TWENTY-EIGHT
A WORKING HYPOTHESIS

The woman approached him. She was even younger than the men and might have been pretty if she cleaned herself up and — in his opinion — had fewer facial piercings. She had what looked like a well-smoked joint and appeared to be half-stoned. She puffed her cigarette as she sashayed around him, sizing him up.

"He don't look too dangerous, Chance," she said to the leader. "Kinda cute, in fact."

Chance drew his own gun and handed her the flashlight. "Search him for cash and anything valuable, Esther. See if he has a wallet." He stared at Michael with dead, lifeless eyes that reminded him of a shark's.

Esther moved closer and reached for Michael's back pocket. He waved her off. As he did, he felt wetness drip down his side. It was likely a scratch from the tight crevice he had navigated.

"You're not getting any money from me," he said.

"Whoo-ooo! You sound tough," the other man said. He had a ragged beard and wore glasses with one cracked lens.

The leader approached Michael, brandishing his gun. To Michael, it had a lethal, utilitarian design and looked like the Glock he had recently seen in a gun display. The man spat at Michael's feet and took a long gulp from the whiskey bottle. "Let's pop him." He pointed at the wall. "We can stand him up there and have target practice. *Poof! Poof! Poof! Poof! Poof!*"

The woman whooped, delighted with the idea. She wore scruffy shorts with a tattoo on her inner thigh that claimed she'd been *Born to be BAD*. "Can I screw him first, Chance? You know, so he can die happy?"

"Hell, no. Baby, I want him sad and mad, right up to the time I waste him." He grinned and pointed his gun at Michael's belly. "Roy, put your popgun away and take the flashlight, then search him. See if he has any rings. And don't take no for an answer."

Roy shoved his gun in his pocket and received the flashlight from Esther. Then he turned and held it under his chin so Michael could get the full effect of his glory. A scruffy beard, a cracked lens, and crude, monstrous features. It all added up to one truly ugly and scary sonofabitch. When Roy grinned, Michael thought of gargoyles. This guy belonged hanging off the edge of a cathedral somewhere.

Chance snorted impatiently. "Roy, stop clownin' around and get your ass in gear."

"Okay, boss. Just having fun."

As if Roy's weird demonstration had conjured them, Michael heard squeaks and the swishing of wings.

"Bats," Chance announced. "Damn. Wish I'd brought my night-vision goggles."

"*I'm* the Batman," Roy crowed in delight. "The Caped Crusader, the Dark Knight, and the enemy of crime!" He danced on his toes and pointed up in excitement. "Man, look at that big mutha."

Michael turned, seeing small brown creatures flitting about, the sounds of their wings reverberating against the walls. A couple of them broke away from the colony and flew over their heads, causing Roy to squeal and duck. Michael glanced at Chance, hoping the leader was distracted and he could charge him, but his gun remained fixed on Michael's chest. No luck there.

He watched the bats flap back and forth. How excited they seemed, as if motivated by an urgent mission. He wished he could join them and fly off, all the way to safety and freedom, to the family he had lost. Chance tried to speak up once, but the bats' frenzy drowned him out. After twenty more seconds, though, their urgency waned and they disappeared as if by magic, perhaps to another realm.

"Okay," Chance said. "Matinee's over. Roy, pat him down."

As Roy approached him, Michael forgot about the bleeding cut on his side. He had something more serious to worry about, the fact that he was about to get killed. He could feel it in the casual tone of their voices, in their sneering disregard for his safety. He steeled himself as Roy checked his hands and wrists and started to paw him over, searching him in intimate places. The slime bag's falsetto babble was even worse than the physical invasion. "Sneaky, sneaky, sneaky. Peeky, peeky, peeky!"

Michael clenched a fist. Damn it, if he was going to die, he'd go out fighting. He'd bash in these bastards' faces and do his best to wipe out their smiles.

There's one more thing I must tell you before I go, Mac had said. *It's the most important thing of all.*

What could it be, and why did he think of it now? What did it matter? He felt Roy liberate his wallet from his back pocket and heard him hoot. Roy peered inside the wallet with the aid of the flashlight, then waved the wallet in the air. "Paydirt!"

"Bring it here," Chance said.

As Roy obeyed, Michael sniffed in disdain. Paydirt, hell. There was only forty-some dollars in his wallet. He tried to focus on what was really important, knowing he didn't have much time and could get shot dead at any moment. What was it? Oh yes, there was that other mystery...

Why did the crack in the wall suddenly widen for me when it wouldn't budge before? It was as if Mac, or some remnant of his friend had looked after him, helping him to open it.

It was a ridiculous notion, but he felt it was true. He also felt a buzzing sensation begin deep in his brain. Mac, he thought, what should I do? Should I test what I feel?

Yes, he imagined Mac saying, *I think you should. You have no other choice.*

Okay, then. He would.

"Shit," Chance said, "there's only chump change here, not even enough to buy a line. No credit cards either. No nothing." He started to toss the wallet away, then his finger snagged on something. He aimed the flashlight at it. "What is this? Looks like a photo. Some kid." He pointed the flashlight at Michael. "Yours?"

Michael felt a chill. "Yeah, it's Andy," he said. "My son." He recalled searching the wallet twice for the photo without success. Now this cheap crook had found it by accident.

Chance flipped the photo and wallet away like garbage. Then he shoved the money in his pocket and returned the flashlight to Roy. "Go back and search him some more. Watch him close so he doesn't jump you. And don't miss nothin'."

"Right." Roy straightened the cracked lens of his glasses. Then he returned to Michael and resumed searching his clothes and body, occasionally poking him with the flashlight and laughing like a hyena. Michael thought of trying to grab the gun from Roy's pocket but knew the chance of turning the tables on this bunch was slim.

In the meantime, the buzzing sensation Michael had felt before grew, spreading throughout his body. Hey, look at me, he thought. I've got a buzz on! He watched Roy kneel in front of him and run his hands up and down his legs and stomach, searching for booty. Since Roy kept shifting the flashlight from one hand to the other, Michael got a good, close view of his paws. Roy's hands were rough and twisted, and they had the blackest damned nails he'd ever seen. They looked like gravedigger hands, and Michael would bet they had lifted many a spade over some poor, bushwhacked bastard's final resting place. The thought gave him scant comfort.

Finally, Roy slapped Michael's thigh and gave him a mocking glance. "That's it, José," he said in disgust. "That measly wallet's all he's got."

"Forty-two shitty dollars," Esther said. "And no credit cards. Maybe I should give him a go, search him really close." She raised her hands. "Magic fingers," she said, slurring the syllables. "If he's stashed something anywhere, I'll find it." To illustrate, she knelt before Michael and explored his crotch. Her fingers moved like spiders, dancing over his groin. She peered up and grinned at him. Despite the situation, she looked a lot better than Roy.

"How do you like it, stud?" she asked.

My body's another magic realm, he thought. Somehow, it's growing stronger and more capable. He eyed Esther's dingy charms, feeling something stir within him.

Chance laughed, but after a few seconds, he stopped. "That's enough," he said. "We got more important things to do than get you laid again."

Esther removed her hands and turned her back to her friends. Michael saw the lustful expression on her face drop like a poorly designed mask. Desperate loneliness replaced it, along with an emptiness that tugged at his heart. She clutched his hand then moved away, leaving him with her yearning and her naked need. He felt pity for her as well as aroused and angry.

Despite the distraction, Michael grew more certain about his new abilities. It was like a deep, wordless knowledge. But he must test what he felt in order to confirm that it was really true. And he must do it *now* before he got himself shot.

He reached out into their minds and smiled when he quickly succeeded. Yep, he'd known he could do it, and the ease with which he did was further proof of his new gifts. Only Roy's mind offered any difficulty because it was messy and bordered on chaos. In fact, the man was half-crazy! It was only a minor impediment, though, and after stimulating a few of Roy's dendrites, Michael planted his psychic switch there too and made Roy's brain receptive, obedient to his will.

Michael raised his hand and sent out a mental command. *Chance and Roy, point your guns at each other.* A moment later, he laughed. "Be careful with your pistols, boys. It's not polite to shoot unless I give you permission."

"What the fuck are you talking about?" Roy said. But he was already pulling his weapon from his pocket and pointing it at Chance, who was doing the same. They stood, aiming their guns at each other's chest.

Esther screamed. "What are you two doing? Are you crazy?"

Michael could tell from the men's screams and terrified faces that they realized they had a serious problem. Yes, indeed, they weren't so cocky now. Chance, the stronger, was able to resist Michael's will and turn his gun a few inches in his direction. Michael, enjoying the men's panic, responded too late, and Chance fired at him. A bullet grazed Michael's shirt next to his ribcage and ricocheted off the wall behind him.

Shit, he could have killed me. Stay alert!

Michael slapped Chance back like a misbehaving child. Chance obediently pointed his Glock at Roy again. When Roy started to whimper, Michael punched his face hard from ten feet away. As for Esther's irritating wail, Michael simply made her shut up and gave her an order.

"Esther, get my wallet and pick up everything that was in it, including the money from Chance, and bring it here. Understand?"

"Uh, sure, honey." While Roy and Chance stood pointing their guns at each other, she carried out his order. "Here it is," she said, "I think I got everything."

"Is my son's photo there?"

She squinted at her hand. "Think so," she said.

"Okay, put everything in the wallet and slip it in my back pocket. When you're finished, go stand with your friends."

After she obeyed, he took stock of himself. His new power felt good, an intoxicating gift he knew he had received directly from Mac just before he died. It was Michael's inheritance, and he had a right to use it any damned way he wanted. He was tired of being pushed around, of running from people who wanted to abuse him and throw him in jail, study and dissect him like a bug. It was high time he got a little payback.

"W-what's w-wrong with us?" Chance sputtered. "W-what have you done?"

The buzzing sensation grew still more intense. It felt as if his whole brain was being rearranged. "I haven't done anything," he replied. "It's you who are going to do it to yourselves."

"What do you mean?"

Michael hadn't tested it out completely yet, but he had a working hypothesis. Just before Mac had died, he had given him all his powers. Not only that, his powers had combined with Michael's, becoming something far greater than they had been before. Now, at last, he possessed much more potent weapons to combat those who sought to capture and control him. Whether they would be enough, only time would tell.

Still, he could give it a trial run now, have a little fun.

"Boys," he said when the sensation was gone, "on the count of three, I want you to fire at each other's heart."

They trembled, their eyes bulging in terror. "S-stop," Chance managed to say, and said nothing more.

"One," Michael said. He paused, smiling.

"Two."

Chance's and Roy's guns wavered a bit. Michael corrected that problem with a blink of his eye, making their hands rock steady. He inhaled deeply, preparing to speak the final number.

Do I really want to do this? Is this really who I am?

Michael shuddered and looked about him, feeling as if he were waking from a spell. He remembered what Cassandra had said before he and Mac left her. *Watch out for windmills.* Her warning referred to perhaps the most famous incident in *Don Quixote* where Don Quixote had foolishly battled windmills because he believed they were ferocious giants. It was a foolish delusion, and instead of collecting the spoils and the glory of a knight, he had caught his lance in the arm of a windmill and been thrown from his horse.

A foolish delusion. Wasn't that what his new powers were if he used them in the wrong way? If he let them use *him*? Not only that, it wouldn't be too bright to leave three dead bodies behind him. They would be an obvious clue that authorities could follow. Unless he made the bodies disappear, of course.

Michael sighed. "Lower your guns," he said.

The men promptly obeyed. "Thank you," Roy said. "Oh, sweet Jesus, thank you so much!"

"Shut up," Michael said. He thought for a moment, then had another idea. As before, it created a buzzing sensation. It felt like a powerful bee was active deep in his brain.

"Listen," Michael said, "I want all three of you to forget I was ever here. Understand?"

Esther got it first. "Just forget you?"

"Right. Forget I ever existed, that you ever saw me. If anyone ever asks what you did or saw in this cave, you won't even mention me because I wasn't here. Got it?"

They did get it. They got the message clearly. But a moment later, the three of them moaned and glanced at each other in confusion. "What the fuck are we doing here?" Chance asked.

"Yeah," Roy said. "Last I remember, we was sittin' down and chillin'. Bangin' Esther and smokin' a little weed."

Michael watched the three of them return to the blanket. They didn't even glance in his direction. He was about to leave when he realized they could provide him with a further service. He went and confiscated their weapons, ammo, money, and flashlight while they drank and passed a joint around. Under the circumstances, it was a good haul. A guy never knew what he might need down the road, and it was wise to be prepared. Chance even had a fancy holster with a cowgirl on it that would come in handy.

When he'd cleaned them out, Michael gave them a brilliant smile they didn't see and marched back and forth in exultation, parading himself before them. He not only could make them kill each other, he had actually made them forget he was here! He'd never thought he could do either. "I want to thank you all for your generosity," he said. "It means a great deal to me."

Enough strutting. Don't go overboard and lose it. He knew he had dodged a terrible threat, one that came from within and involved the sin of pride. Struggling for calm, he summoned the map in his head that Mac had given him. Yes, straight ahead was the way to go. He had a long and arduous journey facing him, and he knew he'd better get cracking if he wanted to see Andy and Laura again, hold them in his arms. But how would he ever succeed with what Cassandra called the government's "bad men" endlessly tracking him and seeking to seize his secrets and powers? Or put another way, how could he find the dragon's most vulnerable spot and drive the lance home with a lethal thrust? Wasn't the dragon too big to have such a spot and too powerful to be killed or even wounded?

Enough with these endless questions! It would do him no good to let doubt cloud the picture, to second-guess every step he took. Michael took a deep breath and started walking. *C'mon, Mac, time's a-wasting. We've got a job to do.*

Damned straight, he imagined his friend saying. *It's about time you got off your lazy ass and did something constructive.*

Michael agreed, but he didn't like being nagged or ragged, especially since his friend was dead. To make sure Mac got the message, he spoke it aloud.

"You're dead, you know. I saw you die and give up the ghost. So stop haunting me. You're dead, dead, dead, not even bubbles in the dirt."

I know, Mac conceded, *but as long as you think I'm alive in some way, that's what really counts. Wouldn't you agree, my boy?*

Mac's smug cheekiness irritated Michael. He started to argue, then realized Mac was right. More to the point, Mac's precise status wasn't the issue. What mattered was that he must use Mac's map to ESCAPE from this cave, then find a way to see Andy and Laura. And he must do it without being caught. Michael knew that the mighty government dragon would be using all its resources to find him. That required him to use all his new and unexplored powers, whatever they might be, to evade it and stay free.

Before he left, Michael went to the blanket. Esther sat humming a song, and he could tell she didn't remember him or know he was there. As for Chance and Roy, they no longer looked dangerous but simply harmless, just two guys on a blanket. They sat placidly sharing a joint, mumbling a few words now and then, completely oblivious of his presence. Roy—aka Batman, the Caped Crusader, etc.—didn't glance in Michael's direction even though his cheek was still bright red from his punch. Michael found himself wondering if most of the world was as tuned out as these men in another way, basically unaware of their countries' abridgement of personal freedoms and their relentless pursuit of individuals they sought to kill or capture. Thinking back, he couldn't think of any examples he'd been aware of.

He turned and headed onward through the cave. Oddly, the oozing cut on his side seemed to have healed. When he lifted up his shirt to check, there wasn't even a scratch beneath the blood. He was also surprised by the fact that he didn't need Chance's flashlight to navigate the cave. He was beginning to see better, the cave's darkness giving up its secrets like an old friend.

The most amazing thing though was that his body no longer hurt. In fact, he felt great, charged up and eager to travel. Let the pilgrimage begin!

It's good to have you back, Mac, Michael thought. *Even if you are dead.*

Mac, whatever his reasons, chose to be silent.

ABOUT THE AUTHOR

John, a retired English professor from Norfolk State University, has published over 200 stories in *The Speed of Dark, Weird Tales, Whitley Strieber's Aliens, Galaxy, The Age of Wonders*, and elsewhere. He's also published twenty books, including SF novels such as *Speaker of the Shakk* and *Beyond Those Distant Stars*, winner of AllBooks Review Editor's Choice Award (Crossroad Press), and *Alien Dreams, A Senseless Act of Beauty, The Merry-Go-Round Man*, and six novels in the *Inspector of the Cross series* (Crossroad Press). Crossroad Press has also published two SF novels, *Dark Wizard* and *Dax Rigby, War Correspondent*. MuseItUp Publishing published *The Blue of Her Hair, the Gold of Her Eyes* (winner of Preditor's and Editor's 2011 Annual Readers Poll), *More Stately Mansions*, and the dark erotic thrillers *Steam Heat* and *Wet Dreams*. John's time-travel tale *Killers* was an Editor's Top Pick at Musa Publishing. Some of John's books are available as audio books from Audible.com. Two of John's major themes are the endless, mind-stretching wonders of the universe and the limitless possibilities of transformation—sexual, cosmic, and otherwise. He is the former Chairman of the Board of the Horror Writers Association and the previous editor of *Horror Magazine*.

John welcomes comments from readers at jroseman@cox.net and invites them to visit his web site at www.johnrosenman.com and blog at www.johnrosenman.blogspot.com. His Facebook author page is https://www.facebook.com/john.rosenman/

Curious about other Crossroad Press books? Stop by our website:
http://crossroadpress.com
We offer quality writing
in digital, audio, and print formats.

Subscribe to our newsletter on the website homepage and receive a free
eBook.